SINCERELY, YOURS

CHARLOTTE BARNES

BLOODHOUND
— BOOKS —

www.bloodhoundbooks.com

Print ISBN 978-1-914614-32-3

ALSO BY CHARLOTTE BARNES

PSYCHOLOGICAL THRILLERS

Intention

All I See Is You

CRIME THRILLERS

The Copycat

The Watcher

The Cutter

PART I

1

2010

I couldn't stand to watch her die. But I couldn't help her either.

There was a quiet crack. If we hadn't been standing stock still and silent when it happened then I doubt we would have heard it at all. A crack, then a pop. Mum looked at me as though I might know the source, but I didn't. I shrugged, and carried on looking through the hanging clothes – ones she'd only brought home with her that day. 'You don't have to steal everything I buy,' she'd said when I made a beeline for the bedroom. It was one of our ongoing jokes, though, how nice it was that we were both the same size – how convenient.

Mum set a hand on my shoulder to halt my shuffling. The coat hangers had squealed from one end of the wardrobe pole to the other. But when we were quiet again, the sound of footsteps – the uncomfortable sucking of a shoe being lifted away from wooden floors – was somehow amplified. It was hard to tell which room of the house the sound was coming from, though.

I opened my mouth – to scream, maybe, I wasn't sure – but Mum clamped her fingers hard across my face. She rounded her lips as though to shush me, but she only mimed the instruction, and made those fiercely wide eyes she used to make, to warn me she was being serious. She took slow and deliberate steps to the doorway; it was open enough to peer through from the right angle. If we hadn't been in the middle of a break-in, I would have laughed at her Scooby-Doo demeanour. She was too beautiful to be anything but a Daphne.

I've no way of knowing what she saw around the bend of the doorway. But she hurried back into the room with a different kind of wide-eyed look. Her finger was pressed to her lips then, as though to underscore the importance of my quiet. She rushed me against the open doorway of the walk-in wardrobe, wordlessly warning me of something – I didn't know what until later. It was only when I was inside the space, squashed mute against soft linens and stiff jackets that she said, 'You stay in here, whatever happens.'

'Mum, I–'

'Sarah.' She fixed a hand over my mouth again. 'Please.' I've never been sure whether she whispered this or only mouthed it. But I nodded my understanding and, as though only in that moment realising the danger of whatever was walking through the halls, I crouched small in the belly of the cupboard. She pushed the door closed as I shrank away from her. But she left a wide enough crack for me to see.

2

The police thought I was joking, I think. In their defence, I don't imagine it's a call they get that often. Or, if it is, the person on the other end of the line is probably biting back on tears of laughter. The only thing I was biting back on was a growing urge to curl up and die next to her, as though I could make myself into one of those loyal dogs – the sorts you read about in the human-interest section of a newspaper. They'd find us both, weeks later: Mum suffocated and me starved to death.

'Have you called an ambulance?' the operator asked.

I stammered over the admission. 'No– no, I– I didn't think to. Should I call them instead?' Through this messy plea for help, this plea for someone who might know what to do, I watched Mum the entire time; she'd always been the one to know how to handle things. 'I saw it happen, though, I saw him.'

There was a long pause. 'Okay, my love, can you take some deep breaths for me?'

'I didn't try CPR,' I said, misunderstanding the request.

'No, no. That's okay. There's an ambulance on the way, okay?' She used hush-baby tones. 'The police are coming, too, so it's really important that you don't touch the body, okay? Can you do that for me? Are you alone in the house now?'

There were so many questions that I didn't know which to answer first. 'He left,' I said, simply. 'I watched him leave too.'

Before she could add anything more there was a thunderclap hammering against the front door – loud enough for the woman to hear. 'That'll be the police, my love, okay?'

'Are you sure?' I thought he might have been back – with reinforcements, ready to do away with the witness.

'I'll stay on the phone with you, okay? I'll be right here.'

On the other side of the front door there was a man and a woman, both in bright yellow garments, with a medical kit slung over each shoulder. It seemed wildly optimistic of them, but I think I was also holding on to some hope. I stepped aside, the phone still pressed to my ear, and let them flood the hallway.

'It's the paramedics,' I told the woman on the phone.

'Okay, the police won't be long now.'

'We'll need to know where your Mum is.'

'They want to know where she is.'

'Okay, my love, I'll let you go.'

Enough people had let me go for one evening. But the line went dead.

'She's in the bedroom.' I think I expected them to know where that was. 'I'm sorry – it's through there, in here,' I moved as I spoke, and it occurred to me then how I was retracing his steps – how all of us were. 'Are we disturbing evidence? Will the police– Can they tell our footprints–'

'Can I get your name, honey?' This new woman asked, in soft tones again.

I hated but needed to be spoken to like a child. 'I'm Sarah. Mum is Evelyn. Or Eve, she doesn't mind Eve, she–'

'Sarah, could you walk me through what happened here?' she interrupted me, guiding me away from the room I'd just shown them to. The man was in the background, busying himself with clicks and zippers and alchemy.

She listened with a neutral face and I remember wondering how she wasn't horrified by my behaviour – disgusted that I hadn't gone out there, disturbed him, maybe died. There was the occasional headshake from her, something that could have been a twitch, but that was the closest she came to a reaction.

At the end of my sad story-time she opened her mouth to add something, but her colleague interjected, as though he'd been waiting for a natural pause. 'Alex,' he called her attention. 'The police are here. I'm going to walk them through the state of play in the bedroom.'

'Okay, thanks.' She didn't even look at him; she stayed looking at me. 'Can we talk some more, Sarah? Is it just you and your mum that are here?'

'My dad, he isn't around.' I could hear a flurry of newcomers in the hallway and I wanted to warn them: *Watch your footsteps; that's where he was.* But they'd probably already guessed. 'I don't have any siblings, either. It's just me. She always joked,' I stopped to let a smile escape, 'she always joked I was enough, that she didn't have enough clothes for– for two.' I thought of the wardrobe, the new clothes, the wailing screech of coat hangers that had disguised his first moments in the house.

'Okay, that's good, that's really good, Sarah. Does your Mum have relatives?'

'None that we're close to.' Her own mother hadn't been around, I remembered.

'She doesn't have siblings either?'

I shook my head and sucked in my chest. 'It's really just us.'

'Alex.' The man appeared again. 'We're going to need to head out.'

From the corner of my eye I saw her throw him a pleading

look and he backed away. 'Do you have any family friends that we can call, honey?'

'The police are going to need–'

'Noah,' she snapped across him. 'Anyone at all?'

'Madison. I could call Madison.'

'Okay, who's Madison?' she asked, feeling through her pockets. She pulled out a scrap of paper and clicked her pen alive. 'Is that someone we could call for you?'

'I don't know her number. My phone is around– My phone might be–' I gestured to the hallway. I'd used the house phone to call them. But when had I last seen my mobile? 'Can I?' I looked from one to the other. The man – Noah – shifted from one foot to the other and avoided my gaze, as though he hadn't been looked at like this before – or maybe he had, but not so he'd notice. 'I'm sorry.'

'Sarah, there's nothing to apologise for, okay? Noah will get your phone.'

'Alex, the police should be the ones–'

'Can you tell us whereabouts it is, or does it have a cover we might spot, maybe?' she asked, as though her colleague hadn't spoken.

There was a set of drawers as you came in through the front door, I explained. He disappeared and I imagined him retracing those same steps again. How many footprints were over the original footprints? I thought of Noah backtracking along the hallway, towards the open front door. He would be walking past the bedroom, along the outside of the wall where the wardrobe cupboard stood – where I'd folded myself. Then he'd walk back. Is that the way he'd left, after he–

'Sarah.' My name sounded strange coming from Noah's mouth. 'I got your phone,' he said, handing it to the woman, 'but the police want to have a quick talk with you. Would that be okay?'

'Now?' I asked.

'Only if you're okay with that.' He looked behind him and I saw his head twitch, as though signalling to someone. 'Why don't we try to get in touch with Madison first, and we can go from there? Does that sound better?'

I closed my eyes to stifle the onset of tears and nodded my head. 'That would be better, if that's okay, I think.' All the while thinking that nothing would ever be better again.

3

They took my clothes. The saving grace being that, while treading through my house, they managed to pluck out some fresh items for me to wear. I told them I hadn't disturbed her; only held her for a minute or two. But they said something about trace contact; no stone being left unturned. I wanted to ask them about the footprints, then, but it didn't seem like the right time. They left me 'sitting tight' in what I guessed was an interview room designed for victims; there were sofas rather than hard-backed chairs, and a box of tissues nearby. It was nothing like the crime series Mum and I had binged, though. But then, watching someone die had felt different to how I'd expected as well.

I slept for an hour or so. When I came around, my neck cricked from the fantasy angle that my head had lolled at, I wasn't sure whether I'd slept at all, or just passed out. Either way, time had moved on, which was both a blessing and a disappointment. *This is really happening then*, I remember thinking, in the seconds before a police officer I half-recognised from earlier eased their way into the room. It occurred to me that even in a victim's interview room there were probably cameras and I wondered whether they'd watched me sleep.

'Can I get you anything, Sarah?' she asked, and I didn't like how familiar her tone was. There was something too friendly about the way she sat opposite me, two fingers pressed to my knee as though to ground me.

But please, let me drift away, I thought as I shook my head in answer. 'I'm okay, thank you.'

'Tea?'

'I'm okay.' Which was a lie because I would, of course, seldom be okay again. 'Can I leave yet? Is there more that you...'

'We're going to need to ask some questions, if you think you're up to it this evening.'

'Is it still evening?'

She frowned. 'It's the early hours.'

And I wondered how a night could last so long.

'We can get some coffee, or even something to eat if you think you can manage it. It's really important we keep your strength up right now.'

'Tea.' I gave in. 'I don't have sugar.'

'Okay.' She pulled her phone out and thumbed in my order. 'I'm texting my colleague, okay. She's on her way to us so she can stop and get tea.' When she put her phone away she gave me a tight smile. 'You don't have to be alone again tonight, okay? We'll have a talk while we're waiting for your guardian – Madison, is it?'

'She's a family friend.' It was disingenuous to call her that. Madison had been in my life for as long as I could remember. Once, she'd even gone as far to joke that if she'd had a child then it would have been me. I knew Mum would want Madison here, for this. 'You've managed to get in touch with her though?'

The door opened and another woman sidled in. 'Tea?' She smiled and set it down in front of me.

'I'm DS Laing, and this is DC Brooks,' the first woman introduced them both, and ignored my question. 'If you're up to it, Sarah, we'd like to have a talk through some of the things that happened this evening, while you were at home.'

People kept making it sound like they were asking me things when they weren't. I knew I would have to talk about it, for as long as they wanted me to. *Why ask?* I thought and sipped my drink even though it was too hot, but at least it was a different kind of feeling.

DC Brooks picked up. 'Can you tell us what was happening immediately before the–' she faltered. 'The break-in.'

'Mum and I were in her room.' I swallowed hard and felt a small pebble land in the back of my throat. 'She'd brought a load of new clothes today. Payday. And – she and I, we're–' I shook the present tense away. 'We were the same size, so I was skimming through her wardrobe. It was a joke we had.'

DS Laing looked like there was a laugh in her. She was old enough to have daughters, I guessed, maybe not daughters my age, but certainly daughters. I wondered whether this was a tradition in her household too.

'And what was it that alerted you to someone else being in the house?' Brooks asked.

'Mum heard something. Well, we both heard something. There was a crack, a kind of, I don't know, a popping noise. Mum told me to stop shuffling the clothes so we could listen, and then – and then she went to the doorway, and she saw something. Him, I guess she saw him, and then she–'

'Did she say anything about the man she'd seen?' Brooks asked, and Laing frowned like it was a stupid question – which it was.

'No, no, she just – well, she hurried, to get me to hide.'

There was a heavy silence wedged between us all then, until

Laing reached over and grabbed my hand. 'You did the right thing tonight, do you know that?'

The floodgates cracked and tears poured through. 'But I didn't– It wasn't– I–'

'You would be dead,' she interrupted me with a mother's firmness. 'And no mother would ever want that for their child, I promise you that much. Your mum saved you, and that's exactly what she wanted to do.'

'But what about– what about what I want?'

She sniffed hard. I wondered whether she might cry too. 'It doesn't matter,' she answered, and she sounded sincerely apologetic. 'Your Mum, she told you to hide?'

I nodded. 'Hide, and don't come out. But when I knew he'd left, I left too.'

'How long did you wait?'

'I counted to four thousand.'

Brooks noted down the number while Laing did quick maths. 'A little over an hour,' she said to her colleague before facing back to me. 'That was smart, Sarah. Waiting like that.' It felt like a compliment, but I couldn't thank her for it. 'Now, I need you to think really hard for me, and I know it's rough, but this could really help us get along. Did he say anything, anything at all, while he was in the room?'

For the fourth or fifth time I thought back through it all. It was like a horror film on playback and forth. But the only audio I had was–

'Sarah,' Laing interrupted me, her hand on my knee again, pulling me down. I wondered what face I'd worn; how much hurt she'd been able to see. 'It's okay if you can't remember anything more right now. These things, they come back to us with a little time. Maybe it's something we can try in a day, or two days, or whenever you're ready. For now, could we talk a little more about what happened before he got in the room, would that be okay?'

'I think so.' My voice shook as though my larynx were pneumatic. I wanted to apologise again, but it seemed only right to save all my sorrys for Mum.

A knock came at the door and an officer in uniform stepped in. 'Sarah's guardian is here,' he announced. 'Should I bring her in?'

Laing looked at me. 'Would you prefer that, Sarah?'

'Does she know– she knows what's happened?' I asked and both detectives nodded in unison. 'Then maybe it would be nice – not nice, sorry. It could be good to have her here, for someone. If that would be okay?' I felt like I was asking a lot, even though they'd offered.

'I'll bring her,' the junior officer said, without awaiting further instructions.

Only seconds later there came another knock. Madison must have been loitering close by. This time when the door opened it was her – tear-streaked and exhausted.

'My darling girl.' She rushed into the room and I stood to greet her. Her arms had been outstretched on her approach and she caught me inside them; my knees buckled, my shoulders shook with feeling, and she squeezed tighter as though keeping my innards in place. 'My sweet, darling girl, I am so sorry,' she whispered, her tears coming in time with my own. 'I'm here. I know it's not the same. But I'm here, and we'll do this,' she spoke quietly into my ear and I wanted to believe her. I counted to a hundred while we both held each other, and I greedily pulled in the smells of her perfume, hairspray, make-up. She and Mum had always used the same brands.

4

It was five days later when the same detectives turned up at Madison's house. I moved straight in with her. I was seventeen and she wasn't listed as my legal guardian – but everyone reasoned that if there were extenuating circumstances for a 'child' making their own decisions, this was probably a good example. The women, Laing and Brooks, had promised they'd keep us up to date with things. But this face-to-face discussion was the first I'd heard of any developments; or rather, I assumed they were bringing developments. They could have spoken to Madison before this without me knowing, I guessed, but from her reception to them it seemed unlikely.

'Anything you say in front of me you can say in front of her,' Madison snapped frankly, in response to Laing's suggestion that I wasn't present for whatever discussion was about to roll out. 'There's not much in the world that she needs shielding from now.' I gave her a thankful smile. She was right; the time for shielding me from the world's evils had long passed.

'Sarah, how are you doing?' Brooks asked, and Laing gave her that same look as before – the one that suggested she might be being stupid. And again, I couldn't help but agree.

'Fine,' I lied. What else did she want? I couldn't sleep through the night, and my clothes were stacked in the corner of the bedroom I'd moved into, as far away from the wardrobe as I could get them. The night before this, I'd woken Madison up with such vocal theatrics that over breakfast we'd talked about ripping the wardrobe out entirely. But sure, I was fine.

'Sarah,' Laing picked up, 'we wondered whether anything more had come back to you, from the night of the attack.' Madison and I swapped a look and the detective clocked it. 'Anything you've remembered could be important, do you know? Even something that might seem insignificant.'

I took a deep pull of air and reached for something. 'His breathing was raspy?'

She frowned. 'Like asthma?'

'I guess?' I shrugged. 'Or like he'd broken a window, crept around a house and then attacked someone.' It was clear that the point of entry had been a window on the ground floor – a mere 100-and-something steps away from where we'd been, at a guess – that he'd broken and squeezed himself through. 'I don't remember smelling smoke. Cigarette smoke, I mean. It just sounded like he was raspy, in his breathing.'

'Okay, and is there–'

'He stayed with her, after.'

'Did he do anything while he was with her?'

I thought. 'No, there was nothing – he didn't do anything. He just stayed. He gave himself a minute, as though he was catching his breath.' My eyes slammed shut. 'But his breathing was better then, I think, like maybe he'd caught his breath – during. He sat on the bed and stayed, and looked at her. It might have been a minute.' The memory was too much so I tried to shake it away but there was no shifting it – we all knew that much.

'This is really great stuff, Sarah, really.' Laing reached across and touched my knee – the same way she had on the night. 'You don't have to push yourself, though, do you understand? If you want, we can arrange for a counsellor to come–'

'I thought she didn't have to push herself?' Madison snapped, and Laing backed away from me. 'She'll get there when she gets there.'

'Of course. I know it's difficult.'

'Do you?' Madison cocked an eyebrow and her meaning was clear: *You've seen a parent murdered, have you?* 'Like I said, she'll get there when she gets there. Is this what you wanted to discuss with her today?' Her tone became formal; it was the same one she'd used when the editor of a newspaper had called two days before and Madison, in her best business tone, had told him to, 'Fuck off and leave us be.' It seemed unlikely that she'd issue the same request at Laing and Brooks, but I couldn't rule it out altogether.

Laing straightened up. I didn't want for us to be on bad terms with each other. She wasn't the person who'd murdered Mum, after all; she was the one who was meant to be finding him, so it was in my best interests to keep her onside. I forced a smile at her but I knew it must look inauthentic. I hadn't smiled in six days and it seemed unlikely that a police interview would be the experience to change it. But she acknowledged the effort, at least, pushed her hair back behind her ears and smiled in return. I half-expected the same hand to reach forward for a hand squeeze or a knee tap, but she kept that in check. It was her maternal instincts, I guessed, that kept making her want to soothe me. I wondered again how old her children were – whether she'd shove them in a wardrobe.

'I can't imagine how frustrating it must be to hear this, but we're still in very early days with the investigation.' From the corner of my eye I saw Madison cock the same eyebrow as before. 'It's hard for us to say anything definitive at this stage, but we wanted to alert you to one or two things that have come to our attention.' She shuffled a handful of papers that had been lying limp on her lap, but she didn't look at them. She was steadying herself, I guessed, and I wondered whether she needed a tap on the knee for some of that magic grounding. 'We have reason to believe the person responsible for your mother's death might have killed another woman in the local area some weeks ago.'

She said it all in one breath, then sucked the air from the room to rehydrate her lungs. There was a hard thump in the centre of my chest and I lurched forward as though her words had physically struck me. Madison was close again, setting a hand on my shoulder and asking, 'Darling, look at me, look at me again now.' She was asking me to watch her breathing, to give me a crash course on how to manage it myself. This was how it felt in the morning, in the middle of the night, during every flashback, when I remembered she'd gone – that she'd been taken.

'Sarah, darling girl, come on now.' She crouched in front of me and held my head steady between her palms. 'In,' she sucked, 'and out. We're swimming, remember, remember we push the water away and we pull it back, to keep us moving forward.'

Mum couldn't swim. But she agreed with Madison that it was a skill I should have. One of my earliest memories of the three of us was me and Madison swimming in a lake while Mum matched the gestures on land. Madison would always extend the offer to adult lessons and Mum would always say, 'I'm not beautiful enough to be a mermaid.' Which I'd always thought was a lie. The three of us would, in a fashion, swim together and Madison would always remind me to push away and pull back. 'You have to use the water, darling girl. You aren't fighting against it, only through it.' She'd whispered something similar in the early hours of the morning two – or was it three? – nights ago, when she'd been reminding me how to breathe in the minutes after a nightmare.

'I'm okay,' I managed, 'I think I'm okay.'

Madison stood and sat next to me then, our outer thighs pressed together. 'So he's done this before?'

'It looks that way,' Brooks answered, giving her superior a break. 'There are certain parts of that previous crime that appear similar to this one. Given the proximity of them, it gives us good reason to believe the same person or persons might be responsible. It seems unlikely that these two incidents would be unrelated.' She spoke in a level tone and I wondered how many times she'd had to deliver that speech or a similar one. 'The previous incident took place nearby–'

'Wait, I'm sorry,' Madison interrupted. 'Persons? You think he's what – part of a team?'

'Not part of a team, no,' Brooks explained. 'But we can't rule out the possibility that more than one person might be involved.'

The edges of my vision were watercoloured and there was a pebble beach forming in my throat. I swallowed hard to clear the mess. 'What about the other witness?'

'What other witness, sorry, Sarah?' Laing answered.

I looked from one detective to the other. 'You said the cases were similar. This first one, and what happened to– what happened at home. So what did the other witness see? Did they see anything more than I did?'

'There wasn't another witness,' Laing said plainly. 'That's part of what we wanted to talk to Madison about. Well, talk to you both about now. We have to consider the possibility that he didn't know he was leaving someone behind...'

5

I'd never been a make-up sort of girl. But that morning it felt like a kind of war paint. Madison had offered to lend me some of her things, but I couldn't stand the smell association so we'd left the house to buy new products together. It had been strange, doing a Mum activity minus a Mum, but Madison was doing her best to compensate for any shortfalls. We went to four different shops to try out five different shades of foundation and three different kinds of mascara, which left us both panda-eyed by the time we'd got home.

'You don't have to do this, you do know that?' she said that afternoon when we landed hard on the two-seater together, full cups of tea and trash television at the ready. She said the same thing again from behind me in the bathroom the morning I came to use the make-up. Her worried face bounced back at me through the looking glass and I recognised her concerns all too clearly, because I'd just spent fifteen minutes trying to carefully disguise my own.

'The police said there's nothing to worry about.' I tipped my head back and spread my eyes wide to get a good angle on my lashes before painting them over in black.

'That's absolutely not what they said, Sarah.'

'Close enough.'

'Absolutely not, again.' She came and stood beside me to look at my real face rather than my mirror image. 'They said to exercise caution and to try to carry on as best as we can until they have more information. That's what they said.' She landed hard on every few words as though underscoring their dictionary definitions. 'It's been two weeks, darling girl. That's no time at all. Why do you think you need to do this right now?'

I yanked at the cord to turn off the mirror light. 'Then when?'

She sighed and stepped away, giving me space to finish, manoeuvring around my getting ready. 'What do you want for breakfast?'

'I don't want–'

'Hush up. What do you want for breakfast?' She raised an eyebrow. I'd come to see it as a staple move of hers; something about the expression made her more intimidating, and she knew it. Madison was wasted really, in not having children of her own. She had the mindset for it. 'Toast, cereal?'

'Toast.' The curtness of my answer didn't register with me until she was halfway out the door. 'Thank you, Mad.' She turned to face me then. 'You know, for...' I gestured to the room around us, meaning: the bathroom; bedroom, sans wardrobe; new make-up; fresh clothes; for sorting out whatever state had been left behind at my real home.

But she waved the gratitude away. 'Hush again. I'll get your toast.'

Something I'd underestimated about the return to college is that I wouldn't be the only person there who knew my mum had been murdered. Classmates who I wasn't on talking terms with beforehand certainly had no interest in talking to me when I went back either. In fact, they seemed to be keeping a safe distance – as though personal tragedy were something that could leap from one person to another. But the classmates who I was on talking terms with, I found out, had been rallied into the president's office.

Landon, Tyler and Jessie were poised, like a welcoming committee, to be a part of the starting back meeting; a meeting Madison had only told me about on the drive in.

'I didn't want you to be worried,' she'd said.

More worried, I thought.

'Sarah.' Tyler was the first to throw his arms around me. He pressed me so tight against him that I couldn't tell whose heartbeat was knocking. 'Babe, I'm so sorry.'

'We're all sorry,' Jessie said, standing in the background, waiting patiently for her hug. Everyone seemed to think they were afforded physical contact during grief, which was one of many things I'd learnt in the weeks before going back to college.

That said, Landon wasn't a hugger. But he did thump me on the arm gently with a balled fist. 'You had the finest mother of us all, Wainwright. 10/10 would have dated her.' It was, I thought, probably one of the nicest notes of sympathy I'd had – and Mum would have loved it.

'Sarah, do you want to take a seat?' President Connors said from behind his desk. There was a plaque across the front branded with his name in case anyone forgot. But he was always trying to be one of those cool teacher types who insisted on students using his first name. 'You're welcome to call me Julian,' he said to every new-starter, who soon learnt that Julian was certainly more generous than what students said behind his back. They were bastards really, but that can be set down to their age. Besides, I'd never been much better.

'Thanks.' I positioned myself between Tyler and Jessie.

'I thought it might be helpful for us all to have this talk together, so you're in a safe space, loved.' Connors spoke slowly, as though I might not understand. But people had been forcing safe environments all over the place since Mum, so this kind of emotional intervention came as standard. 'Other students are, of course, aware of everything that's happened and I'm sure we can count on fellow students to be respectful of the situation. If there are any problems at all, though, you're to go to a member of staff immediately. We won't tolerate any hostility or ignorance in a situation like this.'

Situation; incident; loss. There were so many synonyms for murder. 'Thanks, Julian, I really appreciate that. I'm sure everything will be fine.'

'Everything will be fine,' Landon repeated, landing hard on *will* as though he would personally see to it. 'People won't be assholes about it, Sar.'

Connors laughed. 'Yes, Landon's quite right.'

'If anyone is an asshole, though...'

'I know, Lan.' I flashed a tight smile. 'I'll tell you.'

'Damn right you will.' He gave me the same gentle arm punch again. It was probably the most physical contact he and I had had since we'd lost our virginities to each other the summer before. We'd been so desperate to shed childhood that we rushed through it one evening when no one was looking, only to swiftly go back to normal the following day. Little did we know that adulthood on the other side of our virginities would look like grief, formal meetings, and lack of sleep. I would have held on to my hymen a summer longer if someone had warned me.

After another ten minutes of emotional safeguarding, Connors released us into the outside world so we could walk to our lockers in stoic silence. I got the textbooks I needed and slammed the door closed. 'Jesus, someone talk.'

Tyler laughed. 'How normal do you want us to be?'

'Just – I don't know, just a normal amount of normal.'

'Why the fuck are you wearing make-up?' Landon asked.

A surprised laugh erupted from me; my first in a while. 'That amount of normal.'

'Okay, but really?'

'Fuck off, Landon, she can wear make-up,' Jessie chimed in. 'I think you look really good, Sarah, it suits you.' She slammed her locker closed. 'Of course, make-up is a construct of a patriarchal society and you absolutely don't need it to feel either beautiful or validated by a male-dominated community such as a college setting, because–'

'My Christ,' Tyler muttered.

'What he said but louder.' Landon rolled his eyes while he tugged his backpack on. 'I get it, men are tossers, blah blah, women would be better off without us, yada yada. Take a day off, Jessie. You'll bore us to death.'

'Better than being strangled.' The eruption came from somewhere behind, and all four of us shot round together to find the source: Nathanial Evans. At some point we'd all been friends and there'd been a fallout; one of those that people can't really remember the details of, but they hold the grudge all the same. One or all of us would have the occasional disagreement in a corridor and nothing more ever came of it. But this.

'Evans–'

'Come on, Landon,' he carried on, 'Sarah can take it. At least that's what I've heard.' He closed the gap between us and stood level with my ear as he dropped his voice. 'Or maybe you're more the type to watch.'

Connors called Madison to collect me early, which she dutifully did. There was an adult meeting that I wasn't present for; it made me wonder whether I had more of my childhood left than I'd realised. She left the room but Connors stayed in the office, and with a head nod Madison guided me out into the car park. We were both buckled into our respective seats when she let out a heavy sigh and dropped her head back.

'A brawl in the hallway, Sarah.'

'It wasn't a brawl.'

'Quite right, a brawl involves two people.' She leaned across to open the glovebox and pulled out a battered packet of cigarettes. 'My understanding is that you thumped the kid in the cheek, so hard that he hit his head on the locker behind him. That sound about right?'

I looked out of the window. 'Yes.'

The cigarettes came into my line of vision; Madison was holding the lid open for me to take one. 'It sounds like the prick deserved it anyway.'

'I can smoke?'

'Only in emergencies.' She handed over the lighter. 'And for celebrating minor victories.' While I lit a cigarette – something I'd only ever done in secret before then – Madison rolled down her window. 'I'm glad to have a kid who can stick up for herself. Your mother would be too.'

6

College was difficult. To begin with no one had wanted to say the wrong thing for fear of offending me. After Nathanial, no one wanted to say the wrong thing for fear of a black eye. Although, given a choice of the two, the second seemed the safest for me – particularly given that another week had rolled by with no news from the police, neither about Mum nor the woman who came before her. The weeks knocked together and I became aware of a near tangible worry sitting between me and everyone around me: wedged on the dining table while Madison and I ate; puffing out clouds of black fury while Landon and I tried to be the cool smokers. No one was saying it, but collectively everyone wondered what the weeks would mean; if he waited the first time, how long might he wait for a second?

'Serial killers usually have shorter cooling off periods the more murders they do.'

Madison choked on a mouthful of mashed potato. 'I'm sorry?'

'It's three weeks tomorrow.'

'Who said anything about a serial killer?'

I shrugged. 'You think he'll kill two women and stop?'

'I think he's a deeply disturbed individual–'

'I'm sorry,' I cut across her and she looked relieved. 'I shouldn't have said that.'

'Sarah, you're allowed to say anything here.' She set her cutlery down even though she was only halfway through the meal. It was something I'd started doing, ruining the most basic daily events for people. A lot of my friends couldn't get through a meal in front of me either, with me shuffling food around my plate, thinking about how Mum would never eat again. 'Where did you go?'

I looked up. 'What?'

'You looked like...' she paused to think. 'Never mind. I'll wash up while you find trash on television.' She stood. 'You're off college tomorrow, too, I meant to say.' She said it like it was nothing.

'Why? I didn't do anything.'

'Police interview. They've got some questions about your mum.'

I've got some questions about their police work, I thought as I pushed back from the table. But Madison and I were learning the different ways to navigate each other. If she were prepared to talk about it, she would. The rest of the evening passed without mention of the visit, until she lingered in the living room doorway for a second too long on her way to bed.

'We have to be there for eleven tomorrow.'

'Okay.' I didn't look away from the screen. I stared at that episode of *Drag Race* with the intensity of a hostage at gun point. 'I'll be ready.'

'Sure you're okay down here on your own?'

'Course.' I gestured. 'They're talking to the judges now. I'll be up soon.'

It could have been the same interview room they'd placed me in the first time; in the hours immediately after it had happened. It was hard to tell. And I wondered how many interview rooms they had, dedicated to witnesses and victims. *If this room could talk.* I looked from corner to corner and spotted three different cameras, discreetly flashing their red eyes. Madison came with me and she, too, sat in silence for the wait. There had been two bottles of water on the table in front of us, one of which she'd cracked open within seconds. The sound of it slowly exhaling back into shape was the only noise that passed between us. When the door opened she and I jumped in synchronicity, as though we hadn't been ready for someone to enter – but after everything, I suppose, we should have always been ready.

'Sarah, Madison,' DS Laing said, taking a seat opposite us. Brooks sat alongside her and flashed a thin smile in greeting. I desperately wanted for one of them to accidentally say it was nice to see me, just so I could use the back-pocketed retort of how unpleasant it was to be there – again. 'Thanks for coming in today. I realise it eats into your college time, Sarah, so we appreciate you helping us.'

'I'm helping myself, really,' I replied. Madison squeezed my hand, and I couldn't tell whether it was in support or warning. 'Mad said there were some things you wanted to talk to me about – about Mum.'

'Of course.' Laing shuffled her papers like she had during previous visits and I wondered whether it was a nervous tick. 'We're currently looking for connections between your mother and a victim from another crime.'

'The earlier woman?'

She looked put out. 'It's hard to say for definite what the connections are–'

'The same murderer, I imagine.'

'Sarah,' Madison cautioned me.

'It's okay,' Laing said, even though I hadn't apologised. 'We're looking for areas in their personal lives that might tie them together and we're hoping you might be able to help us with that, Sarah, if you feel you can.'

I wanted to be a petulant child about it. But I also wanted them to find Mum's murderer. It was a hard balance between the two mindsets. 'What do you need to know?'

She signalled to Brooks to take notes. 'Did your mother have any hobbies or social events that took her out of the house on a regular basis?'

'Thursday night yoga. Is that the sort of thing you're looking for?'

'Anything like that, yes. Anything that she did regularly, that may not necessarily be in her diary.'

Madison snorted. 'If you're relying on her diary for information then no wonder you're struggling. She hardly used it.'

'That's not fair,' I answered, 'she would take pages out for scrap all the time.' We swapped smiles. We'd started to have these occasional moments of remembering her; mixed in with the anger and confusion and spite. 'She didn't go every week but she did go to a yoga class now and then, usually Thursdays if she was going, down at the sports centre in town. She mostly worked from home but there's a café – I can't remember…' I trailed off, thinking.

'Monty's?' Madison suggested and I snapped my fingers.

'Yes, Monty's. She'd work there sometimes. I don't know how well she knew the people. Well enough that they knew her order, but not so well that she sent Christmas cards.'

Laing waited for Brooks to catch up before she looked back at us. 'This is something that one or both of you might be able to help with. We haven't found evidence to suggest this in your mother's belongings, so we certainly don't mean to imply it. But was she romantically involved with anyone?'

'No,' Madison and I answered in sync.

The detective looked between us. 'You're sure?'

'She hasn't been on a date in two years.'

'Sarah's father was Eve's longest relationship,' Madison added.

'And that ended on good terms?' Brooks asked, pen poised.

'It certainly wasn't bad terms. Eve fell pregnant and he didn't feel ready for fatherhood. She said she was ready for motherhood. That was all that happened, really. He kept in touch for a while, but he really didn't want a child.'

Laing threw me a look to gauge my reaction.

'This isn't anything that Sarah doesn't already know,' Madison added.

'Although, if I may,' I said, 'it seems unlikely that a man who hasn't had contact with me for my entire life would come back seventeen years in to kill Mum.' The bluntness of the announcement seemed a surprise to the room. 'Sorry.'

'No,' Laing held up a hand, 'you're quite right.' She made a note of something. 'Even in fleeting relationships, though, there haven't been any problems?'

'Fleeting relationships?' I parroted back and Laing winced as though immediately spotting the error. 'What does that even mean?'

'Sarah–'

'No, Mad, I want to know what counts as a fleeting relationship.'

'I'm sorry, Sarah, I only meant–'

'I think it's clear what you meant.'

'Maybe we're finished here for today?' Madison set her hand on my arm. 'Unless you've got any more questions?'

'Sarah, I really didn't mean to imply anything negative about your mother,' Laing carried on as though Madison hadn't spoken but when I didn't take the bait she circled back. 'If you think of anything or anyone who might be helpful, or of interest, then don't hesitate about getting in touch with us.'

'We'll do that.'

The grown-ups handled the rest of the conversation for me. Madison signed us out of the police station and led me to the car, while my arms stayed firmly crossed over my chest to form a protective stance. She didn't force a conversation; she knew me better, I suppose. But she did let me be sad, and quiet, and petulant. Then she let me sob my heart out when we got home.

7

Before Mum died, I would have described kiss-and-tell newspaper stories as something reserved for footballers and other non-celebrities. But apparently claiming to have once shared a bed with a murder victim also had an appeal – at least for a handful of people who happened to have slept with victim one, whose name, I learnt from seeing it splashed across headlines, was Jada Burns. She'd been three years younger than Mum; hadn't had any children; and she'd lived alone a stone's throw away from our house.

There were conflicting reports about what she did for a living; articles in the more local print papers seemed to suggest she was a finance manager but the stories that were being periodically uploaded to patches of the internet suggested everything from a maths teacher through to an insolvency practitioner. The one thing there weren't many discrepancies about, though, was the amount of sexual partners Jada had had which, in a word, seemed to be 'many'.

'The fleeting relationships question suddenly makes more sense.'

Landon knocked my phone out of my hand. 'Why are you even reading that shit?'

'To know more about her.'

'But you won't know more about her, Sarah. You'll just know what some dickhead had to say about her, which isn't the same thing.'

'Are you a feminist?'

He opened his packet of cigarettes and offered them to me. 'Look at me, chivalrous and everything.'

'Spark up for me?'

'Fucking hell, shall I smoke it too?'

'Listen to this,' I continued, scrolling again already, '"Jada was always the one that got away for me. If I had my time again then I like to think things would have worked out differently."'

'I never understand why people say that.' He made a dragon of himself, exhaling hard through his nose before passing me the cigarette. 'Isn't it the most redundant thing to say things would have worked out differently?'

'There's another one here who seems to think she was the best he had. Another one who said they were close friends. Another one, another one, another one.'

'So, she put it about?'

'You're a real prick sometimes, do you know that?'

'I've been told.' He exhaled hard again. 'There's nothing wrong with putting it about. If anything, I wish more women would.'

'Women do.' I clicked out of the news article and opened a fresh tab. 'They're just not putting it about with you. Now, are you going to help me find out more about this woman or not?'

'Sarah, what do you even want to know?'

I keyed in her name. 'I want to know what made her special.'

Jada Burns was one of many people who didn't give much

33

thought to the privacy of their social media. Landon and I managed to find her Facebook and LinkedIn in the space of ten minutes, once we'd sifted through enough profile pictures to work out whether we'd got the right woman or not. From her LinkedIn, then, we managed to work out that she was in fact an insolvency practitioner.

'What does that even mean?'

'It means she made people bankrupt.' I carried on reading. 'Which presumably means there are lots of suspects.'

'How do you make someone bankrupt?'

'It's complicated.'

She'd worked at the same company for the last seven years, and she'd spent ten years at another company before that. Her employment history at least made her seem like a reliable person. All of her specialist skills – time management, written and spoken communication, other generic entries on a CV – were endorsed by tens of people, and there were bitesize reviews at the bottom of her qualifications that explained Jada was 'respectful, consistent and a joy to work with', among other things. There was nothing listed that might give anyone reason to kill her. But I didn't know whether I'd expected it to be that easy.

'Good person all round then. Smoke?' He bit down on a butt.

'I'm fine.'

'Sarah, haven't we looked for long enough?'

'It's been an hour.' I lowered my phone. 'There must be something that made her a target.'

'Any number of things could do that. Murderers aren't known for their logic!'

'Except they are,' I snapped back. 'It's just working out what the logic is.'

I pulled up Jada Burns' Facebook page. I wondered how long it would take for them to remove the profile altogether. *Is there a timeline for these things?* I thought, scrolling through her most recent updates. Mum hadn't used social media; she always said she didn't understand the point. It was one of the few things I'd had to be grateful for; one less thing in her name to close down. Although Madison had handled most things: bills; mortgage; talking to Mum's life insurance company.

'Should I have life insurance?' I'd asked Madison, while she was knee-deep in premium details and paperwork.

'Are you planning on dying?'

She hadn't looked up when I didn't answer.

'Jada updated her statuses a lot,' I said. 'Feeling sad, feeling excited, visiting friends.'

'So she had a normal life is what I'm hearing?'

'She doesn't have a relationship status,' I added, skipping over Landon's question.

'Which makes sense, right? I mean, given everything we've read about her.' Landon pulled out his own phone. 'This is going to be easier with two of us doing it.'

'What's the point in us both reading her profile?'

'I won't. I'll read headlines.'

It was a perverse story-time for us both. Landon and I had known each other since we were knee-high to grasshoppers. I still had memories, tucked away in my back pocket for when I was trying to sleep at night, of Mum reading to us both; always hidden inside our own personal pillow fort, with Mum doing the voices for each character. It crossed my mind that I should start reading Jada's status updates with an accent, or trying to sound more masculine or feminine for the sake of animation. But it probably wouldn't have been appropriate.

I'd started to have thoughts like that; bleed-throughs, from what was okay to what had stopped being okay, as though Mum had taken all these things with her.

'"Reports from police suggest this could be the start of

something much bigger and that young women, sharing characteristics with either victim, should be especially vigilant."'

I dropped my phone. 'Do they mean a spree?'

"'Detective Sergeant Laing is due to hold a press conference at the end of this week, to mark five weeks since the murder of– since the murder of Evelyn Wainwright–"' I heard the crack in his voice when he forced out Mum's name, but we both pretended it hadn't happened. "'–amid fears that the killer will strike again before the month is out, members of the public want to know whether there's more the police could be doing to catch the man responsible."' A long pause passed. 'Do you think he'll kill again?'

Madison and I had talked a lot – maybe even too much – about what the infamous 'he' might do next. He'd been the hot topic around the dining room table, after every news report, on the drives to college. Our speculation around the stranger's likely course of action knew no limits, with my own theories becoming wilder and less likely with every nightmare. But no matter the news reports or police actions, my own answer didn't change.

'I don't know why anyone would assume he won't...'

8

DS Laing hadn't returned any of the three messages that I'd left for her. So I went to the police station. I hovered in the reception area for nearly twenty minutes and made mental impressions of the wanted posters and the warning signs that crowded the space. There was a photo-fit image of a man wanted in relation to a string of robberies; a written and detailed description of a woman who was scamming local businesses for insurance; a flyer, hanging limp and unloved, to advertise a victim support group. The bottom was a fringe pattern, with each finger boasting the number of the person running the group. There were only two left, and I felt a twist in my stomach that might have been sadness. Although 'sad' had become a default emotion so it was sometimes difficult to tell.

'Sarah, I'm really sorry to have kept you.'

I'd been staring so hard at the offer of support that I didn't even realise Laing had walked over to me. 'It's okay. You're working on the case?'

She made her lips into a thin line. 'As best as we can.'

'I've been reading more about Jada Burns.' I shrugged off my backpack and pulled out a handful of printouts. There were webpages popping up all over the place to talk about the murders, and the victims. 'There are men here,' I thumbed the pages, 'who are posting shit all over the internet about women who get killed. How, they wouldn't just be random victims of a violent crime and–'

'Sarah,' she eased the papers away from me, 'this sort of thing happens all the time when a high-profile case appears.'

'So, you know about them?'

She spoke into the pages. 'Not these people, specifically. I only know this happens.'

'Will you talk to them?'

'The people responsible for this?' she asked, and I nodded. 'Sarah, there's not a huge amount we can do about people posting harmful opinions on the internet. I'll take these notes you've made,' she fanned them, as though assessing the quantity, 'but for the time being we're going to have to follow up more on the concrete leads we have here.'

It was the first hint she'd made at there being leads at all, never mind concrete ones. 'No one's told us what's happening.'

'Your family liaison hasn't been visiting?'

'Well, no, she has. But she just tells us the investigation is ongoing.'

'Which it is,' she explained softly as though talking to someone five years my junior.

'But we can't know anything about it?'

She frowned and then stood, a not-so-subtle hint that my time with her was up. 'As soon as we have something that you should know, then we'll be in touch. But for the time being you need to keep doing what you're doing.'

I don't know what I'm doing, I thought, but I nodded like I understood.

'Your mum wanted you to go on having a life.'

'So that's what I should do,' I snapped, 'sort my life out?'

Her frown deepened and I wondered what life experiences she'd got tucked away in the creases of her forehead; whether she knew what an ask it was, that I might have a life after all of this.

'It's Halloween this weekend, right?' she said, as though the date might have skipped my attention. 'You're young. See your friends. Make the most of all of this.'

The horror? I wanted to ask, but instead I said, 'Is it safe?'

'Of course it's safe,' she answered without skipping a beat, using the exact same tone I'd heard her use during television interviews. Somehow, the assuredness of it made me trust her less again.

Madison was late home from work so I cooked dinner for us. Pasta with homemade tomato and basil sauce, served with a side of garlic bread.

'I'd like to go to a party with Landon and everyone this weekend, if you're okay with that.'

'I'm not.' She spooned a heap of pasta into her mouth and made a dramatised sound of appreciation. 'Oh, Sarah, you've done well. I needed a hearty meal after today. Tell me about your day? Much happening?'

'Wait, what?'

'I asked about your day.'

'I asked about a party.'

'Could you pass the bread?' Her mouth was full again; she gestured the bread bowl towards her. 'You asked if I was okay with a party, and I'm not.'

'But why?'

'Because it isn't safe.'

'DS Laing said it was.'

Madison dropped her fork. 'When did she say that?'

'Earlier today when I went to the police station to talk to her.'

'Well,' she hesitated, 'DS Laing is talking shit.'

My eyes spread. 'Mad, come on–'

'Sarah,' she picked her fork up and pointed at me with it, as though she'd use it to conduct whatever speech was coming, 'there is a murderer walking around the streets. He took my best friend away from me a month ago. Now, my foster daughter wants to go wandering around in a room full of people who are wearing masks. Walk me through the logic here, you're an adult. Why do you think you should go to a party?' She jabbed at the air with her fork periodically to underscore certain words, but a handful rang out to me without any extra emphasis: best friend; foster daughter; adult. She speared three pieces of pasta onto the empty prongs. 'I'm not losing you.'

There was a heavy silence between us then. Madison might have been waiting for me to back-chat her, and for a second or two I thought I might. But there were better options.

'Chinese?'

'I'm sorry?' She looked up, but kept her head lowered towards her bowl.

'Halloween takeaway. Do you want Chinese, or pizza?'

'Pizza, I think.'

'Romantic comedies?'

'Exclusively from the 1990s?'

'Deal.' I smiled. 'I'm sorry.'

'Don't be. You're young and you're allowed to have fun. But I'm not losing you,' she repeated, and flashed a tight smile back at me. 'I'll make sure that I finish on time on Friday, so you just worry about getting the films lined up and the pizza ordered. Plus garlic bread.'

'I can go to collect the pizza when you're on your way home?'

She blinked hard. 'Just get it delivered.' She chewed through another mouthful. 'If they deliver it before I get here, use the spyhole...' She hovered like the sentence might continue but then changed her mind. I heard the end of it all the same: *Use the spyhole. And don't let him in.*

9

The pizza deliveryman left the order on the front doorstep and, as instructed, kept the change as a tip. Madison had already called to say she'd be late, but that gave me a freehand to choose the first film: *Notting Hill*. 'One day I'll meet Hugh Grant and he'll fall head over heels in love with me,' Mum used to say, whenever we watched anything with even a flicker of the actor in. She was more beautiful than Julia Roberts though. I wish I'd told her that.

The two food boxes were keeping warm in the oven when Madison rushed in. 'I'm sorry, I'm sorry,' she said, freeing herself from her coat and hanging it on the nearest empty peg. 'Work finished on time but the traffic through town had other ideas and – can I smell...' she made a show of inhaling hard, 'can I smell garlic bread?'

I laughed. 'I put everything in the oven to keep warm.'

'Did you put the plates in?'

'Oh, I– shit, I didn't think.'

She kissed my cheek. 'Just kidding, darling girl, anyone who doesn't eat their pizza straight from the box is clearly a heathen of the worst order. Get comfy, I'll grab the food. Need a drink?'

'Juice, please,' I said, already halfway to the living room.

'Want a beer?'

'I'm seventeen.'

'Hm.' She made a show of thinking. 'Want a beer anyway?'

The opening scenes were playing out when Madison came into the living room, carrying two pizza boxes like a tray, with two beer bottles perched on top. She set everything down on the coffee table and waited for a natural interlude – Hugh Grant's housemate was running down the stairs for our first encounter with him – before she spoke.

'Top box is the garlic bread. I can smell it.'

I tried to manoeuvre the second box free but the front doorbell chiming in the background distracted me. I lost my grip and knocked both boxes onto the floor, their contents spilling but only slightly.

'Hey,' Madison reached out to catch my hand, 'hey, it's okay. Trick or treaters most likely, okay?' She saw me look at the spilled food. 'Five-minute rule. Don't sweat it, darling. I'll get rid of the kids, okay? Just – you just give yourself a second.'

It wasn't until I reached down to collect the boxes and the small avalanche of pizza that had dropped from them that I realised I was shaking. It wasn't a violent shake – like on the night it happened – but a tremor. I held my hand out flat and took deep breaths, waiting for the movements to steady, and I listened to the safety of Madison's voice – 'Cute costumes, take whatever you want.' – to remind me where I was. But no sooner had she made her way back into me – 'Are you okay, darling girl?' – and the same thing happened again: the doorbell; the jerk; the tremor.

'I'll disconnect that damn bell.'

She disappeared again – and again I tried to remind myself to breathe.

After the seventh round of trick or treat visitors, Madison

went as far to put a sign on the door. 'Not celebrating Halloween', it read, and I heard the grunts of disappointment from teenagers when the Post-it note turned them away. Halfway through *You've Got Mail* the letterbox clunked open and closed, and it would have made for perfect comedic timing, had Madison not found a newspaper clipping showing details of Mum's murder lying on the inside mat. 'What a trick' was written in red block capitals, shielding the bottom half of Mum's face.

'Why would someone–'

'Because someone's an arsehole.' Madison balled the paper up. 'I'll throw this. Skip the film back a minute? I'm not missing the good bits.' She tried to sound light-hearted but there was a crack in her voice that I recognised as hurt. By the time she came back into the living room, though, it sounded more like anger. 'What sort of a creature would even do that?' She landed heavy on the sofa. 'I'm going to call the police tomorrow.'

The police were yet to do anything about murder, so it seemed unlikely that they'd be put out by Halloween pranksters. After her third angry outburst – and after skipping the film back through the same minute, for the second time – we settled down to watch the rest of the picture in perfect silence. Madison reached over to my side of the sofa just once, to give my hand a squeeze, then went back to her own space until the credits rolled. The names of the actors were scrolling up and away on the screen when she clicked the pause button.

'Are we done for the night, kid?'

I hadn't noticed the last thirty minutes of the film, so it seemed wasteful for us both to pretend to watch another. 'If that's okay?'

'Sure it is.' She hit the stop button and, as though hitting a switch in me as well as on the remote, I shuddered into quiet tears. 'Oh Christ, Sarah, okay, darling girl.' She closed the gap between us and pulled an arm around me. 'What do you need?'

I shook my head: *I don't know what I need.* All she'd done was turn the film off before the credits rolled; a sacrilege offence in Mum's presence – in which I wasn't, and never would be again. After every motion picture, in the cinema or at home, Mum would stay rooted to the seat until the final screen flashed on; the one with the company logos, that the average viewer hardly ever spotted. She'd missed a deleted scene in a film once, she told me, and swore never to let it happen again.

'Shit,' Madison whispered, more to herself, 'the credits.'

I leaned hard into her and let the tears come. There was a creeping relief spreading up my back, as though the muscles had been holding on to shudders and shakes for the entire day. And they were giving way.

'I'm so sorry,' I sobbed into her chest.

'No, darling, I am. I should have– shouldn't have.' She squeezed me. While I was pressed hard against her she said, 'I should have remembered, because I always bloody hated watching those credits straight through.'

Crying gave way to laughter, then, although the noises were indistinct to begin with. I pushed myself upright and wiped away black tears; my mascara must have been somewhere around my chin.

'She was a pain for it, wasn't she?' I sniffed hard, a redundant effort after heavy crying. It only made me more nasal. 'But she was never going to miss another–'

'Deleted scene,' she finished, and smile. 'Yeah, yeah. I heard it.'

Before I could reply the doorbell chiming cut me off and Madison's eyes tipped back at the noise. She heaved herself up from the sofa and stomped towards the door – 'So help me

God...' – making a beeline for whoever the intruder was. I leaned over to the side table and grabbed tissues, one after the other to blot my nose, first, and then my eyes that, despite the laughter, looked to still be leaking bad feeling. I couldn't switch the crying off once it had started. But I usually at least managed to save it for the shower, or bedtime.

'What do you mean an incident?' I heard Madison say. In a knee-jerk reaction my stomach clenched. 'I'm going to need more than that.' The other person was inaudible but Madison's tone had already changed; she sounded worried, unnerved. 'Well, why isn't DS Laing here herself to explain all of this?'

I scampered from the sofa to the doorway like a dog with its tail lit. There were two officers standing on the porch; they were in uniform, so they mustn't have been Laing's ranking. Two women, and one stood closer to Madison than the other; I guessed this was the one who'd done the talking.

'If we can just come in to explain...' she said, sounding exhausted. She trailed off when she saw me, though, and she took on that awkward look I'd noticed people have. Since Mum, I had an innate ability to make people feel uncomfortable without even trying; something I'd gone notably out of my way to achieve before she'd died. But apparently all I'd needed to do was be the witness to a violent crime, because now friends, classmates and complete strangers all gave me the same initial look-over: blank eyes, a vacant stare, and the foot shuffle that implied they might run – if they thought they could get away with it.

No one spoke. But the longer the silence dragged out, the more certain I felt of their reason for being there. A noise escaped me; not quite a laugh, more like a shriek, the prelude to a whimper. It was a nervous sound that prefaced–

'He's done it again, hasn't he?'

The officer's lips formed a thin line. 'If we can just come in...' she repeated. But I couldn't quite hear much from anyone after that.

10

E sther Thompson was a thirty-year-old woman who lived with her cat on the other side of the city. Phrasing it that way made her sound a million miles away from Madison's house. In reality, Esther was probably a ten-minute car ride away from us when she was being murdered. The early reports all leaned heavily on her having a cat and I couldn't work out why. It might have been to show she wasn't really *that* lonely; or maybe it was the opposite. Maybe they were trying to show her as a premature spinster. It's a wonder that they didn't make her maimed and misshapen by the claws of a hungry cat instead. But I suppose when you're selling murder you've already got a decent enough hook to carry the story.

The officers had asked us not to watch the news until there was more information available; their meaning being, I guessed, that the news didn't know shit about what was happening. But that didn't stop the tweets and the status updates from flooding in; they were the first to mention the cat, to imply the loneliness of the woman. I was only ever a scroll away from finding out more information on the latest victim, so in the end the police gave in. The one who'd done the talking handed me the remote

– 'There hasn't been anything to confirm it was the same attacker.' – with a helping of attitude, and then she went back to guarding the door.

Guard all you like, I thought, flicking on the television, *he didn't need a door last time.*

'Early reports are suggesting that this may be the work of one attacker...'

'The police are yet to confirm...'

'Neighbours of the deceased have spoken to news outlets already on how...'

Madison turned the television off at the socket. 'We're waiting for Laing.'

'She isn't coming.'

'No, Sarah, because she's across town dealing with–'

'Another dead woman.'

She pushed her hair away from her face and let her fingers settle against the back of her neck. 'I'm sorry. I didn't...' I watched her knead at the skin under her hairline, and slowly work down to the points of her shoulders that she could reach. 'I can't imagine how hard this is.'

I didn't say anything. It was hard. But since Mum most things were.

Madison stayed fixed in the centre of the room but stretched her arms out to me, inviting me in. When I didn't move she gestured again, a quiet beckon for me to go over. *Maybe she needs this*, I thought as I pushed myself away from the sofa and clung to her. She squeezed gently, as though too much pressure might crack me open; but the gentle touch had been enough. I held on to my breath like the air in me was gold dust but eventually I exhaled hard, in a rapid shudder that loosened tears I'd been carrying without knowing it. And I wondered whether Madison had somehow known before me; that there were feelings just waiting to pour out. She set a hand on the back of my head, lightly, and shushed. It felt like being nursed – like being mothered.

'I know, darling girl, I know.'

In the background a phone squealed but neither of us moved. It wasn't my ringtone, or Madison's, which only left one other option.

'Excuse me?' the other officer said. It was the first time we'd heard her voice. Madison and I broke away from each other to answer her with a look. 'DS Laing has requested that we take you down to the station.'

'It's the middle of the night,' Madison answered. She sounded curt and I wondered whether the motherly instincts in the hug had bled through. 'Why isn't she coming here?'

'I'm afraid I can't answer that for you. We've just been asked to take you in.'

'Like we're the fucking criminals.' Madison snatched at a hoodie hung over the arm of the sofa and handed it to me. 'Let's get this over with.'

It hurt me to see how much Esther Thompson looked like Mum. They both had the same hair colour – a chestnut brown – and I wondered whether Esther had the same natural highlights in the summer months that Mum had always had. There were deep lines around her mouth in some pictures; in others, there was a wide smile. There were times when she looked animated – when she was pictured with others – and then one or two examples where she looked rigid, as though the photograph were being taken under duress. It looked as though she was wearing a suit in each of those images, though, or a suit jacket at least. *They must have been for work*, I thought, using my fingertips to push them away. It made me uncomfortable, how inorganic they were; they reminded me too much of the pictures someone was about to take of her, on a slab somewhere – ready for the formal identification.

I shook my head to shoo the thought away.

'Are you okay, darling?' Madison set a hand on my shoulder. I'd almost forgotten she was there. She'd dismissed the woman quickly, though, knowing at a glance that Esther wasn't someone she'd recognised. It took me longer, not because I recognised her, just because I recognised something in her–

'She looks like her, doesn't she?'

My head snapped up to Laing sitting across the table. 'You see it?'

She nodded. 'I think there's a clear similarity between them both.'

'Jada Burns, she looked similar too,' I said and Laing gave a slight nod. 'He has a type.'

'It's too early in the investigation to assume–'

'DS Laing,' Madison cautioned, 'I think Sarah is a little too old to have her intelligence insulted with that line.' She cocked an eyebrow, as though daring the detective to challenge her. But Laing seemed to agree. 'Sarah, darling, do you recognise this woman?' She tapped the corner of a photograph, guiding my attention back.

There were seven pictures altogether, including the work photographs. But apart from the shocking similarity between this stranger and Mum, there was nothing. I shook my head. 'I don't think I've ever met her, no.'

'And you don't recognise the name at all?'

'I can't remember her mentioning an Esther. Her phone,' I looked up, 'did you check Mum's phone, for the name?'

'We'll be looking through any connected cases in the coming days,' she answered, and it felt like a stock response. If I caught a news report on a re-run, I could probably find her saying it again to someone else asking a difficult question. 'Given these obvious similarities, it would be remiss of us if we didn't start to look for connections as early as possible. And given that you're the only witness still...'

'No one saw her?' I latched on.

Laing looked down at the pictures. 'No, it seems she was alone when it happened.'

I'd started to think witnessing a murder was its own death sentence. 'I'm sorry,' I said under my breath. I'd lost count of the amount of times I'd apologised though: for not seeing him; hearing him; saving her.

Madison squeezed my hand under the table. 'What happens now?'

'We'll arrange for the two of you to be taken home. If there's anything else we need, or any questions that arise, then we'll be in touch. I wish there was more we could tell you at this stage.'

'Okay,' Madison shifted in her seat, 'and what happens with Sarah?'

Laing shot a confused look between us. 'I'm sorry, I don't–'

'We may as well call a spade a spade here. There's a guy out there killing women. He's three down now, goody for him, and the one witness to one of the crimes is being left unattended. Does that seem – I don't know, sensible?'

Laing looked like she might smile. 'I understand. Sarah, are you back in college?'

It seemed a random starting point. 'Four days a week.'

'Could we have a rough copy of your weekly timetable, do you think? Times when you're leaving, arriving, when you're usually at home and not. That sort of thing? You're welcome to provide something similar for yourself too,' she said, directing the last offer at Madison. 'The officers won't be intrusive unless necessary, but I'll arrange for a car to drive by at regular intervals throughout the day and night. We've done a good enough job of keeping your name out of the media for the minute, and we'll look to continue that.' She paused and ferreted around the inside pocket of her jacket. She pulled out her business card and snatched a pen from the table. 'You're welcome to call any time, day or night.' She slid the card across to me.

'I've got your business card,' I said, but I took it anyway.

'That's my personal number.' She smiled at me, and then looked back at Madison. The two swapped a knowing glance, as though something inherent, maternal passed between them. 'We're doing everything we can.'

'And we appreciate that,' Madison answered for us.

'But it's still not enough,' I said, as I pushed my chair away from the table. No one corrected me, though, and I thought that must mean I was right.

11

Jessie started collecting me from the bottom of Madison's front garden. She was the only one out of us all who could drive, and despite Landon's attempts at calling shotgun – 'Fuck you, I belong in that passenger seat.' – Jessie had been insistent that I was the one riding to college with her. Each morning she collected me and each morning Madison waved us off, as though they shared a fear of me being snatched away by the bogeyman in the thirty yards from door to gate. Madison blew two kisses – one for each of us – and then closed the door like clockwork. We were ten days into this when I said, 'Aren't we all a bit bored of this now?'

'I'm going to need more.'

'Come on, he isn't coming to get me.'

Jessie looked left, right, left again. She was new enough to driving to still obey all the rules. 'No?' She indicated and pulled out of the sideroad, her car clucking from a lack of acceleration as she moved. 'Tits.'

'You're okay,' I reassured her.

'No, I know.' She smoothed out the drive and switched into third gear. 'So, we know he isn't coming to get you?'

'Exactly.'

'It was a question. Not a statement. How do we know?'

I looked out of the window. I couldn't remember the last time I'd walked down the street without a chaperone. 'Wouldn't he have done something by now? It's been weeks since...' I petered out. It was a hard thing to find the right phrasing for.

'Esther.'

Madison had a calendar on the fridge in her kitchen. The month was laid out all open-plan and easy-to-access, with a box to denote every day. I'd taken to putting crosses through them. She asked one morning whether I did that to keep track of the week. I lied and said yes; said I'd lose track of my college schedule if I didn't have somewhere to look for it every day. But it wasn't a day-by-day tally. It was more like a 'number of days since...' At any given moment I could tell anyone, to the nearest hour, when I'd last seen Mum.

'Hey, you with me?' Jessie clicked her fingers next to my face.

I nudged her. 'Keep your hands on the wheel.'

'We're at a light. Did you hear me?' She didn't wait for an answer. 'I said, just because he hasn't done anything yet, doesn't mean he won't. He hadn't done anything, ever, until he did something to that first woman.'

'Jada,' I filled in her blank. 'The first victim was called Jada.' I'd taken to using their names; to making sure other people did too. It seemed important, somehow.

'I'm just saying,' she rounded the corner into the college car park, 'there's no such thing as too careful, and it isn't like the police are in any rush to catch the bloke.'

'I don't think they're deliberately dragging their feet, Jess.'

She snorted. 'Well they're not winning any sprints either.'

Landon and Tyler were loitering at the edge of the car park, near to the college gates, and I'd never been so grateful to see them. I thanked Jessie for the ride and got out before she had the chance to share anything more. It wasn't that I disagreed with her; I was only tired of talking. Madison had banned television during dinnertime and she'd also taken to talking more and more; although it felt like being spoken at, rather than to. She was encouraging me to see a counsellor, so I could talk, talk, talk until my heart was content. That was another problem, though, how everyone was working so hard to convince me I should have something to say.

Jessie followed quietly and looped an arm through mine when we came to a stop in front of the boys. 'How was the walk in today, chaps?' Jessie asked, smiling.

'Fuck off.' Landon grabbed my arm the other side. 'Comfy seat, was it?'

I laughed. 'The comfiest I've ever sat on.'

Jessie couldn't give me a ride home that afternoon. But I'd deliberately avoided telling Madison that. It wasn't a lie so much as it was an omission; I thought I could get away with it on a technicality, if anything got mentioned. There wasn't anything exciting or dramatic involved in wanting time alone. It really was just that: time alone. I walked the long way home from college and listened to the knock of my footfalls against the concrete, comforted by broad daylight – a time of day when fewer crimes were committed, allegedly – and the sound of no one at all walking behind or next to me. It was such a blissful seventeen minutes that I nearly walked straight past Madison's house.

I couldn't stop thinking of it that way; as hers. It didn't matter how many sleepless nights I had there, or how many meals we cooked together. Although I hadn't been to my actual home since the night Mum died, I knew it was something I'd have to tackle at some point. Madison kept making tactical visits there, though, grabbing things as I needed them, collecting the post and paying the bills.

'We'll tackle it all when you feel ready to,' she'd said.

We hadn't even been able to have Mum's funeral yet; thanks to forensics and body release forms and everything that gets tangled inside the mess of a murder. Cleaning out the house before we'd buried her felt too much like filling over her grave before she was in it.

When I came to a stop at the end of the front garden I realised Madison's car wasn't there. She hadn't said she was working a late shift; or if she had then I'd lost the memory of it. Either way, it seemed wasteful to have a quiet house and not make the most of it, so I decided against walking further. Daylight was dimming out and while I thought everyone was being overdramatic about me being left alone, I couldn't altogether rule out the Average Joe dangers of the world – never mind the witness-to-a-violent-crime dangers.

There was a pile of post to push past when I opened the front door. I hadn't officially moved address, though, so it was unlikely there'd be anything for me. Living at Madison's sometimes felt like living off the grid, which was one of the few positives to it all. I set the letters on the sideboard, dumped my bag by the door and made a beeline for the kitchen. 'Work changed my shifts,' the note on the fridge said, 'have Jessie for dinner.' I laughed at the poor phrasing, pulled the note away from its piercing magnet and dropped it into the bin.

While the kettle boiled I stood with my back to the kitchen wall and watched the doorway. It was easier to listen out once it had whistled to a stop. Between every action I took a deliberate pause: opening the fridge; pause; closing it; pause; walking back to the kettle. It was the only way to keep track of the noises in the house. I paused again after closing the fridge and heard a clunk – something like metal on metal – from somewhere outside the room. I felt for my mobile in my front pocket before I ventured out, looking left and right and left again before treading into the hall. I wondered whether Jessie was this nervous whenever she checked both sides and signalled out of a junction.

I took slow and measured steps back towards the front door. He hadn't exactly used conventional means the last time he'd broken into a house I lived in, so I wasn't sure why the door felt like a safe bet. But when I got there – and I saw the paper lying on the doormat – my breath rushed out and I laughed a little. *It's a flyer.* I leaned down to the pick it up. *It's just a flyer. It was just the letterbox.* And it had just been the metal on metal of the lips closing together, that much was true.

But it wasn't a flyer at all.

12

Sarah,

What a strange note to be writing. I've restarted it ten times over to try to find a good way of beginning but I don't think I'd find one so I may as well be direct and get it all over with. I'm the person who killed your mother. There are some people sick enough to make hoaxes out of these things.

So, so you can be certain, I came in through a window at the back of the house and your mother was in the bedroom. I thought I could hear her sorting through clothes. Then I saw her appear in the crack of the doorway. Only for a second. It wasn't until the police let slip there'd been a witness that I thought it must have been you sorting through clothes that night. It must have been you she whispered to. I'd thought it was panic. That she was talking to herself. Not that that makes much difference I don't suppose.

But look, Sarah, I wanted to write to you to apologise. You haven't told the police what I look like which I suppose means you mustn't know. That's good for us both. It means we can hopefully move on from this. But what happened that night, what I did. I never would have done that if I'd known you were there – if I'd known you were watching. It's a terrible thing to have seen and I'm sorry you had to see it at all. I don't know whether the apology means much.

It won't serve anyone well if you tell the police about the letter, Sarah. They can't find me in a room full of evidence so they won't find me from a slip of paper. But take the apology, would you, and know that I really do mean it.

Look after yourself, Sarah, and let this go.

Sincerely, yours –

PART II

13

Madison made a fuss over things in the same way a mother might.

When she walked into the restaurant it crossed my mind that she might have a date lined up for after our dinner. She was wearing a dress I hadn't seen her in before: floor-length, and sparkly in the right lighting.

Overhead, and trailing slightly behind her, there was a cluster of balloons with 'Congratulations' written across them in different fonts and colours. If it weren't for the beaming smile on her face, I would have dropped my head in embarrassment. But I couldn't recall the last time I'd seen a smile reach her eyes so I thought I'd let her have the moment, even though it was meant to be mine.

The waiter – a young man who looked as startled by Madison's efforts as I felt – took her coat and draped it over the seat opposite me, and then he offered to take the balloons as well.

'Oh,' she said, the smile widening even further, which I wouldn't have thought possible if I hadn't seen it myself, 'they're actually for her. Could you do the honours?' The waiter awkwardly shuffled the balloon ribbons from one hand to the other and back again, as though he either hadn't fully registered or understood the instruction. Madison pulled her chair towards the table and made a wiggling motion with her fingers. 'Tie them to her seat, would you? Then everyone can see.'

Oh yes, please, I thought, *let everyone see*. 'Thank you.' I flashed him an apologetic smile. 'Can we get two glasses of house red?'

Madison snorted. 'Bring a bottle of fizz.' The waiter looked between us; baffled, again. 'Whatever the most expensive thing is,' she added, 'bring that.'

'Thank you,' I said to his back as he left the table. 'Did you take an extra pill today?'

She laughed. 'Rude. Darling girl, we're celebrating.'

'Yes,' I looked up at the balloons, 'so everyone can see.'

'If I can't spoil you now, when can I spoil you?' She reached across the table to grab my hand for a squeeze. 'This is a really big thing for you, you know that, darling.'

The truth was that Madison had been spoiling me for years. This was one in a long line of achievements that she'd wanted to celebrate more than I had. I'd come to think of these small celebrations, though, as a way of thanking her; of letting her see that her efforts at motherhood had paid off – even if I wasn't her daughter.

'You could have invited your friends,' she said, in that same mothering tone she'd used since Mum had died. She'd developed it quickly and I'd wondered whether she'd secretly watched Mum for years, learning the nuances of motherhood. They were different parents completely though; Madison had let me get away with loads more than Mum would have done. There had been times, particularly during my university years, when I'd wondered whether this was how my friends with divorced parents had felt; one always making more allowances than the other to make up for the shortfall of them not being together. Although Madison didn't exactly have the same shortfall to make up for – or another parent to beat.

'I'm seeing them in a few days.' The waiter brought our chilled bucket over with two glasses and I thanked him twice. 'I thought it would be nice to be just us tonight.'

'Well, that's lovely.' She poured a generous helping for each of us. 'To the start of many forthcoming successes.'

'Mad–'

'Ah,' she halted me and wagged a finger, 'my drink, my toast.'

I swallowed a sigh. 'To the start of many successes.'

She took a good mouthful, swilled it around and swallowed. 'How's the new place?'

Since finishing university I'd bought my own flat. Small, but big enough. It had two bedrooms, a spacious kitchen diner, and it was on the penultimate floor of a high-rise in the centre of town. You needed either a key or a code to get through the security doors downstairs; unless it was the weekend, then you needed to get through Barney, the security guard. A handful of months had passed since the purchase and I hadn't done the best job of making the place look like home. Although I had managed to get an office set up.

'It's good, yeah, it's really good. I'm struggling with soft furnishings.'

'Like cushions?'

I laughed. 'More like a sofa.'

Madison looked up from the menu she'd been browsing. 'You're still on the floor?'

'I've moved up from the floor,' I looked down my own menu to avoid eye contact, 'and I've upgraded to meditation pillows.'

'But I bet you've got the damn workspace up and running.'

'I work more than I sit.' When she didn't answer I looked up.

'You need to be looking after yourself,' she said, as though it might not have occurred to me. 'I know a home office is important but you can't drive a car without fuel in the tank, darling girl. Your Mum always said...' she petered out. The mood lighting was enough to cover up any tears forming, but I heard the unmistakeable cluck of a lump in her throat. I reached across for her hand but she pulled it away; she must have been closer to tears than I'd realised. 'Your Mum always said,' she restarted but paused for a big breath, 'you have to look after yourself before you can look after anyone else.'

I smiled. 'She did always say that.' I looked back at the menu to stop my own eyes from giving me away then. 'What do you fancy?'

'Well, he's a bit young but the waiter isn't a terrible idea.' My head snapped up and Madison burst into laughter befitting of a teenager. 'Are you dead from the waist down?'

'It absolutely isn't appropriate for my parent to ask me that.' I tried to keep a straight face, but I could feel my lips lifting at the edges. 'But no, I am most definitely not. He just isn't my type.'

'Well, there's a waitress–'

'Mad.'

She held her hands up in mock surrender. 'Fine, don't talk to me about it.'

'I won't, don't you worry.' I looked down the list of pastas. 'Feed me, would you,' I said, avoiding eye contact, 'this is meant to be a party.'

She topped up my glass. 'Then finish that, and we'll order.'

It was two hours later when we stumbled through Madison's front door; giggling like girls on a prom night. We got through two and a half bottles of bubbles over dinner. The remaining half Madison had brought home, after rushing the waiter through the bill – 'We've somewhere to be, sweetheart, could you move along?' – and then rushing me along the walk back, 'Sarah, you don't want to miss it?'

I hadn't answered – because it hadn't exactly felt like a question – but no, I wouldn't have minded missing it. I couldn't tell her that, though, because over the course of the night – over the excited conversations about 'it' – it had become clear how much this really meant to her.

'Sarah Wainwright, crime reporter extraordinaire,' she muttered as she pushed the front door closed, double locking it behind her.

After getting around to the dinner portion of our night together, I'd been able to tell Madison the full details of my new job; recently acquired at an office block on the other side of the city. The position allowed a lot of movement to surrounding areas, though, and it gave me a good in to be among the earliest people to hear of crimes: spates of robbery; arson; murders. 'I'm so proud of you,' she said, for the twenty-something-th time as she felt around the living room for the television remote.

'I'll get glasses.' I excused myself, in the hope that she might be on a different beat of conversation by the time I got back. By the time I was walking back in, though, Madison was glugging the bubbly straight from the bottle. I spluttered with laughter. 'Classy.' She hiccupped as she took the drink away. 'Classier still.'

'We nearly missed it.' She gestured to the television screen. 'Sit,' she said, 'sit and be excited with me.' When I was next to her she draped an arm around my back and squeezed my shoulder so tight that it hurt. 'I'm so bloody proud of you, darling girl.'

'Mad, really–'

'And tonight on the show...'

'Shush, shush, it's starting.'

'...we've got Sarah Wainwright.' There was background applause. They'd held signs up for the audience to make sure they knew when to be excited. 'Sarah is coming along to talk murder and mayhem with us this evening, and we'll be helping her to celebrate not only the release of her debut book,' there came the stirrings of applause as she said this, 'but also the outstanding success of it, as she celebrates yet another consecutive week on *The Sunday Times'* bestsellers list. Please give a warm welcome to Sarah, everybody!' On cue the crowd went wild and I stepped onto the podium to take my place in the hotseat.

Madison took another sip from the bottle before passing it to me. 'So bloody proud.'

14

If I so much as uttered a syllable Madison silenced me with a raised finger. She didn't want to miss a second of the interview, even though the interviewee was sat next to her. So I watched on in silence while the version of me who'd been made presentable for evening television was probed and questioned by an obscenely beautiful woman, famous for that reason alone, such was her level of attractiveness.

When I'd been introduced to Carolyn – the host of the show, that is – I remember thinking how wonderful it must be to be famous for a pretty face, rather than an ugly past. She greeted me like I was well-known for something worthy. The truth was that I was a local hero for *not* having saved someone I love.

'But wait,' I heard the cries from the Average Joes of the town, 'I'm over here not saving people all the time.' It didn't wash, though, because people had already decided that I was a kind of success story for having survived that night.

'Sarah, it's an absolute joy to have you on the show,' Carolyn started. Madison had the television at a deafening volume. 'And to be celebrating your achievements with you, too, I mean, another week on a bestseller list. I can't even imagine how that must feel?'

My throat clucked as I watched my past self fumble for an answer. 'Well, it's a real honour,' I said, 'and, of course, I think it's a really important thing to get people talking about.' I shook my head lightly, in the past, and cradled my forehead as I watched. 'That is, I think it's important that we keep talking about the case, and the victims, and the fact that–'

'There's still a killer on the loose,' Carolyn finished.

'Exactly.'

Madison reached across to squeeze my hand. 'You're a brave woman.'

'So, Sarah, I know you and I talked about this a little before the show,' Carolyn lied. No one had thought to sit me down and ask what I was and wasn't comfortable talking about. But I was self-aware enough to know that a panic attack on television – even pre-recorded television – wouldn't go down well for anyone involved. I sucked in my breath and let it swell in my chest, not leaving space enough for a flutter of nerves. 'Your mother, I'm sure, would be so proud of all that you've...'

'Did she actually ask if that was okay?' Madison spoke over the television.

'No.' I didn't look away from the screen. 'She wanted a good reaction.'

'Cow.'

'It must have been a difficult book to sit down and spend time with.'

Past-me nodded and flashed a tight smile. 'It was. But I think the thing people really forget about the book, and books like it, is that– is that they're real. This isn't a story, I mean, this is and has been my life for a long time. The other survivors in the book, they've lost people to the same killer, and that's a strange bond that I don't think I've even captured, but – but it's definitely a bond that ties us together somehow.'

To date, I was the only witness. But there had been another three murders since Esther. They were all women of a similar age to Mum; in the right lighting they all even looked similar. The second set of victims had been killed two cities away from us. But the home invasion was the same; the method; the timing; the type. He certainly had a thing for brunettes on the right side of forty. Although he hadn't murdered another mother since mine.

'You spent a lot of time with friends and family members is how I understand it?'

I smiled. 'We joked that it became a support system in lots of ways.' I shook my head; 'joke' hadn't been the right word, but I could remember not knowing a better one at the time. 'I spent time with the family members of every murder victim, yes. I learnt – well, there was a lot to learn about these women as exactly that: women.'

'Was that the aim with the book? To show us who these women were?'

'Who they were, in some ways, but also who they left behind. For a lot of us who have lost people to this– this person, for us there's a hole that can't easily be plugged. We're not talking death by natural causes, which is terrible enough, of course. Instead, though, we're talking about something that disrupts the natural order of things, and those of us who're left, we have to live with that and carry it about on our person and...' I trailed out. Past-me shook her head lightly; I remember blinking back tears. 'It's a heavy thing to spend the rest of your life carrying.'

Carolyn reached over to where I sat opposite her and rested a hand on my knee. 'You're an incredibly brave woman to talk about this, Sarah.'

'Not brave enough,' I said, at the same time as past-me said it.

Madison paused the show. 'Do you really think that?'

'Did you read the book?' I reached over for the remote. 'Let's just watch.'

In the book I mentioned survivor's guilt – a lot. My counsellor had walked me through it several times over; sometimes for the book, sometimes as part of our sessions. A few other friends and family members felt the same, though they hadn't been there when the attacks took place. *Imagine how I feel*, I remember thinking, whenever one of them spoke about how they could have done more – if they'd only been there to stop him. It wasn't ever said with judgement, I knew that much. But I'd be lying if I said it hadn't added to the unshifting weight of having watched her – watched him.

'I think there are a lot of people who would disagree with that.' Carolyn leaned back in her seat and looked down at her cue card. 'Throughout the book you comment on your dealings with the police, as part of your mother's case, but also in terms of you investigating the other victims, too. How was that? Did you find the police co-operative?'

I'd made a nuisance of myself. But I didn't care. 'I pestered them quite a lot for this book,' I said and cracked a smile, to lighten the admission. Laing had stopped answering my phone calls in the end, instead leaving rookie officers to follow up with me. The detectives for the most recent three cases had been co-operative though. I'd even helped them, where I could, by talking to the people closest to the victims. The police got their information and I got mine, so it was a quid pro quo arrangement. But I'd long ago stopped being useful to the police in my own city. 'They've been helpful enough over the years. I think the detectives from the first murders got a little tired of me poking around, but that's what non-fiction writers do, isn't it?

When you're writing the truth, you have to make sure everything is as accurate as it can be, otherwise I'll cause trouble for my publisher.'

Carolyn laughed. 'I imagine you're in quite good standing with your publisher these days, Sarah. They must be delighted with the success of the book as well?'

'They really are. Tina, she's my editor, she's a complete godsend. I can't tell you the amount of midnight phone calls she's had to fence from me, and she dealt with them all like they were nothing. I'm really grateful that I got to work with her.'

'No mention of me?' Madison winked. 'Does Tina know you're on this?'

'Funny. Who do you think arranged it?'

Tina had been the first person to follow up with me about the manuscript. During our first conversation we both cried down the phone – me for Mum; her for the thought of her own daughter – and we'd decided soon after that we'd like to work together. There had been lots of time throughout the writing, editing, publishing where she'd sat me down like a mother might and asked questions only a mother would – 'Are you sure this is a good idea for you?' – and we'd discussed the pros and cons from personal and professional perspectives alike. There had even been a handful of conversations that had involved Madison, too.

Before the final announcements were splashed across newsletters, social media banners, and fuck-knows-where-else, Tina had one final sit-down with me. 'Sarah, honey, think hard about this one. This guy is still out there.' She paused, as though letting the information sink in; like I didn't think this same thing, on repeat, every goddamn day. 'You're sure you want to kick the hornet's nest?'

I'd hugged her close and pressed my answer into her

shoulder. 'More than anything else in the world.' And I'd really meant it.

'Your publisher isn't worried about the implications of the book?' Carolyn asked.

'If I'm not worried, they're not worried, and I'm really not worried.' Past-me flashed a forced smile and I felt my stomach turn over. 'I'm happy to be kicking a hornet's nest if it brings light to this string of crimes, if it does anything at all towards stopping them from happening again.'

'Is that your real hope for the book, Sarah?'

I made a show of thinking about the question. 'My hope is that the police will bring the killer to justice before anyone has an opportunity to write another book.'

'Speaking of which,' Carolyn said, turning sharply away from my answer, 'I've heard on the grapevine that there *is* a second book. Can you confirm or deny that for us?'

'Go on, brag,' Madison said, leaning forwards in her seat.

'There is,' past-me said with a half-laugh. 'It will be a little different to the first book, I should think, or I hope anyway. But there's definitely a second book coming.'

'True crime again?'

'That much I can tell you, yes, it's definitely true crime again.'

'Well, we will eagerly await that next release from you.' She turned towards the camera, then. 'We're going to take a little break now, folks, but when we come back the one and only Sarah Wainwright will be doing a live reading for us, to share a passage from her best-selling true crime release, *Those Who Stay*. Don't miss it.'

Madison snapped the television off. 'You're still not going to tell me?'

'About the new book?'

'Of course about the new book.'

'It's a follow-up, I can't tell you more than that.'

She turned to face me. 'Okay, can you tell me whether it's all safe?'

I rolled my eyes and smiled to make an expression I hoped would look playful – because no, I couldn't tell her it was safe at all.

15

Landon sat next to me with his phone against one ear and his fingertip pressed into the bud of the other, to shield himself from the noise of the restaurant. Tyler, Jessie and I sat in silence while we waited for him to finish. Although from his occasional grunts and 'Hmm' noises it didn't sound as though he was a particularly active participant in the conversation anyway.

In the time he'd been on the phone the three of us had perused our respective menus, swapping only quiet whispers about which pizzas and how many of them we were likely to order. Jessie opened her mouth as though to add another whisper, but Landon held a finger up to shush the noise before it had even arrived. Jessie's eyes spread wide and I spluttered a laugh across the table. It felt like old times, but with alcohol and work phone calls.

'Well, I'll talk to her,' Landon finally said, his tone curt. 'I'm with her right now, actually.' He winked at me and I knew what was coming. 'Well, if you'd let me... Haha, yes... Well, it was a celebratory dinner, not a business... Of course, yep... You too.' He ended the call without the formality of a farewell.

'Jesus H Christ. I'm sorry.'

'We're ordering a spicy vegetable, hot meat, and four cheese for the table,' Jessie announced. 'Tyler wants chicken sticks, too, so...' she petered out, and looked down the menu again. 'I'll order?'

Landon looked at me, then Jessie. 'No garlic bread?'

'Okay, and garlic bread.' She stood. 'Anything else, good sir?'

'No thank you, good woman, that'll be all,' Landon answered, using a tone much more jovial than his telephone voice. When Jessie was out of earshot, Landon leaned in a little closer to me. 'Can we talk work?'

'No,' Tyler answered from across the table. 'We said no work.'

'But I've already taken a call.'

'Exactly. Take a night off, Lan. If Sarah can afford to then you can. Right, Sarah?'

I held my hands up in surrender. 'I'm not involved.'

'For such a controversial writer–' Landon started but stopped abruptly when Jessie hit him round the back of the head with a menu. 'Did you get garlic bread?' He tipped his head back to look at her.

'I hope you choke on it.' She kissed his forehead and then walked round to her own seat. 'Now work stuff is out the way, can we get to the part where we're celebrating achievements? You know, now we're all breaking bread at last.'

'Garlic bread, right?' Landon grabbed his beer. 'I'm not breaking regular bread.'

Jessie carried on as though she hadn't heard him. 'To Sarah, who is, the last I checked, still riding high on the bestseller charts, and who will, I don't doubt, be the best crime reporter this city has ever seen.' She raised a glass, and the men matched the gesture. 'These knuckleheads won't say it, but we're proud of you.'

'Thanks, guys.' I swigged my beer. 'And Landon, cheers to you, as well, for landing the job you always wanted.'

'I wouldn't go that far.' He laughed. 'But I came good in the end.'

'I wouldn't go that far,' Jessie mimicked, and we drank again.

Landon grabbed the baton, then, and added, 'And to Tyler, for finally asking out the girl of his dreams and making a life with her.'

'Well, that was a lot nicer than I expected,' Tyler answered.

'Come on, I'm genuinely happy.' Landon drank at a speed that suggested otherwise but no one commented. 'Is that a joint toast, or do we have to find something good that Jessie has done as well?'

'I'm happy with a joint toast.' She reached across the table to grab Tyler's hand. All of us had bottles of beer to swig from apart from Jessie. I wondered whether she was going to bring it up the next time we were all together. Although by then we might have been on a more child-friendly night out. She glanced my way and I cocked a raised eyebrow at her orange juice and lemonade.

'Congratulations to both of you, then,' I added, and Jessie gave me a quick nod. *So, something good did come out of our teenage years*, I thought...

Over too much food and too many beers we talked about what we'd missed. My news – the job, the book and all – was biggest, but my friends knew not to force the issue of talking about it. Well, Jessie and Tyler did. Landon tried to steer the conversation into work as best as he could, using all of Jessie's bathroom breaks – of which there were many – to ask what my start date was at the newspaper; was I writing the new book to a deadline; was I in the city permanently or would I have freedom to visit crime scenes?

'She'll be creating a crime scene if you're not careful,' Tyler eventually intervened. 'Seriously, Landon, leave it. If you're that desperate to talk to her about work then book a meeting in her billable hours.' He downed the dregs of his drink which gave Landon a second to compose himself. Tyler had never been the outspoken one of us all. *But maybe Jessie is having her influence*, I thought as I threw back the last of my own bottle.

'He's right, you know?' I nudged Landon. 'You can at least talk to me during work hours. Why not take me out to lunch?'

He perked up. 'When?'

'I'll call you.'

'Oh, Sarah Wainwright, you've been dining out on that line for years. I've heard you promise other young sweet boys much the same.'

I smiled. 'Okay, so you call me then.'

'I'll do that,' he leaned in a little closer, 'but so help me you better answer or you'll break my heart.'

'I can see we've reached the portion of the evening where we'll need to separate you two out,' Jessie interrupted us, which was likely a good thing. She slipped her coat off the back of her chair and draped it around her shoulders. 'I got the bill on my way back from the bathroom so we're good to go.'

I grabbed my purse. 'I've got cash.'

'Really,' she held up a hand, 'it's on us. We want to.'

'Can we put you in a taxi?' Tyler shrugged on his own jacket. 'Separate taxis.'

'We can be trusted,' I promised, and Landon laughed. 'I can be trusted.' I closed the space between me and Tyler, and pulled him into a hug. 'Let's not leave it so long next time, okay?' I lowered my voice. 'I don't want you to be a dad before I see you next.'

He squeezed me. 'Thank you, Sar.'

'And you,' I moved away and shifted to Jessie, 'you glorious woman, you. Take care of yourself, would you?' I held on to

Jessie even tighter than I had done with Tyler. 'I'm in the city now, which means I'm only ever a call away, for anything. And I'm excellent at holding hair out of the way while you vomit, from years of arduous practice.'

Jessie smiled and looked behind me, to where Landon and Tyler were saying their goodbyes. 'Don't tell Landon yet? We haven't really told anyone and–'

I held up a hand. 'It won't come up.'

'No,' she smirked, 'I doubt it will.'

'Share a taxi with me?' Landon appeared, then, and squeezed me by the shoulders. 'I promise I won't flirt with you.'

'You're a goddamn liar,' I replied, 'but some company in the taxi is fine.'

It only took minutes for Landon to flag down a black cab; testimony to his time spent navigating big cities, before he'd ended up back at home where he'd started. He waited nearly a full minute before he asked, 'Seriously, can I call you?'

'I can't talk about the second book,' I said, looking out of the window to track our journey.

'What about the first book?'

'Sure, I can talk about that.'

'What about the new job?'

I half-laughed. 'That too. Or at least, I'll talk about it once I've started it.'

'And what about the fact that he waited two years between each set of victims, are you prepared to talk about that?'

'I don't know that I have that much to say about that, Lan.'

'You're a goddamn liar,' he matched my earlier tone.

And of course he was right. With a killer murdering in threes, every two years; with an anniversary around the corner; with no leads, still, since the first set of killings. There was plenty left for me to say.

16

The first day in a new job had always felt to me like the first day at school. Only, at school you can tell a teacher if someone is mean to you. In the workplace, people can be arseholes on the sly and not get caught. I tried to leave my caution in the office doorway though. Madison always told me I was too quick to judge people; she even called me on the walk to work that first day to remind me to be kind, and I wondered whether my new co-workers were getting the same warning from anyone.

I pressed hard on the intercom and spoke to the stranger on the other side. I was partway through explaining it was my first day in the office when she cut across me with the buzz of the door being released. By the time I'd climbed the two flights to the main office, I was more than grateful to see Marcus – a face I recognised from my video interview – was waiting for me there. He held the door open and stepped aside to make way for me.

'Welcome to the inner sanctum.'

Behind the door lay a labyrinth of half-empty desks. The spaces that were occupied were packed full of people making phone calls and typing at such a speed that I expected to see wisps of smoke. Marcus led me through the pathway to the private offices at the far end of the room without anyone giving us a second glance. Before we stepped through one of the open doorways, though, he turned to face the hurried workers.

'Let me do this just once and then you won't have to suffer it all day,' he said, before clearing his throat. 'Folks, gimme a minute of your lives, would you?' Those who were typing, stopped; phone calls were instantly hushed. Marcus' power over the room was impressive. 'This is Sarah Wainwright, she'll be sitting in as the resident crime reporter for the paper from here on. If you need her, she'll be in this back office or she'll be out in the city. If it's the latter, and you need her, her number will be listed in the office directory. Any questions?' He looked from one side of the room to other. There was a hand raised near the doorway we'd only just walked through. 'Shoot.'

'*Those Who Stay*?' the woman asked.

'Yes.' Marcus' tone was neutral. The questioner shrugged and then went back to looking over whatever paperwork was on the desk in front of her. 'Right, have at it.' They all fell back to work and Marcus turned to me. 'This'll be where you're based.'

He led the way into a private office – which hadn't been listed as one of the job perks – and retreated to a corner of the room, as though giving me a minute to enjoy the space. The desk was stripped bare, with no visible marks or indentations on it; I wondered how much action it had seen previously before my appointment.

'I get a new desk in for every writer,' he explained, noting my stare. 'I'm a superstitious kind of editor.'

I smiled. 'You worry about bad writing energy?'

'Something like that. It's a bit like sleeping in someone else's bed, isn't it?'

'I'd never thought of it that way,' I answered, but my attention was already drawn to the walls of the room. There were small collages of newspaper clippings, showing famous stories from the city's history. I scanned the headlines to find the reports I belonged in: 'Mother dies in brutal murder'; 'Town terrified by killing spree'; 'Women warned by police'; 'Killer's cooling off period?'

'Ah, and that's a bit like seeing pictures of someone's ex.'

'You have some interesting analogies for these things.'

'I'm wasted on editing, what can I say?' He followed my gaze over to Mum's claim to fame. 'Bollocks.'

I held up a hand. 'It's okay, really.'

'Well, that's the first cock-up out the way. Why don't I leave you to get settled?' He was halfway to the door already. Mum was never a good topic of conversation for people. 'We've got a staff meeting in about an hour, which will hopefully give you time to get settled in. Is there anything you need?'

'Permission to redecorate?' I smirked.

'Granted. Anything else?'

'I'm good, thank you.'

'Sarah, look, don't think me rude...'

My stomach clenched. In my experience people only ever asked you not to think of them as rude when they were about to say something rude – or offensive. 'Haven't you had enough crime in your life? I mean...' he gestured to the walls. 'You're sure you want to surround yourself with this? This city has seen some stuff.'

I know, I thought, *I'm part of its rap sheet.* 'Whether I work in reporting or not, this is kind of where I've made a home for myself now. What with the book and all.'

'Of course, and the infamous second book.' He flashed a tight smile. 'People have been asking me about it. I think they think because I'm your editor now, somehow I might know more than the average.'

I matched his expression. 'It must get boring having to tell them you're my editor at work and not in writing. Was that everything?'

'Yes, yes, it was.' He turned to leave then and collided with an older man, wearing beige trousers, a grey T-shirt and a bright smile. 'Jesus, Joseph, I didn't see you.'

'They never do!' The man laughed.

'Post for me?' Marcus held out a hand.

Joseph waved him away. 'Post for Miss Wainwright.' He pushed past Marcus and into the room to hand me what looked to be a bundle of envelopes. 'Fan mail?'

I couldn't quite summon a laugh, but I tried. 'Must be.'

'Nice to meet you, Miss Wainwright,' the postman said as he retreated without another word. Marcus gave me a curt nod and then followed out too.

The small bundle of letters I dropped on the empty letter-tray on the corner of my desk. It wasn't uncommon to get letters from readers, although they'd historically been sent to my agent or publisher. But the paper had announced my arrival through their social media channels the week before my start date, so it was hardly a government secret.

While my laptop stirred into life I set about rearranging the headline display on the far wall. Some, I didn't mind keeping. The ones about Mum – about him – I couldn't stand to look at every day. I took them down and leaned them against the wall, facing inward. *Soon*, I thought, *I can throw my own headlines up there*.

The phone on my desk chirped to life and sent me out of my skin. It wasn't often anyone used landlines anymore; I didn't even have one fixed in at the flat. The noise had become alien over the years, so I snatched at the handset to bring it to a stop.

'Sarah Wainwright's office.'

There was nothing, only dead air. I sucked my breath in to see whether I could find background noise and there, faintly, there was the in and out breath of whoever had called me. I slammed the receiver back into its cradle and thought, *you don't quite get that satisfaction with an iPhone.* When the phone rang again seconds later, though, I was resentful of not having a caller ID feature to fall back on. I tried for a neutral voice when I answered; experience had taught me that these people usually thrived on hearing you were aggravated.

'Sarah Wainwright's office.'

'I'm calling to discuss details of a crime,' Landon's voice came through the earpiece.

'And what might that be?'

'It's a crime that after a quick peck on the cheek in that taxi, you haven't so much as text to check on me and my broken heart.'

'You're being dramatic.'

'This is me being sincere.'

'Then we may have worked out why you're single.'

'I'm single because I'm hankering after you all the time, Sarah.'

I dropped into my office chair. 'Now, is *that* you being sincere?'

'Come on, Wainwright, give me some credit.'

'I'll give you credit when you earn it. Take me to lunch?' I checked the time. It was short notice but I reasoned that if Landon was desperate enough to impress his boss then he'd make it work.

'Where will I meet you?'

'Front of my office.'

'One thirty?'

'Perfect.'

'Can we talk about the second book?'

'Landon–'

'Off the record?'

'We can't talk about it, full stop.' I hung up, then, to punctuate my point. I couldn't have told Landon – or anyone else, for that matter – about the second book, because I hadn't written it yet. I'd been working on it quietly since the first one hit the bestseller list. But even my publisher hadn't pushed the issue. 'You're a hit, kid, we trust you,' they'd said, which was a relief, given that they'd bought an unwritten book about a string of murders that hadn't happened yet. But I knew they would. Because he'd told me.

17

2012

Sarah,

I promised myself I wouldn't do this again. Write to you, that is. I always knew there'd be more women. After the first – after, well, you know. I always knew it was something I'd do. It was like, Sarah, when you try a new flavour of ice cream or a different type of drink. You expect to turn your nose up at it but the reality is so, so far from that. Instead of turning your nose up it turns out, instead, to be the best flavour of anything you've ever tasted. But at the same time you don't want to taste too much of it because then maybe you won't enjoy it all that much. So you ration yourself, sensibly, to having the ice cream once every couple of years. You know what it's like when you get a taste for something, though, Sarah, and it's suddenly all you want.

There's talk of a book. They're only rumours, Sarah, I know. But I don't know that I know you well enough yet to know the truth in them. Would you write about me? Maybe not. But you'd probably write about your mother. Maybe you'll write about these women, too, Sarah. God forbid, but maybe you'll write about the next ones – and the ones after.

Or maybe they'll catch me first. But I don't know about that one.

The thing is, Sarah, whether they catch me or not, whether it's these women or the next, it feels a lot like you're the only person who really knows me. Maybe that's because you're the only one to see me at my worst? God. There are a lot of maybes here, Sarah. Whatever the truth, thanks for letting me be honest with you.

Remember what I said about the police and the letter, won't you? They won't find anything on the women; a slip of paper won't be the thing to break the case.

Look after yourself, Sarah. Be seeing you.

Sincerely, yours –

18

2014

It had been two years since that second letter, but I carried the memory of it still. It had arrived a week after they found the sixth victim, and I didn't talk to anyone for four days, not even Madison. It took me a while to decide what I would do with it. I'd never told anyone about the first that he'd sent. Telling people about the second would have opened up questions that I didn't have answers for.

The letter had been hand-delivered, like the first, to Madison's house; the same address I'd been registered to since Mum had died, although I'd been living in student accommodation for most of that year. Madison set it to one side for me: 'Stamped but not franked. You should steam that off.' I'd known from the handwriting. But I'd learnt to keep a better poker face than most. I joked about her stinginess and kept the letter until I was alone. Lifting the lip of the envelope and unfolding the paper felt like an act of intimacy, and I'd hated it. I'd stashed the words back inside their casing and sandwiched that between the pages of a book, to make a pressed confession of it. He'd set a precedent in writing twice. When he told me he'd kill again, I believed he'd write again, too.

The job at the paper was everything I'd wanted it to be. I started every morning with a bulletin in my email inbox, compiled mostly by members of the team. They sent over ideas, police reports and rumours, and then I was free to launch myself into which ones were worth covering and which weren't. I quickly struck up connections with crime reporters in the surrounding areas, too, including smaller print papers in the city and one or two new connections a few cities over.

'You're making contacts already?' Marcus asked during a team meeting.

'I've got a friendly face,' I replied, with the most deadpan expression I could muster. 'It'll help to know what's happening elsewhere in the city, to make sure we're covering everything. Outside of the city is just a bonus.'

'Okay. Next.'

It had only been a few weeks but Marcus had already taken to leaving me to my own devices. I'd only had one word of caution after I had allowed an intern to put together a small piece on the statistics of violent crime in the area: 'Remember our readership, Sarah. Sometimes grisly doesn't sell.' But, despite what Marcus might have believed about the paper's audience, there hadn't been any complaints. In my experience of writing, violence sold well.

When I powered down at the end of my second Saturday, I hit the speed dial key for Madison's number to talk to her on the way home.

She answered on the third ring. 'Darling girl, I thought I'd lost you.'

I laughed. 'I'm sorry. It's been so busy, Mad, that's all.'

'Are you happy?'

'Straight to the point.' I crossed the road to avoid a man head and shoulders taller than me with his face hunched out of view. 'I'm fine.'

'That isn't what I asked.'

From the background I heard the murmur of another voice. 'Hey, are you busy?'

'I've got a friend over. I can talk, darling girl, I'm fine to talk.' She lowered her voice. 'I've been thinking, what with the anniversary coming up...'

I'd lost count of the people who'd tried to have this conversation with me. Madison had been the first, two weeks ago via a text message that I'd ignored. Landon brought it up most often out of them all, but at least I knew he had his reasons. After our lunch together we decided to hang fire on a formal interview until the week of the anniversary. It was a callous suggestion on his part but also a completely understandable one. Besides, it was easier to make business out of Mum's death than it was to make a reality of it.

'...what do you think?'

I'd completely missed her idea but, 'If that's what you want.' I fumbled in my coat pocket for my door fob, and then my key. 'I'm just walking into my building.'

'I'll stay on the phone.'

'Really, Mad, I'm fine,' I lied. Unlocking the front door and going into an empty flat still unnerved me, for fear of it not being empty at all. But I'd begged so many phone calls from Jessie in the last two weeks, to avoid this scared loneliness, that I thought it would be a bold move on my part to at least try. 'Text me tomorrow.'

'Will you reply?'

'Love you.'

'Love you, darling girl.'

I distracted myself with thoughts of Madison's company – male, female, romantic or otherwise – while I climbed the stairs to home. The alarm chirped when I opened the front door and I quickly keyed in the digits of the date when Mum and Madison met, to silence it. I slammed the door, bolted the locks, and wedged the key back on the inside hole. The reason was two-fold: I could unlock and leave quickly if I needed to; but no one could force the lock without forcing the keys to drop, and clang, from the inside of the door. Living alone was fine and all, but measures had to be taken.

I held my breath tight in my chest while I stepped quietly around the flat, opening doors one by one before peering behind them, lest any cartoon villains be folded out of view. My bedroom was the last space I checked. There wasn't much to look over, though, given that the room comprised of four walls and a bed. I didn't have a wardrobe. So unless the killer was small enough to origami himself into the drawer of a bedside table, I reasoned I was safe.

With the overhead light blaring, leaving no corner unlit, I landed heavy on the bed and let go of my breath. The last picture that Madison took of me with Mum was on my bedside table, and I grabbed it for our nightly talk. Every evening I filled her in on the latest adventures around the city, most often detailing small-time crimes and petty thefts.

'I still haven't found him,' I said at last, rubbing a thumb over her smile. *I can't believe it's been four years since I heard you laugh.* She was mid-giggle in the image. I could never remember what we'd been laughing over, although I'd spent hours trying to. I set the frame back on the table, weighing down the flattened letters that lived underneath it. I liked to keep everything close. 'Maybe tomorrow,' I said, half-speaking to Mum still, but also to myself, as though making the promise into an affirmation. 'Maybe tomorrow I'll find him.'

On my way out of the room I hovered over the light switch, but I decided to leave the space illuminated for later – just in case.

19

Eleanor the Intern – her full name around the office – appeared in my peripheral vision. I was halfway through typing a long email to a self-proclaimed super-fan, and I reasoned that Eleanor was a patient enough teenager to wait for me to finish. She cleared her throat three times; the fourth time turned into a full cough. But I was finishing up the final paragraph – about how nice it was to hear from fans, and how it wasn't at all strange when they went to the effort of tracking down my work email, only I back-spaced to delete that final part – so I raised an eyebrow and carried on. When I hit the send icon I blinked hard, as though clearing my eyes of something, and then turned.

'Thanks for waiting, Eleanor. Did you need me for something?'

She flashed a sweetheart smile. I wondered whether she was flattered that I knew her name. 'I'm sorry, Sarah, I know you're busy.' I waved the comment away – even though we both knew the truth of it – and her face became more serious then. 'But there's a police officer here to see you.'

There was a shift in my gut somewhere. 'I'm sorry,' I looked down at my diary, 'I don't think I have anything...'

'No, no, she said you weren't expecting her.'

She. 'Did you get a name, by any chance?'

'DS Brooks. She said you'd remember her.'

I did remember her; only she'd been DC Brooks when I'd known her. During the months of putting together notes for *Those Who Stay*, Brooks had been the only person to return any of my phone calls. We weren't friends, of course, but she'd never shied away from talking things through with me either. 'It strikes me that you're a good person to be on good terms with,' she said once during a telephone interview, and I thought the same about her. I suppose we'd both had our reasons. After the second lot of murders had taken place, though, I'd pestered different police stations, different officers. Brooks and I hadn't had enough in common to cover us for any more phone calls.

'I do.' I pushed myself away from my desk and smoothed down my shirt. 'Point her in my direction, would you, Eleanor?'

'Sure thing. Tea, while I'm on my travels?'

I smiled. 'Did anyone tell you yet how great you are today?'

Eleanor let out a nervous laugh. 'You're the first.' She disappeared, then, and I found the time to read another email – not a fan this time, just a concerned citizen – before Eleanor reappeared with Brooks lingering behind her. 'I'll just grab your drinks,' Eleanor said, as she stepped aside to let the officer into the room.

I stood and extended a hand. 'Detective Sergeant Brooks.' I leaned on the *sergeant*. 'You've moved up in the world. Take a seat?' I gestured across the desk, and she landed hard in the visitor's chair.

'Recent promotion.' She looked awkward at the mention of it. 'You haven't done too bad yourself, though, Sarah. Crime reporter at *The Herald*. How did that happen?'

I shrugged. 'It was something I was quietly working towards.'

'I would have thought this was the last place you'd want to be.'

'The city, or the crime desk of a newspaper?'

'Both, maybe. But you're happy here? It's early days, I know.'

'I'm comfortable enough. How about you? You're happy at work?' She threw me a quizzical look. 'I thought, if we were making small talk, it was only right for me to ask. You'll have to forgive me, I can't remember what your home situation was. Partner, kids, cat?'

Brooks laughed. 'Okay, Sarah, you've got me. I have good reason for being here.'

'Colour me shocked.'

'It's been nearly two years.'

'It's been nearly four,' I corrected her. 'But go on.'

'I mean, since the last... We have no reason to think he'll hit this city again. It might be that he doesn't attack anyone, at all, this time around. But it would be remiss if we didn't check in with you, given that you're working here full-time now, and living alone.'

'How do you– Do you know what, never mind. You're the police. I guess it's your job to know these things. It hasn't escaped my attention, though, and I know there's no need for me to get complacent with my safety. I promise that if I see him about to kill someone, this time I'll call on the right side of the crime.'

'Sarah, I–'

'I know. You didn't mean to cause offence.' An awkward beat of something passed between us. 'DS Brooks, can we be balls on the table honest?'

She looked taken aback by the phrasing. 'It'll make life easier.'

'I really don't think I'm in any danger, whether he hits the city again or not. He's had ample opportunity in the last four years to make himself known to me and he hasn't.' My stomach let out a hungry moan, as though reacting to the lie. 'He would have said by now, don't you think, if he were going to be a danger to me?' Even I couldn't tell whether it was gutsy rhetoric on my part or whether I was actually asking for reassurance.

She looked like she was weighing the options up.

'But, to set your mind at ease, I'm very careful, all the time. I'd explain the security measures of my building, but it sounds like you may already know them. I work all the hours that God sends, in an equally secure building. When I'm not working, I'm usually fencing phone calls from friends to let them know I'm okay. Honestly, this man started and finished with me the night he killed Mum.'

But she didn't look convinced. 'Okay, Sarah.' She pushed up from her seat. 'You know where I am if you need anything, though, okay? That's all I really wanted to remind you of.'

'Does that include an interview?' I asked and she smirked. 'If he happens to wind up back in the city for any reason, and you happen to be the big chief that cracks the case.' Her smirk cracked into a laugh then. 'I'm serious, DS Brooks, you're on the frontline of all this if he does end up back here.'

'Which you're certain he won't.'

'But you think that he might,' I tried, and from the shift in her expression I could see I was right. It had been a half-guess, based on her unscheduled visit to me at work. Something must have set her on edge, though, I reasoned; I just didn't know what. 'Is this all to do with the anniversary, or is there more to this?'

'Are you asking as a crime reporter?'

'No,' I snapped, 'I'm asking as the only surviving witness to an unsolved murder.'

She rubbed at the back of her neck and dropped her eyes.

'Sarah, when the anniversary of a crime is coming up, all sorts of crazies come pouring out of the woodwork.'

'It's a good job you were on hand to tell me that because otherwise...'

'Fair point. But I more meant that whatever evidence we think we've come by in the last few weeks, it could be nothing at all to do with the crimes themselves and everything to do with the time of year.'

'So there is evidence?' I latched on. Brooks rolled her eyes. 'Come on, who are you worried about? Laing?'

'Laing doesn't know I'm here.'

'Oh.' I stood and stepped around my desk to close the gap between us. 'So, you're secretly looking out for my well-being nowadays?'

'I didn't say that. I just said Laing doesn't know I'm here.' She took a step back as though to put a healthier space between us. 'I wanted to touch base with you before the anniversary. There is a lot of talk between police stations and teams at the minute. Everyone is on high alert for anything that might happen. You don't– Sarah, you don't have to trust us all the way because I know we're likely not your favourite people, but you need to know we're here for you. I'll tell you as much as I can, but it has to work both ways, you understand?'

Like a guilty teen, my knee-jerk reaction was to ask her what she knew. But I bit back on the panic and only agreed. 'Of course. It has to work both ways.' Then, when she back-stepped again, I added, 'So, what can you tell me?'

It brought a smile, at least, which cracked the growing tension. 'I wish we could part ways on something substantial but there really isn't anything out of the ordinary, given the time of year. We've honestly got nothing more than breathy phone calls and boastful letters.'

'Letters?' I tried to sound neutral. 'People are writing to you?'

She shook her head. 'It's crap, Sarah, really it is. There's nothing to suggest any of these letters are worth a stamp.'

I formed a tight O with my lips and exhaled slowly, to make a show of steadying myself.

'Some of them are horrifically detailed but grossly inaccurate; some of them read as bonkers but mad polite.'

The breath froze on its way out of me.

'"I knew I'd do it again,"' she mimicked, '"and there'll be more to come still. Yours sincerely," yada, yada.'

'Yours sincerely?' I asked. 'You're certain?'

Brooks looked questioning again. 'I'm certain of "yours sincerely"?'

I tried to edit my enthusiasm, or at the very least direct it towards the right thing. 'You're certain there's nothing to them, I meant.'

'Sarah,' she took on a tone that was somehow both friendly and patronising, 'here's how I think of it. If a killer got away with six murders, how likely is it that he'd go ahead and send a letter to the police that are hunting him?'

Seconds rolled by and I sensed she was waiting for an answer. But I only shrugged, and thought, *Maybe as likely as he is to go ahead and write to his only living victim...*

20

"'The police found different ways of asking me the same question. I found different ways of not answering. Although I didn't realise, as a teenager, that this back and forth with the case would be something that I'd carry into adulthood, too. The officers often explained that they were trying their best and I explained their best was never good enough. It was unreasonable of me. But the left behind relatives of murder victims tend to be unreasonable in lots of ways that I came to learn – from my own behaviours, that is, and from the behaviours of the kind individuals who I spent time with throughout the makings of this book. All of us have suffered a violence that, no matter the police work, isn't something to be detained and taken away from us. For the rest of our lives we'll live with the absence of the person who was murdered. If the man responsible was caged, somehow, I'm sure we'd all sleep a little easier. But it wouldn't fill the spare room, or the other side of the bed – or the empty space in graduation photographs that Mum should have been in.'" I took a deliberate pause to mark the end of the reading, and then flicked through the pages of my well-worn book to look for the next sticky note.

'I'll read something from later in the book, too, if that's okay?'

'Please do,' Landon answered. He leaned back in his chair as though preparing himself for a perverse story-time.

I cracked the spine a little further and spread the pages. '"Mum was a riot. I know that a lot of people say that about people they love, but she really was. She'd love to know that I'm describing her like that, too. She spent most of her life trying to be the soul of a room and it wasn't until she was gone that I realised the extent to which she'd managed that. Madison and I often talk, even now, about the space in a room. We don't mean it in a physical way either; metaphysical, maybe. It's easy to imagine, still, how Mum might howl with laughter or cry with empathy; the inappropriate joke she'd tell at exactly the right time, or the way in which she'd waltz in with more food, wine and cheer than necessary (and that wasn't a Christmas thing, but an any-excuse thing). For the man who did this, he was acting on an urge. He saw something – or rather, someone – who he wanted, and he went out of his way to take that person. For those left behind, though, that is, for those of us who stayed, he took away so much more."'

There was dead air for so long after I'd finished reading that I wondered whether Landon was expecting more. I chanced a glance at him and noticed he was staring at nothing at all, his eyes fixed at a random spot on the desk. I cleared my throat to catch his attention and he looked up, then.

'I hit the pause button,' he explained. 'I thought you might need a minute.'

Or you might need a minute. 'Are you okay, Lan?'

He smiled. 'She was just a bloody brilliant woman, wasn't she? Like, Jesus.' He ran a finger under each eye as though clearing away tears. 'She was always the fun one, from all of our parents. I remember rocking up at yours once when I was –

Christ, maybe no older than fifteen. Mum and Dad had argued like buggery, and I'd necked more vodka than I knew what to do with, and not once did she mention grassing me in for that. She welcomed me in, sobered me up, told me to stay the night and packed us both off to school the next morning like it had been any other sleepover.'

I half-laughed. I could remember that night, too. 'She was good like that.'

'Do you need a break?'

'I'm fine,' I lied. But these readings required a good game face, even around the likes of Landon. 'Do you need a break?'

'I'm best just to power through. I can get myself good and drunk after.' He tried to laugh but the sound cracked in his throat. 'So, the good thing about pre-recorded shows is that we can patch all this together. The first reading will open the show, then the interview, then the second reading.'

'And that'll air tonight?'

He nodded. 'It has to be, because of the content. But we'll be uploading the readings to the website and rolling them out across the podcast platform, too.' I raised an eyebrow at the organisation; it looked strange on Landon, who had once somehow managed to forget his own birthday. 'I'm trying to impress my boss,' he admitted. 'My ratings haven't been great, and I want to get bumped to a daytime show.'

I readjusted the over-sized headphones I was wearing. 'So, let's do this.'

He held three raised fingers to count us back into the recording and we picked up as though the first reading had only just happened. Landon asked about the missing mother in life events, how you learn to manage that reality – assuming you ever do. For the first five minutes of the interview he managed to tread across relatively safe topics. He steered talk towards the policing of the case and I huffed into the microphone.

'I know it may not sound like it from some of the tones in the book,' I started, 'but I do genuinely believe the police have done their utmost to catch this man.' I thought back to my talk with Brooks; how good it would be to have her on side for whatever might happen next. 'They're treading unfamiliar waters, like everyone else involved in this situation, and catching a killer isn't a daily event for any police department.'

'Of course. But we're four years on now, Sarah.'

I smiled. 'That isn't a question. But yes, we're four years on. I don't think anyone has forgotten that, or overlooked it. The police are still trying their best, though, regardless of the timeline they're working with.'

'Speaking of time,' he said, already sounding too pleased, 'can we talk a little more about the time of year?'

'Mum's anniversary?' I asked, and I could see it had thrown him. 'The anniversary of the killings, that is. I realise it isn't just Mum's death that happened around this time.'

'Well, that's where I'm leaning here. We're fast approaching the two-year mark. Three murders in year one; three murders two years later. We're another two years on and no closer to knowing who this man is, or where he's likely to hit next. Do you have any theories?'

'On the location, you mean?'

'Exactly. Should we expect him to make a comeback in Birmingham, for instance?'

'I don't think we have any reason to expect that,' I answered, but quickly added, 'although no one expected for a serial killer to cut his teeth here the first time around. So, our expectations of this man are a little out of sync with his behaviours already.'

'Colour me an optimist, but is there a possibility that there won't be an attack at all?'

I scrunched my face up. 'What do you think, Landon? Is he likely to give up?'

'Quit while he's ahead?'

I'd spent the lonely hours of insomnia wondering similar things. A sane person couldn't rationalise the actions of the insane. But I couldn't think of a good reason why he'd give up the game when he was so far ahead. 'Only if he wants to be chased,' I eventually answered. 'If he wants to be chased then he likely feels quite unfulfilled by the fact that no one has found him, or is even close to finding him.' I thought back to the letters, then; how he'd asked me, both times, not to share them with the police. 'If being caught was something that bothered him that much, though, then he would have made it easier for the police.'

Landon half-laughed. 'Is that how serial killers work?'

'Some of them.' During my months of writing and researching I'd stumbled across records for serial killers in all shapes and flavours. Some of them desperately wanted to be caught. 'Some of them do sincerely want to be left alone to go about their business. They're happy with no one noticing them, and they're certainly happy with no one tracking them.'

'Which brings us back to the possibility of more murders.'

'Landon, look,' I took on a firmer tone, 'if I knew where this guy was going to hit next then I'd be at the police station now putting pins on a map. The fact is – well, the sad fact that is, none of us know when or if he'll hit next, and that's why we need to stay vigilant. Sometimes killers get cocksure, they branch out, they try on different areas; sometimes they don't.' I took a deep inhale to steady myself. 'Sometimes they come home.'

'And that sounds like a good time for a break to me, folks. We'll be right back with more from Sarah Wainwright after this short interval.' He held up three fingers again to count us out and then pushed away his headset, leaving it to hang around his neck. 'Sometimes they come home?' he asked. 'Is that a serious worry you've got?'

'Lan, come on. Up until five years ago Mum being murdered wasn't a serious worry.' I sometimes forgot that the honesty you feel comfortable sharing post-trauma isn't always the honesty people are comfortable hearing. 'What the hell do I know anyway?' I added, to try to undercut my own authority. 'This guy could have fallen off the face of the earth months ago, two years ago. Maybe six is his lucky number and he'll stop there.'

'Sure.' Landon picked up his headphones and set them level on each ear. He held up three fingers again and on the count of two said, 'I'm just hoping his lucky number isn't nine.'

21

It was my first time sharing Mum's anniversary with an office full of people. Marcus asked if I was okay once every three hours, while everyone else seemed determined to avoid me entirely. There were hushed whispers at the coffee machine, and tentative offers of letting me pass through doorways ahead of people, as though the slightest misfortune in an average day might send me spiralling. But I'd been preparing for this event since it had happened the year before. It never exactly came as a surprise. What came as a surprise was how quiet the surrounding cities were. I'd had a handful of emails about memorial pieces; things that other journalists wanted me to go on the record for.

Though I kept an ear to the ground, there didn't look to be anything in the way of new incidents. And the closer we got to Mum's anniversary, the more my stomach shifted at the thought that he really might not come back for another spate – even though I knew that should be a source of comfort rather than loss.

I was looking out over the bustle of the office when the knock at the door came. 'Got a minute?' Connor asked. He was,

I'd guessed, at least ten years my senior and still in a job well beneath my rank. But there wasn't a hint of awkwardness about him, and I was thankful for that.

'Pull up a pew. What's the news?' I nodded to the seat opposite mine. 'Something exciting happening in the human-interest archives?' Connor was one of many journalists who seemed to catch the easier goings-on around the city. This was the first time he'd had anything to do with the crime office, and I was intrigued. But it didn't take a genius…

'I'm just going to come out and say it.' He avoided eye contact. 'It would be remiss of us not to run an anniversary piece. We do one every year, our competitors in and around the city are running pieces, and you're tied to the crimes. If we don't do one, then–'

'It looks as though you're changing habits for me,' I finished.

'Am I an arsehole?'

I laughed. 'For this? No. But I don't know what you're like out of work.' He looked taken aback by the joke. 'That wasn't a proposition.'

'I'm not offended, if it was.' His tone was more playful, less worried. 'Seriously, though, the memorial piece. It completely falls within our remit; no one is expecting you to write this thing yourself. I more just wanted to check you didn't have any strong feelings against us covering it?'

I rolled the idea around in my mind. 'It would give us an edge if I wrote it.'

'I– ah – okay, sure. That isn't why I came in here.'

I put my hands up in a show of surrender. 'You're welcome to take the piece, especially if it's something you usually do. But, if anyone is going to commodify tragedy, I feel like morally I'm allowed to.' The suggestion had clearly caught him off guard. In my experience, people were always surprised when you looked to gain something from a shitty thing happening to you. But if anyone had the right to gains, I firmly believed it was me. 'Talk to Marcus? Sit on the idea for a bit. It won't take me long to write, so just let me know before the day is out.'

He rubbed at the back of his neck. 'I'll double check with Marcus.'

'Good idea,' I replied, as though it was his original thought. 'Anything else?'

'Only...' he drifted out. 'If you ever want to know what a nice guy I am outside of work, give my extension a dial?'

I laughed so he knew what a funny suggestion it was. Before I could think of a half-decent put-down, though, my desk phone rang and I was grateful for it. 'I'm sorry, I should take this,' I gestured to the handset, 'thanks for checking in with me about this, though, Connor.' He scooted out of the office with a soundless goodbye as I snatched up the phone. 'Sarah Wainwright's office.' Static crunched through the speaker. There had been three non-phone calls in the days before, with nothing more than static and heavy breathing, and I wondered whether this might be number four. I cleared my throat. 'Sarah Wainwright speaking. Can I help you with something?'

'Sarah...' a voice crackled out. 'Sarah, can you hear me okay?'

'Who's calling, please?' I pushed.

'Sarah, it's Therese Brewer from *The Chronicle*.' A newspaper two cities across the country from mine, Therese had been the first female crime reporter to comment on *The Herald's* social media update announcing my arrival. She and I had instantly bonded over Facebook and shared misogynistic tales in real-time as we encountered them. In other words, she was a friend. 'Can you hear me okay?' I could hear the hiss and spit of action unfolding in the background. 'Sarah?'

'I can hear you, just about. Is everything okay?'

'Sarah, they've found a body.'

The newspaper hadn't run an advertisement about my deep-rooted interest in deaths around the area. But I'd confided in Therese more than once that I was looking for leads on a new wave of killings. I'd told her in confidence, but I reasoned it wasn't the worst information to have floating around either.

'Is it him?'

She hesitated. 'It really is too soon to tell. The police are being very guarded about it.'

'When did they find her?'

'About four hours ago. I called as soon as I could. There's still a lot of action happening at the scene itself. I'm still here. I– I didn't know whether to call.'

'You did the right thing.' I glanced at the bottom corner of my computer monitor. *Not quite clockwork*, I thought, *but the date's a near enough match*. 'I know this is your patch,' I said, feigning apology in my tone, 'but is there any chance at all I could pop over?'

She let out a half-laugh, something closer to a sigh. 'Why do you think I called?'

Therese handed over the details and I scribbled each one across a series of Post-its. There were four stapled together by the time we got off the phone. I told her I'd power down at work and hit the road as early as I could; she said to call when I got there. It would be our first time meeting in person and somehow the circumstances didn't seem surprising.

While my computer blinked into sleep, I threw everything marginally important into my bag and made for the door. Connor – as though he'd been outside, waiting – was the first body I collided with.

'Shit, sorry, Sarah.'

'Were you– did you listen?' I asked, gesturing behind me.

'No, God no. I was on my way back into you. About the memorial piece–'

'Take it,' I interrupted. 'Honestly, it's yours.' I side-stepped him and headed for the door, but over my shoulder I added, 'Thanks for the opportunity, and for – you know, at least mentioning it to me.' I didn't wait for a response, only pushed hard against the swing door to the office and rushed to the stairs. I really was grateful for the opportunity to write about Mum, always. But I couldn't pass up the chance to write about the next one.

22

'Madison, I'm sorry, I don't think I'll make it home for dinner.' I called her from the traffic jam between cities.

'What's the story?'

I told her I wasn't ready to say. 'It'll jinx my chickens if I talk about it.'

She laughed. 'I'm not sure that's the saying but okay. Text me when you're home?'

'Of course,' I said, though I had no idea when I'd make it back.

I'd been stuck in traffic for twenty-eight minutes when I realised I'd been sitting in silence, stewing. I turned on the radio but it didn't offer much respite, with one channel talking about a spate of thefts in the local area – wherever that was, off the motorway – and the next cut in with the best and worst of the 1980s, although I opted for the latter when the rest of the channels gave out nothing but static. When 'Never Gonna Give You Up' was cut through with the sound of my mobile ringing through the car system, I let out a huff of air that I hadn't known I was holding.

'Sarah Wainwright,' I answered because I was technically on the clock.

'Hi, Sarah. Marcus here from *The Herald*. I've got a story for you.' The huff of air was back in my chest but it was nerves this time; I knew what was coming. 'It might be something or nothing, but I've got a missing crime reporter. You wouldn't happen to know anything about that, would you?'

It was hard to gauge his tone, so I went straight in on the defence. 'Boss, I'm so so–'

'Sorry, yeah, I guessed that much. Seriously, though, Sarah, where the hell are you?'

'I got a tip about a new story and I got carried away with myself.' The traffic edged forward another couple of metres. 'I'm so sorry, I should have stuck my head in to say. I got carried away with Connor and then this call came in.'

'Wait, is Connor with– no, ignore me. I can see him through my office window. Have you got Connor working on something?'

'The memorial piece for the city murders.'

There was a long pause and I guessed Marcus didn't quite know what to say. 'Was that his idea or...'

'The story was his idea. He offered it to me initially, but then this call came in.' I checked my watch. 'I might not be back before the office shuts today but I'll be there bright and early tomorrow morning, and I can fill you in on everything then.' I had no idea whether I was even telling the truth, but I needed to give him something.

Marcus fidgeted about on the other end of the phone. I imagined him slumping himself down at his desk, tallying up the different ways he could reprimand me. 'Is this anything to do with the body they just found over in Coventry?'

'You've heard.'

'The editor for *The Chronicle* called me.'

I hadn't worked in the industry for long. But I was fast

learning you couldn't swing a stick in journalism without taking someone's knees out. 'Therese from *The Chronicle* called me. She and I have been swapping emails for a bit about the crime desk and–'

'Look, Sarah, it's good that you're making connections, and I think it says a lot that someone from a city over would throw you a tip like this.'

But... I thought, waiting for the catch.

'But, firstly, you can't go off half-cocked without telling someone where you're going. Leave a Post-it on my office door next time as a courtesy at least, would you?'

'I will, I definitely will and–'

'I'm not done,' he cut across me. Marcus hadn't struck me as the stern kind. I wondered whether he was rushing through the reprimand, then, to try to get it over with as quickly as possible – for both our sakes. 'You also can't go off half-cocked on a story that doesn't concern us yet. It isn't inner city, and we haven't even had confirmation of whether this is part of the city murders string or not.'

You've guessed, then. I felt like a child who'd been caught out; although it hadn't exactly taken a genius. 'You should have waited until there was more information available, and next time, you need to. You get that, right?'

I sighed. 'I do, Marcus. I absolutely get it. I am genuinely sorry. This is my first rodeo, but I should have known better than to dash off on half a story and the off-chance.'

'I really hate being the mean angry boss, so let's not make this a grovelling thing.' His tone was softer then. 'What do you know already?'

'As much as you do, by the sounds of things. They've found a body.'

He was quiet for a beat longer than I expected. I wondered whether the signal had fizzled in the ten metres I'd managed to crawl forwards. But then he asked, 'You think it's him, don't you?'

'Yes.' I answered on gut feeling. The truth was, I had no evidence to suggest it was him. But I also didn't have evidence against it either. It was the right time of year; a close enough city; Therese obviously thought there was something to it for her to have called. But none of that reasoning would hold logic, I knew. 'Marcus, I'm running out on a chance here but when Therese called I just got caught up in the– I don't know, in the development. Not really a development.' For someone who made a living from words, they were all escaping me. I took a deep pull of air. 'I got carried away.'

'Yeah, you did.' He stopped but I sensed there was more coming. 'Sarah, I'm about to ask a question that you absolutely don't have to answer. But as your boss, I feel entitled to at least throw it out there. You with me?'

There was a knot in the base of my belly, creeping toward my thighs. 'Yes.'

'Are you in this job so you can find him?'

Yes.

When I'd told Madison that I wanted to move into journalism – specifically crime – she'd asked a similar question, only she'd phrased it, 'Do you want to have an in?' Yes was the short answer, although I hadn't admitted it to her or anyone else. I'd pulled together a lie about wanting to be able to bring the truth of situations to the readers in a city; something about the mis-reporting around Mum's death, and how she'd been slandered by some papers while others had ignored her altogether.

'You can't change that, darling girl,' Madison had explained, and I'd told her that maybe – just maybe – I could at least stop it from happening again. I'd done everything I could to make crime reporting sound like a noble endeavour on my part. But Marcus had rumbled me – and in record time, too.

Even though he'd told me I could ignore the question, I still wanted to give him a believable answer. But I couldn't think of a lie fast enough.

'Sarah, look,' he started up again, when too many seconds had rolled by, 'I can't even imagine what you went through when you were a kid. I kinda know, because I've read your book,' he paused for a gentle laugh, 'but that's as close as I'm going to get to understanding it all. So, forgive me if I'm being an arse about this and know that, if I am being, it's unknowingly and without intention. But you can't chase this for the rest of your life.'

I thought back to that first letter: '...let this go.'

'Plus, the paper's insurance doesn't cover recklessness.'

It took me a second to realise he was joking. 'Not even a little?'

'I mean, recklessness like eating from Chicks at 1am on a Sunday. But other than that, my hands are kind of tied with the things I can help you out with.'

The traffic rolled forward at a steady 10mph. I'd be in a new city within the hour. 'I'm going to be in Coventry before too long.'

'And you're going to meet up with Therese, hear her out, and drive home.'

It wasn't exactly what I had planned. But I took Marcus' meaning. 'Yes, boss.'

'And you'll be working from Coventry tomorrow, but probably not the day after.'

I smiled. If Marcus had been standing in front of me, I would have hugged him. Workplace behaviour be damned. 'Thank you, Marcus.'

He laughed. 'Don't thank me. I might be going bloody mad. But if there's a chance this is a lead then I understand why you've got to take it. Just tread carefully, would you? Don't make a nuisance of yourself; don't take any chances. Call me when you're heading back to the city and we'll go from there. Fair deal?'

'More than fair.'

'Okay, well, enjoy.'

'Thank you, Marcus, really.'

I disconnected the call in time to catch the last chorus of 'Working My Way Back To You' on the radio, and the irony wasn't lost.

23

The outside of the woman's house was a mess. There were hungry onlookers crawling along the pavement, being ushered along by police officers who looked to be equal parts frustrated and exhausted. I'd called Therese as I'd limped off the motorway, two thirds of a tank of petrol lighter thanks to the stop-start journey; I wondered whether it would be too much of a push to write it off as a work expense. It would depend on what I took home to Marcus.

Therese had moved on from the crime scene – a nothing special house along a street of nothing special houses – and she'd set up camp outside the police station. She had suggested I meet her there, but then offered to meet me at the victim's home. I declined both; I wanted the space to work. But I knew that I needed to give her something to thank her for the tip in the first place.

'I just want to get a sense of the space, Therese, if that's okay.'

She half-laughed. 'I get it, I'm not used to a chaperone either. Call me later?'

I promised her I would. Since then I'd remained fixed outside the home where the victim had lived. Her body had already been removed, that much I'd been able to overhear. But there were officials traipsing in and out of the building every few minutes, most of them sheathed in protective plastics to avoid contaminating the scene. I thought of them pulling apart her unmentionables and peering inside; I could remember it all so well. There were hours of work ahead still.

After Mum, I didn't stay at the house. But Madison went back, only hours later, to get me enough personal belongings to survive a few nights. At the time she didn't tell me how bad it was. It was only years later, when I was pulling together research for the book, she'd finally opened up about it.

'It was like seeing her split open,' she'd said, her eyes fixed hard on an innocuous space in her living room. 'Like seeing her whole life cracked down the centre while people pulled out anything that might have been important.' She shook away the memory, then looked at me and tried to smile. 'They needed to know everything about her, didn't they?'

And now they need to know everything about her, I thought as I watched another case of belongings carted from the house by an officer. After another twenty minutes of watching from afar I called Therese back.

She answered on the second ring. 'Have you had enough yet?' she asked.

'It's still in full swing here. I don't even think they're close to being done.'

She let out a heavy breath and the speaker caught it. 'What must he have done to her, the state the place must be...' she petered out, as though suddenly remembering who she was talking to. 'Shit, Sarah, I'm sorry. I need to think more.'

'Not at all, Therese, really. Plus, if the place is a complete mess then it wasn't him.'

'Why do you say that?'

'Because he doesn't do anything to leave a mess.' I flitted

back to the memory of Mum's quiet death. He hadn't ransacked the house, only my life. 'Listen, I was calling about the police who are here. Did you manage to get much out of them? When you were asking around earlier, I mean?'

'They were being pretty tight-lipped, to be honest. That's why I headed back here. I thought I might be able to cut them off at the source. Did you fancy your chances?'

If the Coventry police were anything like the ones at home then I didn't think I stood much chance. Laing and Brooks had always been determinedly quiet when they were talking to the press on television screens or in print; it was one of the few things they'd done right by me. It took some time for the media at home to find out what my name was – and even then, it hadn't come from the police but an ignorant know-it-all at my college who put two and two together and made money enough for a packet of fags.

'I'm just hedging my bets. I'll check in later?'

'Sure. Are you heading home tonight?'

I looked from one side of the busied pavement to the other. 'I really don't know.'

'Dinner?'

'Please. I'll call to check in.'

I scooted around the busy crowds to get as close to the front door as I could. There were disgruntled nudges all the way, as though I were robbing people of something special. One man even went as far to say, 'Oi,' but I shot him a cold enough look to stop whatever might have come next. The years since Mum had given me a thick skin to handle most madding crowds.

When I was bumping shoulders on the frontline, I started the real digging.

'Hey, do you know what's happened here?' I asked the woman I'd nestled next to. She was a few inches shorter than me, on account of what looked to be the beginnings of a stoop in her stature. There were wisps of grey escaping from the tight bun at the back of her head. She was wearing glasses, but she still looked me up and down with a squint before she answered. I felt as though I may have backed the wrong onlooker.

'Woman died.'

I bit back on a sigh. 'Poor woman. Accident?' I looked back at the house to avoid any further inspection from her. 'Horrible, isn't it, to go unexpectedly.'

'It wasn't an accident.' She followed my gaze then and held a watch on the front door as she answered. 'She was a lovely young woman. I can't think why someone would want to go breaking in like that.'

My stomach twisted. 'God, it was a robbery?'

'That's what they're saying.' She sounded sincerely sad. 'I've lived next to her all these years and we've never had a crossed word.'

I felt a smile twitching and did my best to squash it. *A neighbour*, I realised. 'You were close to her?'

'As close as anyone is to their neighbours these days.' She lowered her voice. 'I called the police when I heard thrashing and banging. They tried to push me out the way, to stop me from going in, like, but I saw. I wish I hadn't, but I saw.'

I recognised the shock in her long stare, then. 'I'm so sorry,' I said, and I truly was. But I still had a job to do. 'So, you saw what had happened?'

She shook her head. 'Nothing to write home about. I saw enough to know she'd slipped away. I don't know who the chap was but there was a broken window out front,' she nodded, 'you can see that one there. And there was blood.' She raised a hand to her mouth and pressed hard on her lips; I wondered whether she was fighting a scream – or something else that stirs with grief. 'Don't let on, will you?'

When she turned I flashed her a confused look.

She nodded behind her. 'Not many people here even know who she was, never mind who I am. Bloody journalists are everywhere and all. I don't want anyone questioning me. The police already said they'll be knocking.' A sob slipped out and she pressed against her lips again; she sucked in a lot of air before she carried on. 'I just want to make my peace with what's happened and see that the kids are taken care of now.'

There had been the beginnings of guilt somewhere in the bottom of my stomach. But something else rose then. 'I'm sorry, the kids?'

'Eloise's little ones.'

'She was a mother?'

'Mother of two. Bloody terrible business for them. They weren't there,' she added quickly, 'they're at nursery and school. I suspect the father's been called. Not that he ever showed his face much.'

'Poor kids.' I set a hand on the woman's shoulder. 'You take good care of yourself, won't you?'

She locked eyes with me. 'I will, love, I will. You look... Do I know–'

'I'm not from around here.' I started to fight my way back out of the crowd. People were as reluctant to let me go as they had been to let me in. With my arms sitting uncomfortably close to my torso, I managed to wrestle my phone from the front pocket of my jeans. I dialled Therese's number on the walk to the car.

'Still nothing,' she answered.

'I'll make my way over to you, then, if that suits?'

'You're done there?' She sounded surprised.

'It isn't him.'

There was a long pause before she said, 'How do you know?'

'Witness saw blood. Well, a neighbour saw blood. She's not an official witness yet.'

'How did you– do you know what, never mind. You've got a nose for crime.'

'And a stomach for food. Can we eat? Then I'll head back to the city tonight.'

'You're not staying on the off-chance?'

I unlocked the car and rested on the edge of the driver seat. 'It isn't him.' There was another long pause, so I added, 'But I'm glad I got the chance to look it over for myself, so thank you for calling. In fact, let me thank you with food.' I forced a laugh. 'I'll come and meet you and we'll go from there?'

'Okay.' She paused as though there was more. 'Okay, sure.' I guessed she must have re-thought whatever she'd considered saying, and had gone with a safer option instead.

'Therese, I know you think I'm taking a chance in leaving. But I'm really not.' I pulled the car door closed and wedged the fob in the ignition. 'He doesn't leave a blood trail, and he's pretty good at not being heard.'

'Okay.' She sounded a little reassured at last. 'If you're sure.'

After I expressed my hunger for the fourth time, we ended the call with a promise that I'd grab her from the police station and we'd go from there. It had been a long drive, and for no good reason, so I thought the least I should go home with was a full stomach. Therese would ask more questions, I guessed. But there wasn't a doubt in me that the murderer in Cov wasn't the man I was looking for. Although it was nothing to do with the method, really, or the time of day, or the fact that there'd been a witness. The real deal-breaker was the children.

The only mother my man had ever killed was mine.

24

By the time I was leaving one city and heading back to my own, it was well outside of working hours – even for the editor of a newspaper. While I was keying in door codes and doing a once-over of my flat, I decided against calling Marcus. Instead, I reasoned he could be my first stop – after dumping my belongings – when I got to the office the following day. I had a sleepless night at home first though. There were too many thoughts – plus the occasional worry about work – and I was glad when the alarm clock chirped to interrupt my stretch of staring at the ceiling. I quickly dressed, grabbed my bags, and made my way through the blur of the city. Work felt like a haven, even though there was a stack of Post-its and scribbles precariously balanced on the edge of my desk. I'd only missed the best part of a day, but it looked as though a lot had happened. My laptop bag had hardly touched the floor when there came a tap-tap from Marcus against my door.

'Have you been staring at the door?' I joked as I pulled my laptop free.

'Please.' He trod in and took a seat in my visitor's chair. 'I've got a security feed set up for the main door. You'd be surprised at the weirdos who've tried to wander in here over the years. Can't be too careful.'

'And yet here I am,' I joked again, and I wondered whether it was nerves.

'I wouldn't say you're a weirdo, Sarah. You're just– fixated.'

My head snapped up. 'I'm sorry?'

'Leaving half-cocked to chase a killer?'

'It wasn't him.'

Marcus shrugged. 'Someone died; you still chased a killer.'

Not my killer, I thought but didn't say aloud because it felt too much like proving Marcus' point.

'Wait, how do you know it wasn't him?'

'Wrong method, wrong type of victim.' I landed hard in my chair and started to flick on my electronics one by one. 'A lot happened here while I was away, though, judging by that stack of messages?'

He nudged them further onto the desk. 'They're all about the murder.'

'In Coventry?'

'Speculation started. One of the local news stations picked up the killing and ran it as a feature. Then,' he gestured towards the pile, 'the crazies started calling.'

I grabbed the stack. 'Has anyone been through them?'

'You're the senior reporter, so, no.' He made it sound like this were an obvious answer. 'I've told Eleanor she needs to be on duty to go through them with you, though, so you'll have an extra hand in it all. There are names and numbers for everyone who called and got an answer. Some of them left messages on voicemails, so there might be less information from them.'

'Okay. Thanks, boss.' I clicked into my emails and started to star my way through the ones that needed to be answered soonest. But after a few seconds I noticed Marcus hadn't moved. 'There's more?'

He raised an eyebrow. 'We aren't going to talk about Coventry?'

I eased my hand off the computer mouse and dropped back against my chair. 'There's really not anything to talk about. Therese tipped me off because – well, because it's the right time of year. She didn't have much information when she called, but she called all the same because we're... I don't know, somewhere between being people who work in the same field and being friends.' I shrugged. 'There's no more to it.'

'Well,' he tapped the pile of notes, 'these people think there is.'

'I have a bunch of emails to answer, then I'll make a start.'

'No hurry, Eleanor is making tea for everyone.'

I shook my head. 'Oh, to be an intern.'

Marcus was halfway to the door but he turned back. 'Being an intern's nothing to do with it. She makes the best brew in the place...'

Eleanor and I were on our third cup when we finally made it to the notes. She was an aspiring writer, it turned out, and she felt shock and awe at being touching distance from a best-selling author. 'Have you any tips?' she'd asked.

Be the witness to a violent crime, I thought. But instead I told her everything people always want to hear about these things: how important it is to practice your craft; attend writing groups; learn the rules before you break them. She'd nodded along eagerly, and when I wrapped everything up with a neat, 'So that's that, really,' she took the hint well enough and offered to make another drink before we got started. I accepted eagerly because Marcus was right; Eleanor's tea-making was far superior.

'Do you mind me sorting emails while we do this?' I asked, my fingers already poised over the keyboard.

Eleanor looked surprised.

'I'm sorry, I'm expecting a lot of cranks, you know? You get a lot, with stuff like this.'

'Oh my God, I can't even. Absolutely.'

I deciphered that to mean that checking my emails was fine. 'Fire away.'

'I think it's my next-door neighbour who–'

'Pass. Next.'

'Oh. Oh, I– okay.' She set the first note down and continued with the second. The third, fourth and fifth. I was midway through replying to my seventh email of the afternoon when Eleanor said, 'Are you sure you don't want me just to go through these on my own?'

I closed the email I was drafting and shifted myself around to look head on at her. 'Go on, let's give the next one a go and then I'll make the next tea.'

She laughed. 'I don't mind being the tea maid for everyone, you know?'

'Marcus thinks you make the best cuppa in the office, you do know that?'

'Oh – oh, well.' She smiled in a bashful sort of way; I thought she must feel genuinely flattered, and I was glad for having told her. 'Okay, well, either way I don't mind.'

'Go on, hit me with it.' I nodded at the sheet she was already holding. 'This looks like a lengthier one.'

Eleanor glanced over it. 'I copied this one down. It was left on the office voicemail and I didn't want you to miss it, or ignore it.' She smirked and I nodded; it had been a fair guess on her part. 'Ready? Dear Sarah...'

Like a knee-jerk reaction, my eyes stretched at the phrasing.

'The woman in Coventry is a really sad state of affairs but people are barking up the wrong tree. You should know that – but maybe you don't. The sincerely yours murders will keep happening, though–'

'Exact phrasing?' I interrupted.

'To which part?'

'Sincerely yours?'

'That's how I wrote it down. I listened to a few times over to make sure I hadn't–'

'Did you delete it?' I was already reaching for the phone.

'The phones only hold a certain amount of messages and,' she fanned the rest of the Post-its, 'there were a fair few left.'

'Fuck,' I said under my breath, but I saw Eleanor writhe and I knew she must have heard. 'I'm sorry,' I tried to laugh it off, 'I'm being intense. Carry on, would you? I'm sure it's nothing.'

'The murders will keep happening, though, promise. Anyway, Sarah, be seeing you.'

I rubbed hard at my temple. 'That's how it ends, right?'

'Looks that way.'

'Can you set that to one side?'

She followed the instruction but asked, 'Are you worried?'

'Not at all, only curious.' I flashed a smile and I hoped to God it looked realistic. 'So, now you know the boss thinks you're the best tea maker in the place, how about we get another round in before we tackle the rest of those?'

'Well, who am I to ignore my natural calling?' Eleanor's face was friendly and open still. 'I'll go and ask the others if they want anything, though, as it's nearing lunch.'

'Christ, see you in half an hour to an hour then,' I joked and faced back to my computer screen. 'I'll tackle a few more emails while you're gone.'

When she'd left the room I reached across the table to read the scrawl of the phone message. I must have read it seven times over before I set it back where Eleanor had left it. In rapid thought, I went back and forth on where to go next – what to do, who to call. The victim in me thought the police; while the writer thought my publisher. But I ruled the second option out quickly enough. Although I'd been sorely tempted to stash the note away and hide it in the same place I'd kept the letters for all these years. But instead I grabbed my mobile from the corner of my desk and dialled.

'How may I help you?' the desk sergeant asked.

'Hi there.' I swallowed hard to steady my growing nerves. 'I need to leave a message for DS Brooks...'

25

Eleanor's handwritten note was stashed in my pocket. I'd kept it out of sight on the journey to the police station, and in the minutes I sat waiting for Brooks. In the hours since calling, I'd treated it like contraband: photocopying it in private and placating Marcus with a 'women's trouble' excuse to get out of the office in good time to make the meeting.

Brooks had called back within minutes and asked for a face-to-face chat about things, and I'd felt as though I were in trouble without her even knowing the reason for the call. Maybe it was an educated guess on her part – and a fair one, to her credit. There was no way for me to explain the significance of the call, the message, without owning up to at least one letter. The walk from work to the station had given me enough time to think of one, but whether Brooks would buy it or not was another worry.

'Sarah?' She caught my attention, peering out from behind the door in front of me. 'Do you want to come up? We'll chat in my office.'

The fours year since Mum died had changed us all, and Brooks was a welcome reminder of that. She was authoritative, measured, members of her team stopped when we walked into the room. When they saw that there weren't fresh instructions coming, they scurried off back to whatever tasks they'd been assigned. I took a good look around the space as she walked me through the beehive of criminal activity, making for the private room at the back. But on my way I saw fallen limbs and burst open bags of drugs, among other offensive items that had been photographed and tacked to the boards around the space. The crime reporter in me took her time; I was unhurried in comparison to Brooks. Until one cluster of images stopped me in my tracks. Not quite well-angled enough to face the right-hand wall of the room, there was an evidence board packed with faces I recognised. But it was Mum's that caught me. Pulled along by a magnet in my stomach, I started to drift towards the corkboard. But Brooks anchored me with a hand on my shoulder.

'Sarah,' she spoke gently, 'this way,' and she angled me towards the office. I felt like a victim all over again. But I took two hard blinks and tried to remind myself why I was there.

'Sorry.'

'Don't be. I asked them to cover it.' She flashed a tight smile. 'Simple instructions are the hardest to follow around here. We've got a couple of good coffee-makers if you want a drink, though, or we can do tea?'

'No, no I'm okay. Thank you, though.'

When we were in the office, she pressed the door closed with more care than the action called for, and I wondered whether she thought a loud noise might startle me. I made myself comfortable in the visitor's chair while she circled and took the seat opposite. She checked her mobile phone, ignored the notifications that were listed on the home screen, and then flipped it over.

'You've moved up in the world,' I said.

She lowered her head and laughed. I thought I saw the beginnings of a blush. 'We've both done okay for ourselves, I think, haven't we? Look at you.' She lifted her head. 'After everything. Sarah, it's really admirable how you've picked yourself up, made something.'

The compliments made me shift awkwardly. I didn't know whether it was because of the praise generally – or because I was about to lie to her.

'Anyway,' she carried on, 'you called to have a chat about something.'

'You asked to see me in person,' I countered.

'You first.'

I smiled, then took a deep breath. 'After Mum died, the killer sent me a letter. I never reported it to the police. I was angry and, frankly, I thought you were all incompetent and incapable and even though it would have done me a favour to tell you, I wasn't in a mindset of doing you favours after Mum had died and you didn't catch the man responsible. I can't even remember what I did with the letter.' She opened her mouth to interrupt my lie, but I paused her with a raised hand. 'I can't undo that action. If I could, I would, because I certainly have a different perspective on matters now. Which is why I'm here.' I pulled the note from my pocket, unfolded it and set it flat in front of her. 'While I was out of the city on business, there was a flurry of messages left across numerous office phones. This was one of them.'

Her lips moved as she read the note. I tried to hear her whisper.

'What makes you think this is significant?' she asked, looking back at me. Her expression was blank; I couldn't make out anger, disappointment, or surprise. I wondered whether she was a mother. My own had had that same knack for holding back feelings, when the offence called for it.

'He calls them the Sincerely Yours murders.'

She scanned the note again to find the phrase while I spoke.

'That's how the killer signed the letter to me. Sincerely,

comma, yours. Obviously, I can't say where the comma fell in his speech, but–'

'Do you have the original voicemail for this?'

I shook my head. 'The work phones only save so many messages and this was one of the ones that was automatically cleared.'

'Bollocks.' She thought for a second and I held my breath, nervous a hard exhale might disturb her. 'Definitely a man?'

'So my intern tells me.'

'Can we get her in here?'

'If need be. I didn't bring her with me because I didn't know what this was worth. Without the voicemail, without the letter.'

She pulled the note closer to her, as though she was nervous I might snatch it back. 'It's worth something, Sarah, so thank you. We'll keep this on file with the rest of our documents.' She hesitated for a second, then asked, 'How much of the letter do you remember, the one he sent after your mum?'

'He told me to try to move on.'

She laughed, but then her face smoothed out. 'You're serious?'

'Deadly.'

'Anything else?'

Even though I'd expected the question, something about it still unnerved me. I made a conscious effort to steady my voice as I answered. 'He told me that he was sorry, and that he wouldn't have done it if he'd known I was there.' I nearly smiled, but I didn't know why. 'He didn't mean for me to see.'

'Sarah, I...'

'It's okay, I know.' I flashed a tight smile. 'I've made my peace with it.' *Another lie*, I thought. 'I'm just sorry that I can't be of more help.'

She folded the note over. 'This helps, though, and that counts.' When the note was stashed out of sight – hidden inside a cardboard folder to Brooks' left – she looked me straight in the eyes. 'We need to talk about the killings. You've heard about Coventry?'

'Bits.' *Another lie.* I hated how easily they were coming.

'While the country was flocking to reports of the Coventry murder, which wasn't our guy, there was a murder happening in Hereford. It's around an hour and a half away by car,' she added, answering a question I hadn't asked. I wondered how much the distance from point A to point B mattered. 'Woman in her mid-thirties, lived alone, no children, creature of habit in terms of her work and social life.'

I nodded along with each tick on the list. 'You think it's him?'

'I think it's him.'

'What do you need from me?'

She nearly laughed. 'I need for you to keep out of the way, firstly. Secondly, I need for you to be taking care of yourself. If this is him, it's one of three, as we damn well know, and if he's getting in touch with you about it then there's a reason for it.'

I can't do that. 'Okay, I can do that.'

'You can't,' she said, hearing the unsaid. 'But I'll– we'll be keeping an eye on you, to make sure you're safe and in the city.'

'I can't leave the city?'

'I wouldn't recommend it.'

'But, just so we're clear, there's no way of you stopping me? Or, I don't know, reprimanding me, if I choose to?'

Brooks smiled. 'If only. But no, there's nothing I can do.'

I stood up and smoothed down my shirt front.

'I don't want to add your photograph to the board out there, though, if I can help it,' she added.

'It's okay.' I picked up my bag. 'I'm not his type. But thanks for the warning and the openness. It goes without saying this is all off the record, in case you were wondering – or, I don't know, worrying, maybe.'

'I appreciate that. You take care now. Keep in touch, won't you?'

'Sure,' I replied, although I wasn't sure why I would.

I was halfway to the door when Brooks pulled me back in. 'Hypothetically, just in case I was wondering or worrying. The note you've brought me today, you've made a copy of that for your own records?'

Brooks smiled and I reciprocated the gesture. I'd lied enough already, I decided. 'Two copies, actually, just in case. But it's off the record, for now.'

'Until you need it for a book?'

I laughed off the accusation on my way out. But for the whole walk home I wondered what Brooks knew – or thought she knew – about my plans for a sequel.

26

Madison walked into the living room balancing a tray loaded full of what she'd assured me would be light snacks.

After a call from Brooks in the afternoon, forewarning me about a press conference planned for later in the day, I'd decided to land myself on Mad's front doorstep and take refuge. I'd downplayed the trip as a sudden impulse – 'It's been ages since we spent time together at home.' – and she'd gone along with it up to a point. But her over-willingness to prepare a full-blown meal, and have me pick out an accompanying romantic comedy, was a clear red flag that her carer instincts had kicked in.

'I know you said not to go to any fuss–'

'I think what I actually said was that I wasn't hungry,' I said, not looking up from the letter I was reading. There had been a pile of post sitting on the corner of my desk at work since day one, and it had felt like the perfect workload to bring to Madison's. From the corner of my eye, though, I saw her shoulders slump, so I set the paper down. 'But I can pick.'

'Well,' she set the tray on the coffee table, 'that's what I was thinking.' She kissed my forehead before shuffling past and landing in the seat next to me. 'Besides, you look like you're losing weight, darling girl. Are you remembering to eat in amongst all this – whatever this is.' She flicked a sheet of paper that I'd discarded on the To-Dump pile.

'They're just letters to the office.'

'Fan mail?' She picked one up and I snatched it back from her.

'Some of it appears to be, yes.'

In the weeks before this, I'd managed to convince myself the letters were all concerned locals hounding me for news coverage. But the further in I waded, the more it looked to be letters from delighted locals, voicing their happiness that an 'expert' was taking over the crime desk for the paper. I wondered what made me an expert, exactly: the history with violent crime, or the more recent history of writing about it. Either way, there had only been a handful of letters to throw away – nonsensical ramblings from people who were concerned about their neighbours, relatives, strangers, and what criminal activities they were up to – versus the few kind letters that would be scrapbooked. *Any day now*, I thought, *when a few hours open up with nothing else at all to keep me busy*. I had good intentions.

'Darling girl,' she bit into a vegetable spring roll and spoke around the cracks of pastry, 'you're welcome here always. But why are you here?'

I feigned outrage. 'Well, if you don't want my company...'

'Funny. But come on.'

I dropped the letter I'd been trying to read. 'Brooks called me earlier. She's got a press conference arranged for this evening and she said I'd be interested in the content of it.'

'Professionally?'

'Personally.'

Madison coughed and flecks of food sprayed out of her

mouth. 'Oh, Christ.' She rushed for a napkin, one of two wedged into the corner of the food tray. 'Sorry, I'm not used to having company these days, you see.' She was trying to lighten the mood, I guessed, so I forced a smile. 'Darling, I'm glad you're here for this. What time is it on?' She leaned across me to get to the remote. 'And, the more pressing question of it, when are you moving back in? I'm off work tomorrow.'

'Mad...'

'Sarah, just – please, think about it? That's all I'm asking.'

'Deal. Pass me a mini quiche.'

'Cheese and onion or cheese and ham?'

I picked up the same letter for the third time. 'Surprise me.'

There was still an hour to pass before the televised press conference. I'd told Madison I wanted to watch it, but I didn't want to make a feature of it. If she had things to be doing, she should get on. 'We need to keep going like normal,' I'd said, with my head buried between pieces of paper. She agreed but still didn't move from my side. She filed her nails, painted them, and then stripped the paint to start from scratch. When I side-eyed her she acted defensive and said she didn't like the colour, but I'd seen her use the tactic before. During the days of us sharing a house, more than once I'd watched her kill time with manicures over cleaning; it had been one of my favourite differences between her and Mum.

It was ten minutes away from kick-off when I balled up a letter of complaint and threw it on the rubbish pile.

'Can I have a cup of tea?'

'Sweetheart,' she shot up from the sofa, 'of course. And you're not hungry?'

I'd eaten three vegetables spring rolls, two potato pancakes, and three mini quiches without being hungry at all. So no, I definitely wasn't. But I reasoned it would keep her busy for a beat longer at least. 'I think I might like something sweet,' I lied. 'Maybe a pudding, or something? Do you have ice cream?'

She thought. 'Why don't I pop a lattice in the oven? Apple? We can have it with ice–'

'Perfect,' I interrupted. 'That sounds perfect.'

When she'd hurried from the room – visibly delighted at having something to do – I turned the television on. I caught the end of a news report about changes to schooling policies in the area, before the stern presenter announced they were cutting across to their crime reporter for an unexpected update from our local constabulary.

I cut open the lips of another letter and watched from over the top of the sheet.

'We're coming live from outside...'

'Is it on?' Madison shouted in.

'Nothing yet. I'll shout when it starts.'

'DS Brooks has called a conference to discuss the so-called Trio Killer...'

Is that what they're calling you now? I half-read the letter – one praising me for my honesty and thanking me for my book – before I set it on the fan heap with the rest. I was near the bottom of the pile, then, the letters that had been sitting on my desk for the longest, and I tried to pay closer attention to anything I might need to write an apology to. But then Brooks appeared, in a pressed blue shirt and dark grey blazer. Her hair was wild, free, and I imagined her running her hands through it ten times over ahead of leaving the station for the announcement.

'Thank you to everyone for being here this evening. It's a pressing matter, as I'm sure you've guessed, given the speed with which we've pulled this together. So, we appreciate your attendance and your patience. The details, we know, have been thin. However, we now feel we're in a better position to offer an update and, in truth, a caution.'

My stomach rolled. The sound of the oven door closing cut across my concentration and I flinched. I opened another letter, my hands moving on automatic.

'You may or may not have heard about the recent murder of a young woman in the Hereford area...'

'You were meant to shout me when it was on.'

'...the constabulary in that area were initially concerned this murder was somehow linked to the murders that many of you will likely remember, as having originated in our own city. The Trio Killer, which I believe is the moniker he's been dubbed with...'

'It's not very catchy, is it?' Madison's tone was flat, unimpressed.

'...after working closely with the Hereford team, we now have reason to believe that the most recent victim is likely to be a victim of the Trio...'

'Christ.'

'...in the coming weeks we'll work closely...'

'Sarah?'

'...to ensure the safety of everyone in that area, but also the safety of women...'

'Darling girl?' Madison set a hand on my shoulder to grab my attention. I looked at her but her edges were watercolour. I pulled in a mouthful of air, another, another, but I couldn't find a place to put the air once I'd swallowed it.

'Sweetheart, follow my breathing, okay? One in...' she petered out and made a show of belly breathing. Between breaths she paused to remind me I should be copying her.

But Brooks carried on in the background. '...we're advising people to stay vigilant...'

'Darling girl, let me take this?'

She tried to ease the letter free from my hand but my fingertips had tensed on its edges. *Would there be fingerprints left?* I wondered. *If I took it now, would it help?* I felt a tremor in my hand that shook the paper loose into my lap, but I snatched at it before Madison could. *Would it make a difference*, I thought, again and again, *would it mean he hadn't killed her? Should I tell someone that he'd warned me...*

27

Sarah,

First day at a new job. Or at least, I'm hoping this will get to you on your first day. I thought of flowers but that seems to set a strange precedent, even for our strange... bond. Is it a bond when one person wants to move on and the other won't let go? I wonder.

I've tried to imagine how busy you must be today. When I think of you that way I wonder whether you'll get this letter at all. Perhaps it will sit at the bottom of a pile of fan mail until you finally dig your way through to me. Do you get fan mail, Sarah? For the book, I mean. I do – for what I do, I get fan mail. Not directly to me, of course, Sarah, because how could anyone manage that when no one is capable of catching me. But on the internet, there's a lot of fan mail; a lot of people wondering why I do what I do. I like to read the theories people have. They're wild, some of them. Dead wrong, most of them. Maybe after these next ones someone will be closer to guessing me – getting me. But I don't know about that, still. I've found a new city, though, pretty place, Hereford. Maybe their police are better; maybe they're superheroes. Speaking of which...

You're doing so well for yourself, Sarah. I know it's not my place but it's been something like a privilege to watch you. Despite *everything, you're really managing to make something of yourself; what with the job and the book. I read it, by the way. I told myself I wouldn't; it felt too much like torture. But it was such a good window into you, Sarah, like slipping a key in your chest cavity and taking a look at the pretty and important things you keep there. You must be terribly brave to have shared all of that with the world. I bet you felt brave, didn't you, sharing it all? I imagine you must have got a kind of kick from it; from everyone telling you how excellent you are, Sarah, and oh, you are. You really are doing so well. So why haven't you let go of me yet?*

I know why you're at the paper. At the crime desk. Writing a new book. I understand it all, Sarah, but it won't help you. I'll be seeing you – but don't expect for it to work the other way. Because I've got this far easily enough...

Take good care now, won't you?

Sincerely, yours –

PART III

28

2016

Sarah,

You've been doing better than I thought, Sarah. I don't know how you worked it out but there you were – touching distance. It would have been so easy to give myself away and see you properly, although I've wondered if that's what you were hoping for. How did you work it out, though, or was it a lucky guess? See, I know my system because I'm the person who made it. But no one else in the world could know. And yet, there you were.

I'll tie myself in riddles with it, Sarah, really, I will.

Whatever your magic reasoning was, I can't have you that close again. So, consider this a Dear John, dear Sarah. You've scuppered things a little for me now, but your tenacity is something I've admired over the years so I suppose I can't condemn you too fiercely for it. I'm sure you'll keep looking for me. But mark this as the start of my hiatus in your notes, won't you? You got the city right, but you won't find the women here. Who knows when you'll find the next women, or how many there'll be. The victims might accumulate.

But that's me being cruel, Sarah, because deep down you probably know it doesn't work that way. You'll wonder, though, won't you? You'll carry that wonder through every anniversary until

145

my comeback tour. And it'll all be as much a guessing game for me as it is for you because no one really knows how long I can go without it now, Sarah. So, maybe this will be good for us both...

Maybe this distance will help you.

Take care, Sarah.

Sincerely, yours –

29

I've learnt that Madison isn't exactly keen on surprises. But when it comes to big birthdays, I've never really cared much about what Madison is keen on. Since Mum, every birthday has felt important. So, despite protests in the weeks leading to it, I was determined to throw Madison an embarrassingly lavish birthday party, orchestrated by me and my friends, for the enjoyment of Mad and her friends. Landon made a PowerPoint presentation packed with photographs of Madison through the ages; Jessie and Tyler were in charge of the guest list (or Jessie was; Tyler was in charge of keeping the twins occupied). Meanwhile, I was in charge of decorations, refreshments and the cake. The surprise element arose because Madison thought we were planning a home-cooked meal with her closest friends. By the time the night rolled around, Jessie was juggling a guest list of nearly fifty people, all of whom were eager and waiting to shout, 'Happy birthday!'

'You little shit.' Madison clipped me around the shoulder with the back of her hand and then pulled me close enough to kiss my forehead. 'You said we were having a few friends over for dinner.'

'We are.' I gestured to the room full of people in front of us; the handful balanced on the stairs; the others wedged in the hallway. 'It turns out you have a lot of friends.'

Madison catapulted herself into the crowd with the same smile and zest that I'd always seen her wear. She even managed to take it in her stride that we'd plastered fiftieth birthday banners in every room of the house.

'You weren't meant to tell anyone,' she protested to begin with.

'We didn't,' Landon lied, 'people just guessed.'

'Because I look fifty?'

Landon looked from me to Jessie and then back to Madison. 'I– ah. I mean...'

Madison burst out laughing. 'You're all right, Lan. Get me another drink, would you?' She thrust her half-empty glass in his direction. 'Then we'll call it even.'

Madison had become the mother of my friendship circle. Jessie, distanced from her own parents by a good few hundred miles, had leaned on Mad throughout her miscarriage – and the unexpected pregnancy that followed. Tyler had leaned on her during marital problems with Jessie, after Madison had sworn on pain of death to keep his worries a secret; although she'd told me, reasoning that I didn't count. Even Landon had come to lean on her; though I hadn't known exactly what for. In a lot of ways, she did everything Mum used to do; only we were adults, and she still wasn't Mum. But I'd made my peace with that.

Two hours into the party, we finally got around to cutting Madison's cake: a blue and white fifty I'd had made. There was chocolate sponge and vanilla buttercream inside the five and vanilla sponge with strawberry jam in the zero. Madison made a big song and dance about sampling each before anyone else was allowed to. She wouldn't admit to it, but I knew it was so she could pick a favourite. She spent the next hours steering people towards the zero, which meant she thought the five was the better cake.

'She thinks we don't know.' Landon leaned against a nearby door frame. 'The five is the obvious winner.'

I smiled. 'Maybe other people just don't know her well enough.'

'Probably a good thing. Otherwise they'd steer clear of the zero.' He shifted closer and gave me a nudge. 'Are you okay with all of this?'

'What do you mean?'

He gestured to the bustle around us. 'Birthday celebrations, the big fifty.'

'Mum wouldn't have been fifty.'

'No, she would have been forty-one. But probably thirty-one, probably for the third year running.'

A sad laugh passed between us. 'She'd still want this. It's just that she would have been the one making the plans and inviting the friends and–'

'Eating the best cake,' Jessie interrupted as she came to a stop behind us. 'Everyone doing okay over here?' She looked between us and we both nodded in turn. 'I'm going to have to make a move,' she pulled me into a hug, 'because the twins are– well, you know, you've met them.'

'Have a baby, they said,' Landon joked as Jessie leaned into him.

'Give my best to the birthday girl?' She nodded in Madison's direction and I turned in time to see her taking a shot with her boss. 'I wouldn't want to interrupt.'

'Thanks for everything you did, Jess.'

'Any time.'

While Jessie pushed herself away from us, launching across

the swimming pool of bodies that had come to take up the hallway, Marcus was making his way towards me. He'd been my boss for three years, and a close friend for about two and a half of them. When I'd dropped the party invite on his desk, though, he'd seemed surprised.

'Bloody brilliant party, Sarah.' He kissed my left cheek, then moved towards my right. But when he noticed Landon he changed his mind. 'Thanks so much for the invite, really. I got to chat to Madison for a little while earlier, too, and she was telling me all about your new book.' I narrowed my eyes at the lie and held a stare until he started to laugh. 'Okay, she told me nothing about the new book.'

'That's because she knows nothing about the new book.' I landed a playful fist on his arm. But at the mention of the blessed new book, I felt like making it a more sincere punch. Marcus chased me about my private writing projects as often as he could, for no other reason than sheer nosiness. 'When I give my publisher a draft, I'll tell you everything.'

'Big guy, you bear witness to that, right?' he asked Landon.

'I sure do,' he replied, his tone flat, 'big guy.'

I threw Landon a raised eyebrow and then tried to make my tone overtly friendly, as though I could somehow compensate for his. 'Landon and I need to be on goodie bag duty in the kitchen, Marcus, so we'll have to dash. Thanks again for coming, though.'

'Of course, of course. I'll see you Monday, Sarah. Nice seeing you, Landon.'

'Don't cock measure with my boss,' I snapped as soon as we were out of earshot.

'I wasn't.'

'I sure do, big guy,' I mimicked, taking on Landon's flat tone.

'Well, bloody big guy.' He cracked open a can of gin and tonic. 'Big guy, indeed.'

It was the early hours of the following morning when Madison's house fell quiet. She and I had taken it in turns to thank guests in the end, hoping our slurred gratitude would be a sign for them to get moving, and largely it was. Landon had been last out the door, after he'd hung on to see whether I wanted to share a taxi – even though we lived in different directions.

'Whatever your intentions,' Madison had garbled, leaning heavy against him, 'you can save them for another night. She's with me.' Landon had graciously accepted the knock-back; it had been my easiest experience of turning him down.

'I'll call you tomorrow about the show,' he said, halfway out the door.

'You won't because she doesn't work Saturdays,' Madison shouted back, but Landon didn't show any sign of having heard. Madison liked to think I didn't work Saturdays, even though I'd been working six days a week for as long as I could remember. She worried, though, so I let her think what she needed to.

Once Landon had gone and the clock rolled around to two thirty, I set a hand on her leg and gave her a gentle squeeze. 'Happy birthday, Mad.'

'Thank you, darling girl.'

Madison gave a hard sniff and I turned around in time to see a tear rolling out of the corner of her eye. I reached an arm around her and pulled her in to a tight hug, and she let the side of her head drop against mine. Her shoulders jerked as the tears came faster and soon she wasn't moving at all, but holding her breath between each sob. When she came up for air around the tears she was gasping – like someone was choking her.

The cries were free-flowing for a while. I can't remember how long it lasted. But when she wiped her face with her palms, that came away muddied with mascara, I knew she was finished. She pushed herself upright but stayed close enough for me to keep my arm around her; my hand hugged against the ball of her shoulder. I squeezed and sighed.

'I miss her, too.'

30

I hadn't got used to the experience of waking up next to someone. It seemed strange, how you could go from knowing someone in a professional capacity all the way through to knowing how their hair looks after sex – and then how it looked the next morning, too. Although staying over was a relatively new thing. I'd argued it was a step too close to intimacy; that we were better off tiring ourselves in a shared bed and sleeping in separate ones. But that had opened up a line of questioning that, as a reporter, I should have seen coming. In the end it had been easier to agree to the occasional night of sleeping next to a warm body, rather than having a difficult conversation and, worse still, ruining a good set-up. Finding someone else who didn't want a public relationship – in The Golden Age of Social Media – had felt like finding gold dust. Although we both used the R-word in a fast and loose way. Neither of us really wanted one of those either.

At an ungodly hour one Sunday morning, Wren's phone vibrated across the bedside table with fury enough to wake us both up. Her cheek was pressed against the flat of my back and I felt her stir, but not fast enough to get to the handset. Despite knowing the source of the noise I remained wide-eyed and rigid until she'd rolled away. It still happened, sometimes, when an intrusion startled me enough. She set a gentle hand on my shoulder and massaged at the skin, as though physically trying to loosen my posture one point at a time.

'Sarah, are you with me?'

I rolled over then and made a comedy sketch of stretching. 'Christ, what time is it?'

'Too early.' She leaned forward to kiss my arm. 'I'll go and deal with this.'

'Stay in bed. You'll freeze if you get out.'

We'd reached the time of the year when the heating should be kicking in. But it was holding out for another degree to drop. She looked to the handset and then back to me. She didn't say anything, but from the tight smile I knew it was a call she wanted privacy for.

'I'll be right back.'

'You could tell them not to call on a Sunday.' I tried to sound light. 'It's the Lord's day, after all.'

'I'm not sure spending the day in bed with another woman really fits into that.'

'Pff.' I rolled over and buried my head in the pillow. 'Work doesn't either,' I added, but not loud enough for her to hear. Wren had been my only reason for taking Sundays off from work. It was a sore point, then, that her work could always get her: first thing in the morning; last thing at night; once in the middle of the night, although she thought I hadn't heard her take the call.

'I'll bring tea back with me.'

I could tell she was near the doorway from the throw of her voice. I grunted by way of replying and tried to feign disinterest – until the door closed. There's no way I could pad across the laminate flooring unheard. But I sat upright and scrambled to the end of the bed, hanging as close to the open crack of the doorway as I could crane myself.

'DS Brooks calling... Can you put me through...' She flicked the kettle on. 'I'm not in the office today, no... The paperwork should be on my desk... Is this something that needs to be done today, or are you that short of work?' Her tone was curt. Whatever they'd called about, it wasn't him – or about him. 'The court case isn't scheduled...'

When Wren and I started sleeping together, we established the ground rules early on. She wouldn't ask about my work and I wouldn't ask about hers. If anything ever did slip out – or, for example, if someone were to overhear something they shouldn't one Sunday morning – then it was always off the record and not something the speaker would publicly attest to. She had idly joked about drawing up a contract to outline the terms fully, but the suggestion had fallen down the back of her bed somewhere.

Another ground rule had been that we wouldn't tell anyone about us. Wren was a determined police officer and I was a pain-in-the-rear journalist; we weren't exactly a match made. But we had enough in common to talk over a takeaway every now and then, and the sex was excellent. Beyond that, neither of us had put much thought into the pairing. Although we guessed that others would have something to say.

It happened for the first time in the weeks leading up to Mum's anniversary in 2016. Brooks had been in touch to see whether I'd heard from him. She'd turned up late at my office one evening, on the off-chance of catching me there; from there she'd walked me home. She'd left with her tail between her legs in the early hours of the following morning. On her way out the door she asked, again, whether I'd heard from him: 'Would you even tell me if you had?' *No*, I thought. But I said, 'Yes,' because our relationship had changed in sleeping together, and I reasoned there was even more need to lie to her then.

'...I can't come in today, no.'

I threw myself back on my side of the bed seconds before she opened the door.

'You're welcome to call... No, this evening...' She carried a cup of tea in each hand. 'Call Wilson if there's a real problem...' She mouthed *Sorry* and then dropped on the bed next to me. She wasn't fully committed though; her legs were down, her feet on the floor, as though she might run out on official business any minute. 'Okay... Sure thing... I'll catch up with you tomorrow.' She disconnected the call and sighed.

'I'm not asking,' I said, with my hands cradled around my mug of tea.

'I'm not telling. Do you want to go out for breakfast?'

I paused mid-blow. 'Pardon?'

'Breakfast. Do you want to go out for it?'

'Have you taken leave of your senses?'

She laughed and rubbed hard at her forehead.

Wait, my mind shifted over to suspicion, *what have I missed?* 'Is there something you want to talk about that you want an audience for?'

'Wouldn't I take you to the station for that?' She raised an eyebrow. But I wasn't feeling playful. 'It was just an offer for breakfast, Sarah, outside of my house. But we can eat here.' She pulled her legs back into bed and under the duvet. 'Why don't we do dinner one night this week?'

'I'm busy.'

'I didn't say a night.'

I blew my tea again before taking a mouthful. 'I'm busy all of them.' I could see her disappointment from her profile. 'I thought you were worried about people seeing you with me because of the case.'

She half-laughed, half-sighed. 'What case?'

'Wren–'

'Forget it.' She leaned over and kissed me square on the mouth to stop whatever was coming. The moment might have been saved but the morning was ruined. Brooks had a nasty habit of assuming the killings had stopped – and it frustrated her that I disagreed. We avoided talking about it directly. But at one time or another we'd both fenced interview questions on the topic and our opposing views were obvious. In her defence, though, she didn't have the information I did.

'I'll make breakfast,' I offered. I was looking for an excuse to get out of bed.

'Well, I'm not going to turn that down.'

I swung my legs out of bed and took a sharp intake as my feet landed on the cold floor. Wren had offered to buy me slippers for when I was at her house, but I couldn't think of anything more domestic.

'I keep forgetting to say,' I started, when I was facing away from her, 'I won't be around next Saturday night. I'm with Landon.'

'You won't come over after?'

'It'll be late.' I padded towards the door without adding any more to the excuse.

'Isn't it the weekend after that you're out of town for a while?'

I stopped and tried to flit back through my bank of most recent lies. Wren had either caught me in the middle of a falsehood, or she truly believed I'd lost track of weeks. Given her profession the former seemed the more likely option, but she wasn't confrontational enough to pull me up on it – at least, not while I was walking around the bedroom in her underwear.

'Work.'

'Christ,' I made a show of remembering, 'is that then?'

'I might be wrong.'

'You hardly ever are.' I stood in the doorway but faced into the room, so I could afford her the courtesy of eye contact. Any more time spent hiding my poker face and there really would have been no chance of fooling her. 'I'm sorry, I didn't realise I'd got stuff back-to-back weekends. There'll be other times, though. It's just work, you know–'

'I don't know, no,' she interrupted me, but at least she was playful with it. Before I could answer, she cocked an eyebrow and smiled. 'You better make that a good breakfast, Wainwright, that's all I'll say.'

31

I collected my post from the delivery room on the ground floor on my way to the office. I didn't wait for it to arrive on my desk anymore. I'd made it known around the office, too, that anything mis-directed should come to me as a matter of urgency. 'Crime is time-sensitive and all that,' I'd joked and people had bought into it. But the truth was I wasn't prepared to miss a scoop on him again. We were only two months away from it being his time of year – Mum's time of year – and I knew the break in killing couldn't last forever. I skimmed through the envelopes on my way to Marcus' office but, with no sign of the handwriting I'd come to know so well over the years, I wedged the squat pile into the side of my laptop bag and marked it as a job for later.

'Knock, knock.'

'Who's there?' he asked, without looking up.

'Hatch.'

'Hatch who?'

'Bless you.'

He looked up then. 'Sarah, that might be the worst of the bunch.'

'I really don't feel like my comedy is appreciated around here, Marcus.' I wandered in and took the seat opposite him. 'Is there someone I can complain to about that?'

'I'd advise going straight to HR. But of course you'd have to knock to get into their office, and...' he petered out and shrugged.

'That was quite good for you.'

His computer monitor pinged and he side-eyed the screen. 'Oh, that'll be Chandler Bing asking for his sarcasm back.'

Marcus and I had built a rapport based on a shared interest in true crime, Yorkshire tea and terrible humour. Our morning routines typically involved some combination of all three. If he arrived first then I would go to his office and vice versa. He often had something that he wanted to be covered under the crime heading; I often talked him into letting me pass it to an intern for learning experience.

'You'll want to give this to Eleanor, I suspect,' he said, handing over a Post-it.

I took the note. 'Eleanor hasn't been an intern here for twelve months.'

Marcus narrowed his eyes. I felt as though I could hear him physically riffling through mental paperwork, searching for the right name. 'El – something?'

'Elliot.'

He clicked his fingers. 'That'll be it.'

I looked over the note. In Marcus' scrawl were the details of local break-ins; all the victims were women. *Why would I pass this to an intern*? I wondered, pocketing the note. 'Can I take it myself?'

'If you don't have anything better to do.' He flashed a tight smile. 'Expecting him?'

I forced a similar smile in return, grabbed my bag and stood to leave. 'Wrong time of year. But it sounds like an interesting thing to poke around in, and I think a female reporter looks better than a male intern.' It was an easy semi-truth to tell. I turned and headed for the door without further instruction, but Marcus pulled me back.

'It's a PC who tipped me off, Sarah, so tread carefully.'

'Always.'

'Brooks is probably your best bet.'

I was glad to be facing away from him. 'Why?' I turned then. 'She's the lead?'

'Bound to be, isn't she?'

Of course she is. I nodded and carried on my way to the office. Thinking, maybe it isn't too late to pass it to an intern after all...

The break-ins had already been covered by a handful of small papers in the area. I didn't know how it had flown under my radar for so long. But from everything I'd read online it looked as though the police were looking for a run-of-the-mill panty-sniffer. I winced at my own use of the term – but I had to call it how I saw it. Brooks had been quoted in one or two reports already, so Marcus' guess about her involvement was right. I couldn't decide, though, whether that made me more or less inclined to follow up the story myself. After hours of back and forth – and another chat with Marcus, who wanted to know whether I'd be out in the field for the story or working from my office – I decided the only safe middle-ground was to give it to Elliot and closely supervise his work.

'This seems like your sort of thing,' he said, half-reading through my notes. He looked up in time to catch my raised eyebrow. 'I don't mean – I just meant...' He took a deep breath in. 'I didn't mean anything bad by that. Only that, it seems potentially big, and you usually keep that stuff for yourself.' He shook his head. 'Rightly so, I mean, because you're the senior reporter. Not senior because of your age either but–'

'Please stop.' I smiled.

'Thank you.'

'I just think it'll be a good chance for you to get field experience. I'll happily supervise, particularly given that you're a male intern handling a case that impacts primarily on women. And, of course, it's likely to be a man committing the crimes, so–'

'Why?' Elliot interrupted me, with the flat tone of a man ready to defend his gender.

'It's just statistics, Elliot, don't take it personally.' I waited for him to push back but he decided against it. 'Your best way in is going to be to contact the police. Now, I've done a little digging around...' I talked him through the process of contacting Brooks – or trying to. She was a hard woman to get a hold of, and the task of trying was one I was desperate to delegate. She and I had managed to miss any uncomfortable brushes against each other in a work capacity – through strategic distribution of workloads on my part. Although there had been one occasion where I couldn't avoid contacting her – and she tactically avoided the phone call, getting one of her juniors to get back to me instead. A minor incident, but it had made me realise how desperate we were to keep our sex lives apart from our work ones; which is why we worked as well as we did.

'She won't find it strange that she's getting a call from an intern?'

No, I thought, as I handed over the slip of paper with Brooks' office number scribbled on it, *because she'll understand why I've done it*. I shrugged. 'You're here to learn the ropes. There's no reason why you shouldn't be contacting the police about cases. Not if you really want to work on the crime desk, but then I suppose–'

'No, no, I do want to work here,' he interrupted.

Good boy. 'Okay, great. Well, why don't you go ahead and give her a call and then head back my way when she gets back to you?'

He hesitated. 'You don't think she'll talk to me on the spot?'

No, she'll let it go to voicemail and then call you back – if she wants to. 'Sure, there's always that chance, too. Maybe make some notes before you call? Bullet-points of what you want to ask her, that kind of thing.' I flashed a smile. 'Can't hurt to be prepared.'

'Thanks, Sarah.' He backed out of the room and I almost expected a bow when he got to the doorway. 'Look, before I go, can I ask you about something? It's kind of personal.'

Since I'd joined the newspaper applications for intern positions, with an emphasis on crime coverage, had sky-rocketed – and my salary had gone up a notch or two because of that, too. Whenever Marcus put out an opportunity, there were even more applicants than the time before. Applications had to be capped on the last round because he and I hit a limit on how many pleading emails we could read. Elliot must have been among the brightest, although by the time he'd started with us I couldn't have picked his CV out of a line-up. Since he'd started, though, he'd been quiet, friendly and eager to please; although his tea-making was nothing on Eleanor's, but I'd managed to overlook that. Quiet and friendly aside, though, every intern arrived at the stage of wanting to ask a personal question, and it was always one of two: What are my chances of this turning into a full-time position? Although this wasn't their favourite, it had been high on the list of some. The other one – the more likely one – was:

'The second book you're writing...'

My stomach turned over.

'...is it about the killer?'

I narrowed my eyes. 'What killer?'

'You know.' He shuffled awkwardly. He was right to feel awkward; his phrasing was terrible. '*The* killer.'

I thought carefully about how to word my response. 'No, Elliot, I don't think there'll be a permanent position at the paper. We'll be looking to recruit a new intern.'

His head jerked. 'But I didn't ask...' The deer-in-headlights look came seconds later. His expression made me feel a little like I'd dashed his hopes and dreams. I imagined how he might think back to this moment as a learning curve one day. I flashed him a tight smile and then glanced around my desk to find my reading glasses. He left without another word.

Seconds later another intrusion. 'Why does Elliot look like he's about to cry?'

I looked over the rim of my glasses at Marcus in the doorway. 'Beats me.'

'What did you do?'

'Why do you assume that I did anything?'

He thought for a second. 'You're right. What did he do?'

'He asked the killer question.' I laughed. 'Literally.'

'Oh, Elliot.' He glanced down at an A4 sheet in front of him. 'Anyway, real issue. I've got you down for holiday from the middle of next week.'

There was a long pause where neither of us said anything.

'I'm sorry, did I miss a question?'

Marcus laughed. 'Sorry, I more just wanted to confirm. Anywhere nice?'

'Out of town for a couple of days, that's all.' I looked back through my lenses and carried on reading over my notes for a fresh story. Marcus lingered in the doorway. I didn't know what he was hankering after, but I wasn't going to bow to it.

'Sarah,' he caught my attention in the end, 'you'll be careful?'

Marcus and I never talked about my extracurricular activities. But he knew. I never worked out how he knew exactly – but from the way he looked at me sometimes, I felt it.

I nodded my understanding. 'Always.'

32

The lovechild that blossomed from mine and Landon's morbidity turned out to be a godsend for more reasons than either of us expected. After his first interview with me, his show went from strength to strength and he was bumped to a prime-time slot, as well as orchestrating the late-night interview series that I'd been a part of.

For me, though, our work together gave me something to keep my publisher happy with. The long-awaited second book was slow in the making, but the powers that be were kept at bay by the fact that my book was a constant bestseller. There had been fluctuations over the years. But every anniversary that rolled around warranted more coverage and then, to capitalise on our new-found statuses in the city and afar, Landon and I teamed up for Canonical: a true crime podcast. Not only did the opening episode hook a number of loyal listeners, but we gained more coverage as the weeks and months rolled on – thereby securing my book the sales it needed.

Canonical grew from a late night and too much gin; the circumstances under which all good creative plans are hatched. Landon and I were watching a serial killer documentary – we called it research, but in truth we were drunk and sad and it seemed a good idea – and midway through I slurred, 'Why is it always the killers, Landon?' From the opposite side of our cushion fort he looked at me, glass-eyed in a way that made me wonder whether he might cry at the question. 'I mean, why is it the killers? Why doesn't anyone remember the victims?' I pushed my heavy form from the floor and crossed to the other side of my living room to grab a picture of Mum. She was young in the image – it had been taken by Madison before I was even born – and her happiness glowed. 'No one even remembers her name.'

It was another two hours later when Landon, loaded on pizza crusts and slightly more sober, picked up the same picture. 'Why don't we make them remember?'

Canonical was into its second year. We were regularly approached by advertisers, too, because our 8,000 downloads a month made us a good investment. From one month to the next we had everything from alcohol brands through to escape room experiences.

Landon held out a brochure. 'We've been invited to this.'

'Deathfest?' I looked at the front cover. The title was deliberately bloodied, with the font dripping into the description underneath. 'A weekend full of panels, workshops and film showings to showcase the best and worst of serial killers.' I dropped it on his desk. 'I don't want to feature that on the show.'

'We're not featuring it,' he said through a mouthful of crisps, 'they've invited us along as speakers. We're kind of a big deal.' He shrugged. 'Who knew?'

I looked over the leaflet again. 'Do you want to go?'

'Not especially. But I'm free that weekend and I'll do anything for money.'

'Good money?'

'Jury's out. I've emailed them to see what the offer actually is.' He dropped into the seat at the opposite end of the desk. Landon's boss was kind enough to let us record each episode in an unused part of the radio studio once a month – on the condition that every show started with Landon's dulcet tones announcing our location. 'Are you in town that weekend?' Landon was one of the few people who had noticed my disappearing acts.

'I'll check.'

'Still not going to tell me who the mystery lover is?' But he hadn't quite guessed the right reason for the absences.

'Cute try. But no.'

'As long as he isn't too much competition for me.'

'Oh, Lan,' I pulled on my headphones, 'as though anyone could be.'

'Right answer.' He held up three fingers to count us in: One, two... 'Good evening and welcome to another episode of Canonical. You're here with your hosts, Landon Hughes.'

'And Sarah Wainwright.'

We talked about Amelia Brown. She was a young woman who was murdered by a serial killer in the 1950s, somewhere just outside of London. Her killer was an urban legend; a monster never caught for his crimes. When we'd picked her Landon had asked whether it was too close to home and I laughed it off: 'Why do you think I chose her?' The reason for choosing Amelia was that she was the killer's final victim before he dropped off the grid. That should have been reason enough for people to remember her name, and yet most news reports insisted on calling her 'the final victim', as though that had become her official moniker in death. Throughout the research for the episode I'd become so angry that I'd had to take regular breaks and the recording itself prompted a similar reaction.

'Smoke?' Landon asked.

I pulled a cigarette from the packet with my teeth and talked around it. 'I'm trying to quit.'

'Try tomorrow. We need a break.'

Outside, I lit cigarettes for us both and exhaled hard as I handed Landon's to him.

'Are you okay?' he asked.

'Of course. Why?'

'You're coming across as pretty angry.'

I laughed and smoke tumbled from me. 'I am angry, Landon. Aren't you?'

He kissed my temple. 'You have more reason than I do to be angry.'

We didn't talk about Mum as often as we used to. But Landon often reminded me that I had the option of talking about her.

When I didn't say anything, he opted for idle chit-chat. 'Where are you heading on your next work-slash-sex party weekend?'

'It isn't a sex party.' I inhaled hard and pushed the smoke out with my speech. 'It's just a work thing and I'm meeting some friends while I'm there.' After so many monthly trips and unexplained absences, the lies came easily. 'I'm going up north for the weekend. I shouldn't be gone longer than four days or so. It's partly a research trip as well.'

'For the show?'

I shook my head. 'For the book.'

'Ah, but of course.' He dubbed his cigarette out and threw it in the nearest bin. 'So,' he started, using an enquiring tone that I recognised too well, 'it was Cardiff last time, wasn't it? When you left the city for the weekend, I mean.'

I didn't mind them knowing where I'd been. But I never

wanted them to know where I was going. Friends and family have too many worries and I'd never wanted to pack their concerns in my overnight bag. It had been easier to pass it off as a cloak and dagger work trip. Easier, that is, until Landon slipped into interviewer mode.

'Yes.' I offered him another cigarette and he accepted. 'Why?'

He waited until he'd sparked up before he answered. 'There was a murder there.'

Something pulled at my insides. 'I'm sure there have been a lot over the years.'

'Nice try. But I mean the weekend you were there, there was a murder.'

I'd seen reports about the murder when I'd arrived home from the weekend. I was never sure whether I was relieved or disappointed to see these things though; to be so close, and yet...

'I think I might have seen something about that. Did you want to cover it?'

'Hardly worth covering.' His tone was antagonistic. 'It was just a one-off, wasn't it?'

The question wasn't a question; it was a trap.

I made a show of shivering and moved away from the wall. 'I'm going to head back in.' I pulled my hoodie tighter around me. 'I'll see you there.'

'Mhmm.' He avoided eye contact and took a long drag of his cigarette.

When I was back inside, I knew I had a good two minutes for Landon to finish his cigarette and climb the stairs. In the privacy of the recording studio, I landed hard in my seat and pulled my bag up from the floor. There was a small compartment on the inside that I unzipped and felt around in. The well-worn envelope came out and when I unfolded the lips, the first of the innards was a scored map, its centre loosened from months of being opened and closed. He – whoever *he* was – had sent me a roadmap of his targets, months and all, like a boastful plan. The map had that frayed feel that paper gets when you spend too much time with it. But if I was lucky, I reminded myself, I wouldn't need it for that much longer...

33

2016

Sarah,

I know it's been no time at all. But it hadn't occurred to me before that I might miss it all this much. You're the only person I can talk to about it, Sarah, and I'm sorry for that. There isn't anyone closer to home, though, and I do have to talk to someone. I thought skipping a year was okay. I thought it was safe, even, because you were so close, Sarah, so much closer than you knew. I think of that sometimes – when I'm missing it all. Do you even know when you saw me, Sarah? Have you gone back over those days to see whether you can pick out a new face – one that might look like a monster?

You were there for work, I think. There'd been an incident that you thought was worth covering for our local paper even though it wasn't a local problem at all. Then, Sarah, when I think of it that way, I find it all so uncomfortably coincidental that I wonder whether you were there for work at all or whether you really did know that I might be there. Oh, I tie myself in riddles with it.

This is what time away from things does to me. I've always wondered what it would be like if I were to stop and go about my business like anyone else – like all the other un-special people. But if you're special then there's no escaping it, no matter how hard you try. I wonder if that's how you feel, Sarah, whether you feel special because of what happened to you. Although it didn't happen to you at all, really, did it; it happened to her. They were the best, those first women. It's almost worth coming home for – to try to recapture the magic of it all. But then there's even more chance of bumping into you.

When I get like this, Sarah, I wonder whether I might quite like to bump into you. Then, there's the intricacies of that possibility: whether I'd want you to know that it was me; whether we'd bump into each other at all or whether it would be a carefully constructed series of events that led to us knocking heads at last. The latter sounds more like us. We're both too conscientious to let it be an accident, aren't we?

Your work looks to be keeping you busy. Although you must be wondering what I'm up to. Do you think about me a lot, Sarah? As much as you think about your mother, I wonder. It would be terrible if you thought about me more. But I've heard your latest project; your little offering to the likes of the people who follow me. From that, it sounds like you're more interested in the victim than the killer. If that were completely true, though, then you wouldn't still be looking for me. You'll have to forgive the assumptions, the presuppositions, but I'd bet good money on them being right. Maybe you'll prove me wrong. Maybe this letter will go with all the others, straight into the rubbish. Or maybe they'll go into a safe place where you'll revisit them and look for clues, to make a Nancy Drew of yourself. But, of course, if you plan on being a Nancy Drew, then you'll need more clues...

Take care, Sarah. Be seeing you.

Sincerely, yours –

34

2017

The overnight bag I threw into the back, while the box of cardboard folders took pride of place in the passenger seat – as though I might crack the case through osmosis. I liked to have everything close to hand when I was leaving the city. My out-of-office was switched on and anyone calling my landline at home would get a generic 'I'm out of town for a few days' voicemail, too. I liked to be as transparent as possible when I was going somewhere, in case he decided to up his game from letters to emails to – however else he might contact me. Of course, he knew that I'd be travelling to him; he'd rigged it that way.

I pulled out of the underground car park from my building and exited into the harsh light of the day. The world was turning into a new season and even though we hadn't quite knocked on the doors of autumn, yet, the trees looked as though they were thinking about it. On the journey out of Birmingham I tried to take as many scenic routes as I could, to give my lungs the chance of breathing something fresh – foreign. It was going to take me nearly two hours to drive to Oxford – thanks to traffic – so I wound the window down and tried to enjoy the trip. If I took in enough cold air, I could clear myself of the realities behind the adventure. But a glance at the passenger seat always brought me back.

Somewhere just outside of Banbury the traffic rolled to a complete stop and my thoughts slowly accelerated. I wondered whether he was already there, or whether he was stuck in traffic somewhere, too, cruising in from a different direction. I was no closer to working out what his starting point was from one trip to the next. But his frequent references to 'home', 'our local...' and other intimacies in his letters left me guessing that we might hail from the same starting point. It was one of the things I'd focused on most in the letters: where he came from; where he was going. Away from the letters, I tried to decipher details of our accidental meeting; the one that scared him away. I went through re-runs of the weeks surrounding it all – when the killings should have taken place, that is – and I tried out different cities, different stories I was covering. But I couldn't work out where I'd seen him; or, more accurately, where he'd seen me. But something about nearly coming face to face had been too much for him at the time. Although the tones in his letters since had suggested otherwise, and there had been plenty of letters to choose from.

In the months since his missed kill, he'd written to me at work on twelve different occasions. Whenever a letter was delivered there would be a flurry of phone calls, too, anonymous numbers that held on for a second or two – long enough for me to huff my irritation – and then the line would fall dead. I had no way of knowing whether it was him. But I'd stopped believing in coincidences.

The car crawled forward for a third of mile, rolling steady at eight miles per hour, then we all slowed. I pulled the handbrake up and reached across to my glove compartment where the emergency cigarettes were stashed. On my way back to an upright position I rested my hand on the box of documents, only for a second, as though checking their security. They were safely wedged with the seat belt awkwardly strapped around them, too. Since all this started I'd found it difficult to draw a clear line between being safe and being paranoid. I rolled the window down and sparked up. I decided about three months ago that I didn't mind being paranoid, though, as long as I was alive. As we inched forward I took in greedy mouthfuls of smoke and let them pour out of the open window.

'That'll kill you one day, you know?'

I looked to my right where the holler had come from. There was a man, slightly older than me, with his passenger window open. He was leaning across to shout his warning which, from his playful expression, I assumed had been said in jest. He wasn't unattractive; from this distance I could see a greying around the sides of his hair, but he had the smooth features of a man in his mid-thirties, and silver suited him well.

He laughed. 'I said, that'll kill you,' he repeated, as though I hadn't heard him the first time. I had, though, loud and clear. But I couldn't find the line between safe and paranoid; I couldn't stop thinking, *It could be you*.

The hotel was a nice enough place. I didn't treat myself like a queen on these trips, but I didn't make myself uncomfortable either. I pulled my overnight bag out of the back seat and left the box strapped into the front. Until I was checked in – where I could unpack it properly – I wanted it left somewhere safe.

There was a squat queue of couples in front of me at the check-in desk, so I took a safe-paranoid look around the foyer while I waited. The exits were clear enough, and there were cameras in very visible places; it was obviously secure, which I took comfort in.

'Miss?' the receptionist called my attention around. He

looked late teens – the age I was when this started, maybe – and I wondered whether this was his weekend job.

'Sorry, miles away.' I smiled.

'No trouble at all.'

'The cameras,' I gestured to the small black cups that were suckered to the ceiling around us, 'they're on constantly, I assume, hooked up to cloud storage of some kind?'

His eyebrow arched at the question. 'I can't say that I know, miss, I'm sorry.'

'Not a bother. Is it something you can find out?'

He looked unnerved. 'Are you staying here, miss?'

I laughed. 'I'm sorry, yes, I am.' I dropped my bag on the floor between my legs, as though marking a settlement. 'I'm a crime writer, up here for a conference for the weekend. It makes you hyper-secure, this business.'

The young man reciprocated my amusement, but his laugh was tinged with relief. 'I can imagine. You must have heard some real horror stories in that job.'

I'm starring in one, I thought as I fumbled through my bag to find my purse. 'I've got a room reserved for three nights but I only paid the deposit over the phone. Can I pay the rest now?' I placed a credit card on the counter between us. 'I'm afraid my card is under a different name to the one the room is booked in. Is that going to be a problem?'

His eyes stretched. I saw a flicker of excitement in him. 'Like an alias?'

'Exactly.'

'No problem at all, miss.' He slid the card the rest of the way towards him.

In the trips before this one I'd tried to track him down the old-fashioned way, as though I could swap professions long enough to crack a case so long-standing. But I'd overheard enough of Brooks' work calls to know how unlikely that was. He liked women of a certain age, though, with a certain physical appearance; I hadn't needed the letters to work that out. I'd studied them, though, looking for hints and moments of weakness. He'd talked to me about the women in the months since his last attack, too. I knew a little more of what he liked – and of course I already knew what he didn't like. He still hadn't attacked another mother, so I knew mine must have been a weak spot – or, although I couldn't fully get my head around the idea, maybe she was even a regret.

'So, S. Wainwright for the credit card,' he said, punching in my details and pulling me back into the room. 'And what name is the room booked under, miss?'

'E,' I said with a forced smile. 'Evelyn Wainwright.'

35

Like all men, he had a type. He didn't talk much about physical attributes in the letters. But from the news reports of previous victims – from my intimate knowledge of my own mother, too – I knew there was a certain type of appearance he was drawn to.

I wouldn't say that I wore too much make-up, but certainly too much make-up for him. A genetic throwback, Mum's deep brown hair had skipped over me entirely, leaving me instead with a blonde that could have come from a bottle – something I'd spent most of my teenager years vehemently denying. But I'd grown into the colour throughout my teens, and it had darkened by a shade or two in the years since. I wore clothes for comfort – jeans, T-shirts, over-sized jumpers – unless I was going out for a special occasion: dinner with friends; a book launch; an awards ceremony (I had a high bar for what constituted a special occasion, or rather, an occasion worth wearing a dress for).

Mum, on the other hand, had loved the chance to make herself over. She wasn't dramatic or drastic with her efforts. But she certainly had a few nice outfits to hand; ones that I'd made every effort to steal from her in my youth. I sometimes wondered whether that was why I steered so hard against being 'dressed up' when I was finally old enough to wear what I wanted. Mum, flash with her clothing to pair neatly against what could only be described as natural beauty – no make-up required – was his type. They'd all been beautiful; they'd all made good cover girls when the papers printed their obituaries.

I sat in front of the vanity mirror in the hotel room and started with a make-up wipe. The shade of my skin was naturally a little darker than Mum's. I'd bought foundation a shade lighter than I might normally choose. All the make-up I'd brought with me was lighter, in fact, to create the image of having not tried to look beautiful – when the truth was that was exactly what I was aiming for: easy pretty. I dragged the wet wipe first across my forehead and then each cheek, rubbing hard to scrub away the tan colour and leave behind a blemish of red. It looked a little like I was blushing.

In the bathroom I washed my face clean of the soft chemicals from the wipe and took a hard look at my blank face. *This is stupid*, I thought and then nodded as though agreeing with myself. But I knew the man was a planner. Whoever he was targeting in Oxford, he already knew her; her habits, where she was going to be for the next few days. He'd told me when to be in every city and this one was no different; a red circle on the map with a month written next to it. The specific dates were a given between us by then. He always attacked in the middle of a month; between the thirteenth and sixteenth and I relished the thought at being able to ask him why – why then? But to create the opportunity to ask him, I knew I was going to have to get his attention away from whoever the woman was. And if I was going to distract a creature of habit, it had to be with something he couldn't resist.

I landed hard in the cradle of the seat in front of the mirror and started. I skipped eyeliner entirely and moved straight to long-lash mascara, giving me a bright-eyed look. There were two light shade eye shadows to choose from in the collection I'd brought with me and I opted for the one with a little sparkle, because he wasn't completely opposed to it. Every decision I made in the minutes after taking my own face off and applying another was strategic; I wanted to make myself into someone he might kill. *No*, I shook my head and corrected the thought. I wanted to make myself into someone he had killed. In his letters he made no secret of knowing that I was in the same cities at the same time as him. 'I knew you wouldn't resist,' he'd said once, and he'd been right. He'd left clues for each city in each letter; a breadcrumb trail to crack. It was a journey that had never taken me further than a two-hour drive out of Birmingham. And if he knew I was tracking him, I wondered whether maybe he knew where I was – or rather, where I was staying. Maybe he even knew the name I was using. This wasn't the first time I'd checked in as someone else. But it was the first time I'd checked in as Mum.

I traced my lips with a pale lip-liner as a guide and then drew on a smile with a pale lipstick. After I'd applied a topcoat of gloss I puckered a kiss at myself, and I saw Mum.

It was a knee-jerk reaction, almost, but I grabbed my phone then and pulled up a blank text to Madison's number: 'Made it to the city safe. Free for a call?' It delivered straight away and I held on for the blue dots to appear to indicate an incoming reply but nothing came. It hadn't been an emergency. But something had turned over in my stomach at the sight of myself, and the longing for home – a reminder of home – had been instant. I could have called Landon or Jessie, Tyler even, but it wouldn't have been quite the motherly touch I'd needed. *She'll call*, I reminded myself, because she always did. Madison was better at calling back than Mum had been. I frowned at the comparison and pushed the thought away. I threw my phone in my bag and went back to the last of the makeover. I was nearly there – only one more step – and Mum hadn't raised a quitter.

The squeal of the room phone ringing behind me made me jump. I hadn't given the hotel details to anyone at home, though, so there were limited possibilities about who might be calling. When the phone didn't let up, I crossed the room and approached the handset with measured caution – as though it might somehow lash out at me itself.

'Hello?'

'Miss Wainwright, it's Sean from the front desk.' The kid who'd checked me in. 'I hope this isn't a bad time.'

He let the statement hang like he'd asked a question. 'Not at all. Is there a problem?'

'You told me to call through to you if anyone called the hotel.'

I felt an uncomfortable clench in my abdomen, so fierce that it stretched down to the tops of my thighs. 'There was a phone call about fifteen minutes ago now. I'm sorry I'm only just calling, you see, there was this really tricky situation down here with a woman who'd followed her husband and he didn't know–'

'The phone call, Sean.'

'The phone call,' he repeated, as though it were a trigger phrase. 'It was a man. He asked whether there was a Wainwright booked at the hotel.'

I wondered whether he'd done this for every city I'd visited; called the hotels, asked for a Wainwright on the off-chance. But if he'd watched me well enough he'd know the right hotel, I reasoned. The name, though, the name was always different…

'And you said?'

'I said, yes, a Miss Evelyn Wainwright, just like you told me.'

I smiled. 'Perfect. That's great, Sean, thanks so much for letting me know.'

'Anything else you need, Miss Wainwright, you just call. I'm here until midnight.'

I decided that I'd tip him on my way back to the hotel. Because if I didn't make it back then he'd be the only person with something worthwhile to tell the police. I took a hard look in the mirror and noted all the similarities, and then I pulled out the last weapon in the arsenal: a mid-length wig styled into a bob, in a deep chestnut kind of colour.

36

The restaurant was about as busy as expected, for a major city on a Saturday night. I'd requested a table for two, though, preferably by a window; I wanted to be seen. When I'd pushed my way through the smokers out front – taking in greedy mouthfuls of their pollution as I went – I announced my booking to the woman who was working front of house.

'Wainwright,' she repeated, looking down the list in front of her.

'That's right. Evelyn.'

'Ah,' she raised a finger, 'got you.' She snatched a menu from the stack alongside her and said, 'Follow me, Miss Wainwright. We've given you a window seat, as requested, with a beautiful view of the outdoor courts at the front of the building.'

I didn't care what my view was. I was more interested in the view I'd make. 'Thank you.' I took the menu and dropped into a seat. 'I'll take a large glass of dry white wine, if you don't mind,' I said before she had the chance to ask. I flashed a tight smile and looked at the menu, to signal we were finished, and she graciously took the hint and slipped away. It wasn't that I wanted to be rude; I just didn't want the small talk. It wasn't easy to say whether this was an evening out for business or for pleasure, so it was best to avoid the question. I kept my head buried in the pages of the menu so when the waitress arrived, with my wine glass perfectly centred on her tray, I was ready to order.

'Fregola puttanesca, please.' I waited while she jotted down my main. 'If I could get a black coffee, after the meal not part of the meal, that would be great. Keep the wine coming, too, would you?' I gave her a soft smile. 'I better make the most of a night away from the family, hadn't I?'

She laughed. 'I won't let that glass go dry.'

'You're a star.' *That'll cost me another tip*, I thought as I handed back my menu. 'That's everything for now, thank you.'

In my bag I had everything I might need for a night out alone. There was my e-reader, for a less suspicious choice of reading material. But there was also a cardboard wallet crammed with photocopies of the most recent letters. I felt around in my bag for a highlighter and a pen, but the first thing I came across was my phone. I pulled that out and rested it on the table, and then dived back in. The letters were colour-coded from the time I'd spent with them already. The blue details were location-based; the yellow was person specific to women he'd mentioned; the orange, I uncapped to catch any miscellaneous details I'd missed along the way. I skimmed to the back of the folder. The papers were organised in chronological order, with the oldest letters at the back. At least a night alone gave me a good opportunity to start reading through them all again, without Marcus wandering into the office or Landon knocking on the front door with a bottle of rum in hand. There had been times where their interruptions were exactly what I'd needed. But the closer we got to the anniversary months, the more I needed the solitude to work.

I'd started to imagine it as work, too, as the letters became more frequent. *This might be the sequel you've been waiting for*, I'd thought more than once, as though I could legitimise my behaviours as being something to do with creative licence. I knew I was sailing close to something dangerous though; not so much an average wind as a thunderstorm, rumbling and cracking overhead. 'You're asking for trouble,' Mum would have said, if she were able to.

I circled the date of the first letter in orange to remind me what colour-coded read-through I was on. I was hardly through the first paragraph when my mobile pulsed on the table: Incoming... Madison.

'Miss Wainwright speaking,' I said, using my best posh voice.

Madison spluttered with laughter at the other end of the phone. 'Darling girl, like you don't check your caller ID before you decide whether to answer every call.' She knew me too well. 'I saw that I'd got a text from you?'

'It was just for a chat. No reason.'

There was a beat of silence. 'Try again, darling, but give it more feeling.'

I let out a noise somewhere between a laugh and a huff. 'I missed home.'

'Good! Why don't you come back, and we can have a girls' night?'

'Because I haven't even been here a night yet. I'm booked for the weekend.'

'Work won't mind. Marcus loves you.' Madison was another person who believed these little trips to be work-related. I never thought far enough ahead to imagine what I'd do if the people in my life were to have a conversation with each other. 'Or I can come to you? Where are you this time? Is it far?'

I imagined I could hear her already grabbing her car keys. 'Mad, really, I was just – I don't know. I was having a moment. I'm honestly okay.'

'You said you're there for the weekend?'

'All being well.' I'd paid for three nights but I'd stay longer if I needed to. I never managed much sleep in the nights I was away. Most of my time was spent fixed to social media channels and news outlets, to try to catch the first whispers of anything sinister taking place. 'I should be home by Monday lunchtime if all goes to plan.' *If he sticks to a weekend schedule*, I edited my explanation but held it to myself.

'And you'll make time to see me, will you?' She sounded sceptical.

'Mad, don't I always?'

She hesitated. 'Not lately, darling girl, no, and that's okay.' She hurried through the second part of her explanation, as though she needed me to know that it *really* was okay. 'You're busy and I'm busy, and there have been times when I've cancelled, too. But let's do it soon? I don't want our contact to be restricted down to birthdays and anniversaries.'

Mum's anniversary was only around the corner; two months away. But for something like the death of a loved one, I'd found that anniversaries came in months, sometimes, or seasons: 'This is the month that I lost Mum...' like it was a thirty-day event, which always made them feel a little closer than they actually were.

'Why don't I come over when I'm back?' I suggested.

'In the evening, after work?'

'If that suits you?'

'Oh, darling, absolutely. If you're sure? I imagine you'll come home to a lot of work.'

I laughed. 'Has there been a lot of crime in the day I've been away?'

'No, silly,' she shared a half-laugh, 'I meant writing up the notes from – from whatever it is you're doing while you're away. I don't want to get in the way of that.'

It was the first time I'd felt a stab of guilt for the lies I was telling. Madison hadn't pushed for details. But as the trips became more frequent there'd been a growing nag in the back of my mind that she maybe didn't believe my reasons for being out of the city. There wasn't much that I kept from her. In the style of a typical child, though, I kept this from her because I knew what her reaction would be. It was dangerous, and to most people, I suspected it would seem unnecessary. But this wasn't a petty squabble with a school-friend; this was a life-long grudge. And habits that long-standing were hard to break.

'Maybe I can talk to you about my work? I know I'm a bit cagey about it.' If I felt brave enough to tell her the truth, at least I'd made an opening, I decided. If I changed my mind, there was enough crime in the world for me to bluff my way through half an hour of talking about it. 'Not too much, because, snore.' I tried to lighten the offer.

She laughed. 'Darling girl, nothing about your work is boring to me.' I felt that same stab of guilt again, then. 'If you'd like to talk about work,' I heard a smile crack through her words, 'but we can talk about anything at all, always. You can even tell me about your romance life, if you're feeling *that* brave when you get home.'

I rested my forehead in the cup of my palm and realised I was sweating. 'Who did you talk to?'

'Well, you're an attractive young woman. How could you *not* have a man?' She rushed to add, 'Or a woman. A woman would be fine, too. Maybe even better, in my experience. I mean, not in my personal experience of women, but, in my experience of–'

'Why don't we talk when I get home?' I cut through her embarrassment. It may have been a day away from home, but Madison was right about how long it had been since we'd seen each other. In her fumbling monologue on my maybe-romantic life, I missed her so much it made my belly ache. 'I'll call as soon as I'm back.'

'Okay, darling girl. Take care of yourself while you're away.'

'You take care, too, Mad.'

'Always, darling. Love you.'

I sucked in hard before I rushed my reply. 'I love you, too.'

It was always hard to say; to anyone. But especially to Madison. I loved her like I might love a mother, and that's what made it difficult. No matter how hard I tried, though, I couldn't escape the worry that each phone call might be the last time I talked to anyone. It wasn't anything to do with the visits out of town. It was everything to do with my last night of talking and laughing with Mum about clothes that I was about to steal from her. Those final moments had carried me through especially dark and painful points. Since then, I'd always wanted my last conversations with people to count. Morbid though it may seem, these trips away weren't exactly risk-free. If I was putting my life on the line – a life I owed so much of to Madison already – the least I owed her was a reminder that I loved her.

37

The drive home took longer than I'd expected it to. I left Oxford late morning, on the misguided idea – or rather, ideal – that that would mean missing the work traffic in and around the area. But no such luck. It took even longer to make my way back into Birmingham, but at least I hadn't been accosted or criticised along the way – even if I had been smoking out of my car window for most of the journey. I sandwiched cigarettes and Polos around each other, as though that might ease the stress of there not having been so much as a flicker of action while I was away. I must have missed it. But I didn't know how, when I'd spent each evening with the news on the television – albeit muted – and the radio playing so loud that I wouldn't sleep through any breaking bulletins. The local newspapers had updated their websites, with very few changes to the crime sections across them all. Not only had there not been a murder in the city – or, if there had, it had miraculously gone unreported on – but it looked as though there hadn't been much crime full stop.

When I pulled up in the safety of the garage underneath my building, I grabbed my phone to set up a search engine alert:

'murder' + 'woman' + 'Oxford'. There were two missed calls from Marcus and a voicemail. Getting out of the car felt too much like admitting defeat for the journey, so I stayed put and connected to the message.

'Hi, Sarah. Elliot has been asking questions about the– what do you call them – ah – the break-in stuff, the things he's meant to talk to the police about. Anyway, I know you're not in but give me a call, would you? I don't know what to tell the kid.' There was a long pause, then, when I thought the message might have ended without a farewell. 'I hope you're okay. I hope you're safe. Bye now.'

I hit redial and pressed the phone to my ear. Marcus answered after two rings.

'Talk of the devil.'

'Have I caught you with Elliot?' I let my head drop back against the seat behind me. 'Maybe I can just talk to him? I don't know why he didn't call me himself if he'd–'

'DS Brooks,' Marcus interrupted me. 'DS Brooks and I were just talking about you.'

I swallowed down a bubble of nerves that I couldn't quite explain. 'Brooks is there?'

'Looking for you, I believe.'

Why hadn't she called? 'About the break-in stuff?'

'Is there something else for her to talk to you about?' he asked, and I could hear the smirk. But I was unsure what information the smirk stemmed from: his knowledge of me and Brooks; or his knowledge of me and what he thought I'd been doing over the weekend. 'Should I tell her to come back another time, or...'

I bit down hard on a bullet. 'Put her on.'

There was a long pause and a shuffle while he handed the phone over.

'Sarah.' She'd obviously expected me to be there. I wondered

– worried – what Marcus might have told her. 'I wasn't sure whether I'd find you here or out hounding one of my colleagues.' I could hear her smile.

'Neither. Has my intern been hounding you?'

'Not exactly, but his voicemails are so...' she trailed off and I left space for her to think. 'Awkward. So awkward that I thought I'd come and talk to you both.'

'Elliot can't talk to you alone. His head will explode if he meets a real detective.'

She spluttered a laugh.

I imagined Marcus' face, watching the one side of the rapport between us. *What questions will come out of this*, I thought, leaning forward to rest my head on the steering wheel. 'If he's being a pain–'

'Not a pain, Sarah. He just doesn't know what he's doing.'

'I'm back in the office tomorrow. I'll be working from home for the rest of the day if you want me.' It had been a stressful weekend. An afternoon with Wren Brooks would be a good recovery, I thought; not even for the sex, I realised, but for her company. 'Or you can stop by the office later in the week.'

'The former sounds like the better option.'

I smiled. 'I'll see you later.'

For the rest of the day I fenced emails from Marcus and missed four phone calls from Elliot who, I guessed, had caught wind of Brooks' visit to the office. I was well into the afternoon when I remembered to text Landon to let him know I was home safe. I ignored his quick reply – 'Get lucky?' – then pulled up a blank message to Wren. I didn't need an exact time for when she might arrive. But I did need to get my paperwork filed away and into my safe, stashed away inside a fake cupboard in the back corner of my home office for safekeeping. She replied within minutes to say something had come up at work, but she'd text when she was leaving. I swallowed the urge to ask what had happened, for fear that it would sound like the journalist in me asking, which, in truth, it likely was. I typed what I hoped would be a non-committal reply – 'Okay, see you whenever.' – and then went back to work emails.

The day was cruising to a close when I came up for air. I'd replied to emails from various colleagues at the paper, as well as replying to my publisher about a string of events – anything to keep them off my back, I decided, before hungrily agreeing to their suggestions.

With still no word from Wren, the next job needed to be to pack away the folders parked in the hallway. I heaved the box into the office and dumped them in front of the open cupboard. One by one I pulled them free and stashed them in the safe. For every other folder I paused for distraction, reading back through letters, notes, more letters; newspaper clippings; wild theories. It was only the sort of obsessive behaviour that I'd taken up when I was planning the first book. But I was losing conviction in the belief that this had anything to do with a sequel.

'Where am I going to find you?' I said aloud to no one as I thumbed through a packet of colour-coded copies of letters. Like an amateur forensic examiner, I'd even started to highlight words with a regional meaning; phrases that might clue me up on where he was from, or places he'd been. The man had to have a paper-trail, I reasoned, and I was right. 'But the man and the killer are two different people.'

I wedged another folder in the safe, then another, and watched it slowly fill with years of trauma until I'd run out of evidence to try to hide. Minutes later, I forced a stop in the work. I collected the pile of post that had gone untouched for the afternoon and wandered to the kitchen, phone in tow, to make tea and call Madison. The promise to ring as soon as I was back in the city had fallen between the cracks of other demands, but that wasn't a surprise to me and likely hadn't been to her. With Wren coming, too, I decided that an over-the-phone catch-up would be better than no catch up at all. I dropped the squat pile of letters on the kitchen work surface, wedged my phone between my ear and my shoulder, and filled the kettle. When Madison didn't answer, I finished making tea and carried my handset through to the living room. I cradled the heat of the mug in my hands and tried not to think – or, tried not to think about him. But I knew it wouldn't stick.

I thumbed down to Madison's number and called again.

'Hey, Mad, it's me,' I spoke into her voicemail, 'I'm back home safe and sound. The afternoon sort of got away from me.' I forced a laugh. 'You know what I'm like. I'm around for a couple of hours now, though, so if you're free then maybe give me a call? Catch you later. Love you.'

A heavy sigh rushed out and I rubbed at my temples. It was just a phrase; there was nothing disloyal in it. But using the words had made the thinking/not thinking/thinking even worse. I took what was left of my tea back to the kitchen with me and skimmed through a playlist on the walk. With *Nothing but Thieves* humming in the background, I started to flick through the post – starting with the flyers for new takeaways that had opened in the five minutes that I'd been away.

'How many takeaways does one city need?'

I scooped them into the recycling bin and letter by letter flicked through what was left. Each envelope boasted a window frame with my name inside – apart from one right in the centre of the pile, which was handwritten.

In a cinematic style, then, the music cut out and gave way to a phone call: Wren Brooks. I took a step back from the letter and eyed the phone with a similar suspicion. But if he'd been here –

if he could get *in here* – I decided that having a police officer on their way might not be the worst thing.

'Wren,' I answered just in time, 'hey, when are you going–'

'Sarah, I just got a phone call – Jesus...' She paused and pulled in a greedy breath, and I felt my knee buckle beneath my weight. 'I just got a phone call from a friend at the hospital. It's Madison...'

38

Dear Sarah,

Sometimes, Sarah, when I'm thinking of you, which happens more often than I'd care to admit these days, I think of how unfair this all is on you. I can't imagine what it must be like to carry this around how you do. Although there are probably ways for you to make it easier. These letters mustn't help much though, which I know is selfish of me. Maybe I'm a selfish person, Sarah, I just don't know. We're too close to ourselves to see our worst faults, aren't we? I'm impulsive, I suppose, but not so impulsive that I'll dash off to a new city without doing my research on the place. That's something you've worked out for yourself already, though, isn't it, Sarah, thanks to the comeback tour.

The problem with tours though, Sarah, is that the dates are always changing. Have you ever had that happen? There'll be a date or a location listed and you'll think, yes, excellent news, I can make that; or I can be in town for that; or I can take time off work for that. You'll make all these plans around this one specific date and location – which is fine. But then, out of nowhere, there'll be a problem with the venue; the lighting; the back-up dancers. Who knows! It could be *any number of complicated reasons that prevent a tour happening how the organiser has planned for it to. Sometimes, Sarah, people just change their minds about things.*

And that's another thing that must make this hard on you: I always know something you don't. I knew where I was going to be the night your mum died – and all the other women. I still think about that night, Sarah, if I can be honest with you – the night with your mother. I don't think about it how I think of the other nights – or the other women, I suppose I mean – because your mum was just so special, don't you think, Sarah? Of course, you'll agree. Is there a young woman in the world who doesn't think their mother is special? The silver lining in this mess of ours, Sarah, is that you had a second mother ready to step in, didn't you? From what I've gathered, Madison doesn't have children of her own, though. Is there a reason for that, do you know? From afar at least she seems like a doting mother. She doesn't know what you're doing, though, does she, Sarah? I think you've been keeping all of this from her – keeping me from her. Then that makes me wonder, is it because you want me to yourself, Sarah? Or is it because you don't know what you want me for?

Maybe you need to spend some time thinking about that.

I'll be sorry to miss you this weekend, Sarah, because I really do enjoy whatever this mess is that we've made for ourselves. I have business elsewhere though; a change of schedule to the tour, you might say, something to keep me closer to home. Still, I'll call ahead to find you in Oxford, Sarah, to make sure you've arrived there okay. Maybe you'll salvage something from the weekend, some downtime. You really do need the break from things, Sarah, because you work so terribly hard – not just at the paper, or the comeback novel. Hey, when are we going to see that second book of yours anyway, Sarah; when will I have given you enough material for it? I'm amazed we're not there yet. Although it did take a mother the first time around...

You've already lost one though. It would be remiss of you to lose two.

Safe travels, Sarah. Be seeing you.

Sincerely, yours –

PART IV

39

'Witness comes forward...'
It was days later when I realised I'd made a mistake when I killed Evelyn. That night, I'd left the house like nothing at all had gone wrong. But the headlines knew what had happened.

Even then, without knowing for certain who it was, I had the clearest image of where they must have seen me. The woman – Eve to her friends so the early reports claimed – had said something before I'd gone into the bedroom. I'd assumed she was talking to herself. They do that sometimes, when they start to panic; talk themselves through the steps of hiding from me. I try to ignore it when it happens and I'd ignored it that night, too. But she hadn't been talking to herself at all, I guessed, as I started to read through the beginnings of the newspaper reports. She must have been talking to someone.

I clicked from one article to the next to try to find more details.

'Nasty business,' the cleaning woman at work narrated from behind me. It was too late for me to click out so I agreed with her, offering a hearty nod as I carried on looking through the screens. 'They're keeping that witness well out the way.'

'They certainly seem to be.' I didn't look away from the computer and she eventually took the hint to move on.

The articles didn't tell me anything that I didn't already know about Evelyn – apart from the fact that she liked to be called Eve. It made her too real, so I tried to skip over the detail whenever it came up, which was more often than I expected it to. It said a lot about how little information they had, though, and I took some comfort from that. Whoever the witness was, they hadn't told the police enough to catch me.

I repeated this cycle of looking through the newspapers every day. It was an easy enough endeavour to pass off as normal browsing. It was my lunchbreak; I was entitled to skim through the internet over a sandwich. With every lunchtime, though, more information filtered through. One day I was eating a tuna and mayonnaise sandwich with aged lettuce and vicious red onion, cheese that could have been used to erase pencil, and that's when I saw the reveal: a child.

'Police have since confirmed the witness to Evelyn Wainwright's murder was her daughter, Sarah Wainwright...'

'Sarah.' I rolled the name around in between mouthfuls. 'Sarah Wainwright.'

'Detectives are working closely with Sarah Wainwright to ascertain what she can confirm, relating to her mother's murder. A statement is due to be released later today to outline the next steps in the investigation with this witness in tow...'

I wasn't anywhere near as nervous as I thought I perhaps should have been. If anything, there was a strange sense of relief. Initially I thought it belonged to the reveal of the witness; if the police hadn't banged down my door already, they seemed unlikely to on the testimony of a child. But that wasn't where the relief had come from, I realised. Instead, the relief belonged to being seen...

Sarah was a child of the social media age. Even when she wasn't posting – which she often wasn't, in the days and weeks after her mother's death – her friends were still active enough for me to have a sense of what was happening. Without her uploading fresh material, I found myself drawn to a back catalogue of bad photographs and typographical errors that made up her accounts. She didn't have especially advanced security settings in place – another thing befitting of her age – which made it easy enough to go through her history. But when I arrived at pictures of her and her mother together – 'Day out with the bestie' – I back-clicked out of the profile and took a comfort break. There were other people, other things to be checking on.

I found it hard to pull away from Sarah, though, even though I knew the risks of staying close. The letter was an indulgence, a careless one at that. But the more she was reported on as the child of a murder victim, the more I – the guilty party, the puppeteer – felt the need to reach out. It wasn't redemption; no person in their right mind would forgive what had happened. It was a kind of closeness, though, and I needed it. It was selfish of me. But maybe I was a selfish person.

The letter – handwritten, even though no one appreciates penmanship anymore – would make or break my relationship with Sarah, I decided. She might read it and go straight to the police, or she might do exactly what I asked of her. So, I watched carefully in the days after it arrived. She didn't seem to be taking extra care with her whereabouts – if anything, she looked even more eager to be left alone. But her friends and her surrogate – Madison – made it hard for her to get any breathing space. I could see Sarah struggling with that. But even through the struggles, there still weren't extra news reports; there was no headline flash about contact with the killer. I knew, then, that Sarah and I might have something.

Time stretched out between us in the years that followed. I did my best not to crowd her, to let her grow and advance despite it all. But there were times when I experienced such a swell of feeling – it might have been misplaced pride, or something like it – and I couldn't stop myself then. When there was talk of a book; when there was an interest in a journalism career; when there was talk of a sequel, before the first story had even hit the shelves. It occurred to me, then, Sarah was holding on to me as tightly as I'd held her. I liked that. All my women had felt special before. But after Evelyn, I lost track of who was more special: the women, or the one who'd watched.

40

2017

In the minutes before people die, their faces fall into different displays of feeling: hurt to disbelief to denial to – quiet. Evelyn's expression had been one of panic for most of the time that I was with her. Initially I'd assumed it was her fear of death. Later, I realised it would have been her panic at whether her daughter was next. It's just like a mother to put someone else first like that. That's why I never would have attacked her if I'd known. Since Evelyn I spent more time with women before letting anything happen. Sarah had been easily missed from the outside of Evelyn's home – a teenager with an active social life especially – because I hadn't been able to be there all the time. And I still couldn't be there all the time. But I made a point of being there enough to know whether there was anyone else in the household who might suffer the fallout of my actions. It was one thing to ruin one person, but to let someone else carry the weight of that felt like an unnecessary cruelty.

When I wasn't watching the women, I was busy making a concerted effort to be around for Sarah as much as I could be, especially during times of crisis. When she pulled out of the garage underneath her building, I recognised her mother in her for the first time. They both wore the same panic.

I pulled out from the street opposite and followed from three cars behind. I'd got used to this safe distance. Although I wondered whether she felt the same creeping sensation as I did at close proximity. It didn't seem likely, but still.

The radio was white noise to our car chase. I half-listened to news reports relating to the local area – further break-ins; plans for citywide developments to the road structures; opportunities for a regional festival – all the while thinking how much better Sarah's reporting was. She had a cutting style that she took into every article with her. I admired that. From the way she carried herself I imagined that she might talk in the same way that she wrote: firm and to the point, never saying more or less than she needed to. That's how she'd appeared in television interviews; although it wasn't how she sounded on podcast episodes, so I knew there was a balance somewhere.

She was driving like a lunatic, though, and this wasn't the first time I'd followed her, so I knew from experience that she wasn't a reckless driver. When she made a sharp turn left, then right, left, left, and right again, I understood the aggression – the panic: The Queen Elizabeth Hospital. She pulled into the first empty parking space she came to, leaving me to loop around the multi-storey's layers until I found a spot.

With a smaller sense of urgency than Sarah's own, I took the stairs down to the hospital's entrance. She wasn't there; I don't know whether I'd expected her to be. But the knucklehead paramour of hers – I had no way of knowing for certain, but I'd guessed that there was a history there – was standing outside with a cigarette between his lips and his phone pressed between his ear and shoulder. He fumbled with a lighter as he spoke.

'She called me on the drive in...'

I hated the thought of Sarah using her phone while she was

driving, especially when her concentration had been so frayed already. Whatever her reason for being here, then, it wasn't because something had happened to this one; an idle fantasy that had crossed my mind more than once.

'I don't know, Jessie...'

So, person number two was safe.

'She's gone straight in... I'm smoking... Fucking right I'm smoking...'

'Excuse me,' someone pushed, and when I turned to avoid them I found myself face to face with–

'I'm sorry.' My words were so hurried they knocked into each other. 'I didn't–'

'No bother.' He turned away from me. 'Brooks called her... I don't know... Jess, I – I just don't know, okay?... Maybe you can come down, or Tyler...' I heard his words catch in his throat, as though feeling had made a mixer of his voice box. 'I can't see her go through this again, Jess, I can't.'

Someone dropped a small weight into my stomach. I grabbed the nearest railing outside of the hospital to steady myself, vying for space with a patient being propped up by a metal walking frame. They already had something to hold on to, I reasoned my need was greater. I listened as knucklehead repeated the same denial – 'I can't... I can't watch it happen to her a second time over...' – all the while thinking, *No, neither can I.*

Over the afternoon and into the evening I moved my car from one spot to another, to another. When I could sit in the passenger's seat and crane my neck for a view of Sarah's car, I decided to wait it out until I saw her leave. Another two hours passed before that happened. When she walked into view, the boy had his arm around her waist; it wasn't a romantic gesture, though, but more of a structural decision. He looked as though he were holding her upright. Their faces were cherry-blotched with the aftermath of tears. He looked worse than Sarah – but she was well-versed in this loss, I thought. She pulled away from him and leaned against the boot of her car. When she was free-standing, she only lasted seconds before her knees cracked beneath her weight and she slid down the paintwork, landing in a crouch at the back of the vehicle. He dropped in front of her and held her head pressed against his shoulder; her whole body stuttered with feeling. I felt a strange tingling at the roof of my nose, almost between my eyes. I wondered whether sympathy tears were a recognised phenomenon; *is this sympathy, then?* I thought.

After a full two minutes of watching them feel things I undid my seat belt and slid my seat back for leg room. My hand rested on the doorhandle. It was an automatic gesture; I couldn't recall having moved.

'And what do you think you'll do if you go over?' I asked under my breath, before dismissing whatever idea had been brewing. But I wanted so badly to be there for her.

41

Dear Sarah,

Sarah, I'm just so sorry. For someone so young, you've known so much loss, and so intimately, too, I can't imagine what it must be to have people die around you – not like this, anyway. I've tried to keep up with the news, Sarah, but there's little information available. You may be glad to know that; take some comfort from the little coverage this loss has gained for you. I'm sure you have fans who are aware of what's happening. They'll be feeding on the matter, no doubt. But, Sarah, you must grieve in the way that feels best for you. I don't suppose it's my place to tell you that. You must already know these things. You're a woman of the world, aren't you?

I will say, Sarah, that in the cluttered forum spaces of the internet, there are flickers of unpleasant things being said. I've no idea of the details of Madison's death. What I can say, though, is that it wasn't me, Sarah. My last letter was sent not so much in jest, but more in a teasing way. You should know me well enough to know that I wouldn't take a second mother away from you. Of course, it isn't careless of you to have lost a second one either. I wish, Sarah, that I could take that back. If only I'd known what might happen.

Although I know so many people feel that way about so many things when they lose someone.

In all these thoughts, new and old about what's unfair to you, Sarah, it strikes me that one of the unfairest things of all is that I can always reach you – but you can never reach me. I wish there were a way around that, because I imagine – no, I like to imagine I might be of some use at the moment. After all this time together, Sarah, I'm almost a familiar face, aren't I? It's selfish – although we've already decided I'm a selfish person, haven't we – but I wonder whether you've thought of me at all during these weeks. Have you clung to the comeback tour as something to keep you rooted, or have you cast it out entirely as something with no belonging in your life anymore? It feels dramatic to suggest it, even, but I'd be lying if I said the worry hadn't crossed my mind.

I suppose we'll find out the answer soon enough, won't we.

I do hope you're being kind to yourself, Sarah. Handle all of this with great care.

Sincerely, yours –

I was two people behind her in the queue at the coffee shop. Since Madison I'd found sleeping harder than usual, and I'd sworn off caffeine entirely to try to help it. My medication should make sleeping easier, too, but even that didn't seem to ease the night-time struggles of it all. Still, when I edged closer to the front of the queue I started to eye up the listings of herbal tea and fruit smoothies, for the sake of ordering something – for the sake of, perhaps, being closer to her for a minute or so while we waited at the end of the counter for our drinks. I half-heard her order – '…with two shots, please.' – and thought she must be struggling to sleep, too. I'd seen the lights on at her house well into the early hours of the morning for the last few evenings. But you never could be sure whether it was someone up past their bedtime, or someone who'd been too tired to even turn out a light. The make-up she wore had covered the evidence well. It was more than she normally wore; more than I liked her to.

'What can I get for you today?'

I looked at the menu boards with wide eyes. 'Something with low caffeine.' There came a snort from the end of the counter – her. 'I'm sorry?'

She laughed. 'No, I'm sorry. I'm on the opposite end of the caffeine spectrum.'

'Hard time sleeping?' I was torn between grabbing the opportunity to talk to her and shying away from the contact. The woman behind the counter appeared with a takeaway coffee cup that she set down on the counter. 'Hence the giant coffee.'

Another laugh. 'I need something to get through the day. Bye now.'

The goodbye trailed after her and I didn't reciprocate for fear of appearing too involved. Instead, I stayed rooted to the spot, ordered my peppermint tea, and patiently waited for the cup to arrive. Outside the shop, though, her car was still parked ten strides away. Wherever she'd gone, it wasn't far.

It was the first time we'd spoken.

I pulled in a hungry amount of air and smiled wide on the exhale. This was a special moment and I needed to give myself enough time to remember it, before the adrenaline made it impossible to recall the intricacies. On the walk to the shop I'd noticed a post box, so I re-traced my steps until I came across it again. I'd carried the letter in my pocket for so long that the corners had started to wear blue from the denim of my jeans. This wasn't the first time I'd tried to post it. Since Madison, every letter I'd drafted felt inconsequential – incomplete, somehow. I knew there wasn't anything I could say to improve things for Sarah, though the letter at least might be a welcome distraction. With the envelope resting on the lip of the post box, I pulled in another greedy breath before letting the paper slide through the allotted space.

On the walk back – to where her car might still be parked – I wondered whether Sarah would notice the city where the letter had been franked...

42

Alison Harris was a finance officer at a private hospital in Leicester city centre. According to her LinkedIn profile, she'd been there for nearly ten years. According to the expression she wore when she walked into the building every day, she hated it. But she always looked so much happier when she was leaving. Alison worked regular hours, which made it easier to learn things; much easier than it had been with Sarah – or Evelyn.

I watched her tread into the building with a glum expression. Her hair looked darker in the autumnal sunshine and I liked that; it made her look different to the others. Her shoulders were hunched over underneath a jacket that looked too big for her, and I wondered whether she'd lost weight since I first saw her. When she was inside the building, I knew that I had a set number of hours to get my work done – including a visit to Alison's house. If I could get back to the hospital for lunchtime, though, there was a real possibility that I'd find her at the same coffee shop that she'd been visiting lately – the one where we'd spoken. My belly rolled at the memory.

Her house was a drive away from the city, so I left to get my car from the side street where I'd stashed it. It took nearly twenty minutes to get out of the centre's traffic and I wondered, not for the first time, whether this was a contributing factor to Alison's sadness when she arrived at work every day. But then, the happiness at going home alone for an evening with a microwave meal and too many glasses of wine – if her recycling bin in the garden was a fair indicator – was another thing I couldn't quite understand about her.

I left my car one residential street away. Her house was buried inside a winding burrow of cul-de-sacs and sideroads that I trod through, before arriving at her garden gate. She never locked it, which seemed a reckless decision for a woman living alone. I pushed gently, opening the way into the property. I closed the entryway behind me, in case anyone should pass, and then slowly walked along the path. Alison always took care with the garden. There were plants in bloom, still, despite the recent changes in temperature. She knew the right time of year for things to seed, I guessed, and it showed in her neat borders and bright colours that clashed with the day. It was due to rain.

I tried the backdoor, although she'd never been careless enough to leave it open. The house – all of this, in fact – felt familiar, despite my sporadic visits. I hadn't spent as much time in Leicester as I had in other areas. But the opportunity had arisen to spend at least a weekend in the city and I'd thought of Alison, thought of Sarah, and packed a bag.

I pressed down the handle of the backdoor and leaned into the hinges of it. Even though it was locked, I thought, that didn't mean it wouldn't give way under the right pressure. When my shoulder landed against it, though, it didn't budge at all, and I mentally crossed it off the list of entry points that might prove useful. Window by window I tapped my way around the downstairs of the house. But I struck luck on something I hadn't seen before. On my last visit there had been a set of garden furniture; chairs and a table. They had now been packed away in preparation for the winter months. In moving the furniture, though, Alison had unveiled a squat window towards the bottom of an outside wall; a basement, I assumed. I lowered myself down and pressed a gloved hand against the pane – and it opened.

I was careful to leave everything as I'd found it. During the walkthrough my phone vibrated and caught my attention – a new article uploaded at Sarah's workplace, but not one that was written by her – which alerted me, too, to the time. The morning had fallen away in the cracks between Alison's floorboards.

I'd explored the kitchen, downstairs bathroom, the living area that looked to double as an office. There were lots of hospital logos on the paperwork and I decided she likely knew more about the order of things better than I, so I left them as I found them.

When I saw the time, though, I realised the rest of the house would have to wait for another day. I didn't want to miss her leaving for her lunch.

The side street in the city centre that I had parked in for the morning was clogged with other vehicles when I got back to it. It was a blessing in disguise, I realised, because spending the whole day in a well-populated area wouldn't have served me well. I pulled a cap from my glove compartment and searched for a nearby multi-storey instead. When I'd parked the car I checked my phone again – still nothing written or posted by Sarah – and decided to go straight to the coffee shop. Alison would have left work already, ten minutes ago if not more, and I didn't want to waste the lunchtime.

The pavements from the car park to the coffee shop were alive with people rushing through their lunch hours. Three people apologised – a grunted, 'I'm sorry,' in passing – but four others said nothing at all as they knocked shoulders with me. I could be pick-pocketed and not even realise in a city this busy. When the thought dangled in front of me, I found I was reaching for my phone – clutching it in my palm until sweat beads formed – and checking for my wallet with the other hand. The coffee shop itself spat out a flurry of youngsters with their high-caffeine drinks and avocado smoothies, but when they'd cleared it was easy to see straight into the building. I looked first to the queue, where I had bumped into Alison before, but when I failed to find the wave of her dark hair I scanned the room at large. It was her silhouette I noticed first, a hazy outline of a white shirt, disturbed by strands of hair. Like a spasm of the mind, I imagined grabbing it by the fistful.

There was a man with her. They weren't standing and talking, either, but sitting and having lunch. I hadn't seen them together before and there'd been no mention of a new relationship on Alison's social media. In a rush I flicked back through the house as I'd seen it earlier; there were no signs there, either. But I hadn't made it to the bedroom, where all manner of male trinkets might have been stashed away. I needed to get back there in the afternoon, I decided, then, to make sure I knew my options – knew what I was going to find, when I eventually made it to Alison.

Under normal circumstances, this might have been enough to scupper a plan. But as I watched them – Alison, with her slim figure and pale complexion; him, with his angular shoulders and slim legs – I thought for the very first time: *I could take them both.*

43

When I walked into the office on Tuesday morning a wave of good mornings came at me from various points throughout the room.

I hadn't missed much, Phil told me, while I was trying to brew my morning coffee at the drink station. 'Sandra landed a big deal with PhotoTech so that's something exciting, I suppose.' He tried to sound like it wasn't exciting at all. But that was largely because Phil had also been bidding for the PhotoTech advertising contract. It must have irked him to his core that she'd beat him to the punch. Phil had always been the type of man who couldn't stand to be bested by a woman. I'd always disliked that about him.

'How was Leicester? Did you get what you needed?' he asked, as I was trying to walk away. I swallowed a mouthful of coffee, even though it was too hot, to buy myself another second or two to think of an answer.

For a full hour I had watched Alison walk around her kitchen making an elaborate dinner. I'd never seen anyone go to such effort to dine alone. So it wasn't a complete surprise when she disappeared out of sight – to answer the front door, I assumed – and then walked back in with the same man from the coffee shop. Two dates in a twenty-four-hour period seemed keen. But they were both enthusiastic by the looks of their body language. They sat at the kitchen table drinking red wine, like something tumbled from the opening credits of a romantic comedy. My stomach lurched over when Alison got up to check whatever was in the oven. She bent over – I couldn't work out whether she was being deliberately slow, to make a show of the action – and he watched her. I didn't like how he looked at her, though, as though he were hungry for something – something else. Another half an hour rolled out with them like this. I watched them get to know each other: the feet knocking beneath the table; the way Alison kept pushing her hair behind her ears, leaving her powdered face pale in the overhead lighting, and open to adoration. More than once I had thought of going in through the bottom window – still loose, as it had been earlier. But I hadn't been able to work out the practicalities of overpowering two people; even if one of them did happen to be petite.

'It was a bit of a wash-out,' I said, and shrugged. 'Worth trying though.'

'What was the product again?'

I didn't know whether Phil was asking to be reminded or asking to check whether I'd give the same answer as before I left. 'It's a private hospital up that way, looking to do a big revamp on their advertising campaign, but I didn't like the look of the place.' I made a grimace. 'You know when something doesn't feel right about a company? I just couldn't see us working with them.'

'Shame. Next time, eh?'

He turned away, then, and I felt a wave of relief at how easily he'd let it go.

With my morning coffee, I skimmed through the online pages of *The Herald*. Every morning there was a print copy distributed with the post, but until that arrived I'd have to make do with the digitised pages. The crime section looked sparse and I wondered whether Sarah wasn't yet back at work. But that seemed unlikely. She needed it, after all. I picked through page after page looking for her until I was two thirds of the way down my mug – and then I found her in the obituary section.

'Hey, you're back.' Terry, the person well-known throughout the office and, I guessed the city at large, for his ability to state the obvious. 'How long have we got you for this time?'

I smiled. 'I'm meant to be hitting Nottingham next month but I'll be in Birmingham until then I should think. It's nice to be on your own stomping ground for a while, isn't it? No place like home and all that.'

'Yeah.' He sipped his own drink and I downed what was left of mine. 'Must be nice to spend some time with Cassie as well, I'll bet. She must miss you while you're out and about all over the place.'

'I don't know about that. I sometimes think it's what keeps us together.'

We shared a laugh, then, in the way that men often laugh about their wives.

He nodded at the screen behind me. 'Did you know her?'

I tried to make a show of looking flummoxed. 'Oh, shit, no I didn't. I must have clicked into it by mistake.'

'Well,' he took another sip, 'don't let me keep you, fella. See you at lunch?'

'I'll be there.'

When he was a clear distance from my desk I turned and faced the screen again. Sarah had written the obituary herself, which I imagined to be both a crushing and cathartic experience. She'd picked a picture of Madison that looked to be at least ten years old. She was laughing, with her arms flung around an equally happy looking companion – Evelyn. I wondered why Sarah had done that.

> Madison Hewitt passed away aged 50. She is survived by her foster daughter, of sorts, Sarah Wainwright, who Madison took under her wing at a young age. Madison was the only daughter of Harry and Olive Hewitt; she never married and had no children of her own. Although after taking in Sarah, she became a mother to a motley crew of teenagers, all of whom will miss her dearly.
>
> Madison was a kind and gentle individual with more friends than she realised. These were friends she acquired during years of varied careers and free time that was spent volunteering. During her life, she worked as...

The entire obituary was written with the fondness of someone who had known her. It would have been difficult, but I imagined Sarah piecing the article together with her so-called motley crew of friends. The boys would have contributed little but the other girl – the mother – she would have been helpful. I skimmed through the details of Madison's life and felt my own weight of sadness form somewhere in my larynx. When people around me continued with their 'Good morning' routine, I could only bring myself to nod by way of replying for fear of the noise that may come out otherwise. When I saw that I was nearing the end of the announcement – one paragraph at most left to read – I felt a notable relief. Until...

> From the author to the deceased: Madison, it's been a lifetime of experiences. Thank you. I can only hope that one day I'll be seeing you. But until then,
> Sincerely, yours –

I wondered why Sarah had done that.

PART V

44

Tina had had the opening chapters of my new book for nearly a month when she sent me a late-night email. I'd kept as busy as possible – with the paper, with the podcast, with the impending arrival of another Jessie–Tyler offspring – but when my editor emailed me nearing midnight one evening, asking for a phone call, I replied straight away: *Are you free now?*

She said she wanted to talk with a clear head: *Can I call you tomorrow?*

I agreed in record time and told her to call whenever she could; I'd make myself available. Sleep was out of the question after that. I sat cross-legged on the floor of my makeshift home office, with my laptop in front of me. There was a green dot next to Landon's name on his social media page so I knew he was also flirting with the wrong side of midnight.

Free? I asked him.

He replied: *What for?*

So I called him.

'I might have been in the middle of someone,' he answered after two rings.

'It can't be very good if you're answering the phone to me.'

'Well, maybe it is good, and I just prefer talking to you all the same.'

I laughed. 'Then it must be *really* bad if you prefer an after-midnight crisis with me.'

'Oh, if it's a crisis you're having then I might reconsider.' There was a hum of music in the background. I heard Landon shuffle around, then the sound cut dead. 'I'm all yours.'

'I don't think Tina liked the chapters.' There was a long pause, as though he was waiting for more information. 'She emailed me earlier tonight asking if we could talk over the phone about it all.'

'And that must be a bad thing?'

'Does it sound like a good one?'

'I mean...' I heard him shuffle around again. 'As I haven't read the chapters–'

'Nice try.'

'I'm just saying.'

No one had read the chapters. In the months after Madison's death I'd started to compile everything I had: theories; hard and soft evidence alike; and, most importantly, the letters. There were copies of them everywhere: on my laptop; home computer; even the work desktop. The closer I got to a finished manuscript the more I worried about something happening – not to it, but me. Tina only had the first few chapters because I'd resolved to take it to another publisher entirely if she decided they couldn't represent the work. It wasn't finished, but it was close enough that I could sell to another house if I needed to.

I heard Landon spark up and speak through a mouthful of smoke. 'Is it a sequel?'

'What do you mean?'

'You know what I mean, Sarah.'

'It's about violent crime. But I didn't talk to the same victims or anything.' It was the same party line I'd given to everyone:

Landon; Marcus; even Tina for a time. I'd given the book a mythical status and convinced myself that talking about it was a way of making the entire story collapse in on itself. But now it was a living, breathing near-formed thing – and I was going to have to think of a new lie to describe it.

Landon exhaled hard to empty himself of the toxins and then spoke slowly, as though addressing a child – or an idiot. 'Is it about him?'

~

Tina called at nine thirty the next morning. I crossed my work office and closed the door.

'Sarah.' She pulled in a mouthful of air. 'How are you?'

'Oh, I'm fine, you?'

'No, Sarah, try again. How *are* you?'

Since Madison people had done this, leaned hard on asking how I was. Since Madison, I hadn't known how to answer. 'Can I have a question on sport instead?'

She laughed. 'I understand. I'm fine, thank you. Although we've got a real shitstorm brewing here with an author who's– well, I shouldn't be telling you this, really, but there we are. With an author who's making claims to have had intimates with a celebrity; the celebrity is denying it, which they would because they have a spouse.' She sighed. 'Remember when literature was literature and not... hearsay?'

Tina never told a story unless there was a moral. I wondered where she was going.

'That sounds difficult.' I pulled the emergency cigarettes from my top drawer and moved to the windowsill. 'Will you drop the book?'

'Christ, honey, who knows. But that's why I needed to talk to you about this opening. These chapters you sent over, Sarah, they're damn good writing.'

I paused with my lighter midway to the cigarette end. It felt like a waste of an emergency stash, if Tina were about to give me good news. 'Yes?'

'You're claiming this killer is still active.' She took a long pause and when I didn't confirm or deny the claim – she had the chapters; she knew – she carried on with her worried tones. 'But do you have hard evidence of it? Evidence that will make its way into the book, for instance?'

'I've got all the evidence I think I need.'

There was a long pause. 'Then I'm going to need to see it.'

'I can bring down an external hard drive with copies of the letters on.'

'You're not storing this stuff on the cloud?' Then, before I could answer, 'Oh.'

'I'm just trying to be careful about where I'm storing information, Tina. You know what us writers are like,' I said, trying to brush off the beginnings of her concern. 'I've got copies saved on different machines, but I'd prefer for the letters themselves to stay off the internet for the time being.'

'As long as you're being safe, Sarah. I don't just mean with– you know.'

It was impossible for me to tell her I was being safe without telling a blatant lie or two. For the sake of her conscience, though, I knew she needed to hear it. In my experience, people hated the thought of knowing someone else was being reckless; they felt as though they were somehow liable. But in the years since Mum – more so, even, in the year since Madison – people had concerned themselves with my safety. I wondered whether, after losing not one mother but two, there was a covert rota drawn up between the grown-ups in my life, where they'd all agreed to do their best not to die and to make sure I didn't either.

I pulled in a greedy amount of air. 'I'm being as safe as I can be.'

'Mhmm.' Tina had a string of thinking noises she'd made during previous meetings; I recognised this as one of them, so I held my quiet. 'I'll need the letters, or a sample of the letters, for my own peace of mind. And I need a timeline. How close are we to having a finished draft of this?'

'I've got everything apart from the last few chapters.'

'And you're still working to the outline you sent me?'

'I'm hoping to.'

In Tina's inbox there was a chapter-by-chapter breakdown of the book, as it read, alongside chapter plans for the remainder of the story. The final portion, then, was subject to change. But everything else had happened: canonical victims; unofficial ones; ones that he'd planned at the time of me drafting. I'd be handing the police a gift-wrapped manuscript, half-written by one of the most prolific serial killers they'd ever seen.

'Sarah, how can you be sure about all this?' Tina asked. Her voice was full of worry. 'How are you sure you'll catch him?'

I thought back to the first letter he'd sent after Madison. I'd make sure that it was included in the batch that went to Tina. But to pacify her until the hard drive of documents was handed over, I simply explained, 'Because he needs me to.'

45

Sarah,

I didn't take kindly to you using my words against me like that. I've never done anything to hurt Madison, Sarah, you must understand that. I think you've misjudged me so much to date. How could it have been at my hand? I can even go as far to tell you where I was, Sarah, when Madison fell ill, so you know for certain that I wasn't with her: I was outside your building. You rushed from the front door and down into the car park. You pulled out into busy traffic without a thought. You broke the speed limit on the way to the hospital, although I didn't know your reasoning at the time. Then, when you arrived, the boy appeared to support you; the one from your show. He stayed with you the entire time and he tried to get the girl, and the other boy, to come to visit you but they couldn't, or wouldn't. I didn't hear enough to discern their reasoning for it. But there you are, Sarah, now you know for certain I wasn't with her because I'd been spending all my time with you — like I have been for years now, and I'm only just seeing it.

The weekend when we missed each other, when we should have been in Oxford together, my spouse was ill and I couldn't leave the city. Does that surprise you, Sarah, that I have someone? I wonder whether it makes you sad at all, or angry, even. There are times when I feel guilt over them – not because of the other women, Sarah, but because of you. There have been so many hours whittled into minutes for them, when I should have been present with them, but instead I was finding a way to be with you.

After Madison, Sarah, I stuck to my original plan: to Leicester. I knew you wouldn't be there, though, or that you were unlikely to be. I pursued a nice woman, who I've spent a little time with over the last six months or so, and I was close, Sarah, so close to spending an evening with her – and someone else, too, for bonus points. Then, quite unexpectedly, I found myself crouched outside her kitchen window wondering what the point of it all was. It was nearly an existential crisis, Sarah, so I found what I thought might be my crisis trigger: your absence. What is the point, I asked myself, if she isn't here to see it? In that moment I realised we'd tipped into a strange kind of relationship, Sarah, and I've spent some time sitting with that before writing this. The last letter I sent will have alerted you to my visit to Leicester. There won't be another visit out of the city for a month now – despite what the tour schedule says. So I'll be here; breathing the same air and treading the same streets as you. Which brings us back to the topic of fair and unfair and – it's always been unfair on you, Sarah. But I'm going to level the playing fields now. I'm going to find a way for you to find me...

Until then, Sarah, please do take care. I'll be in touch.

Sincerely, yours –

46

Marcus escorted a heavily pregnant Jessie into my office. He walked closely behind her with his arm outstretched, as though she might give birth right there in my open doorway. I was midway through a phone call with a source – 'Let me call you back in thirty minutes or so, would you?' – to discuss a robbery at an art gallery in the city centre, but it was nothing that couldn't wait. I pulled out the visitor chair to an angle, to make it easier for Jessie to back into. She settled down with the discomfort of a woman who'd been carrying a heavy load for too long. I nearly laughed. *Haven't we all, though?* I thought as I stepped back around to the right side of the desk.

'This is a surprise.' I sat opposite her. 'Drink? Birthing pool?'

She laughed; a tired laugh, though, which made me wonder whether the pregnancy jibes were wearing thin, eight months into the gestation. 'Can I get a tea?'

Marcus leapt into action. 'I'll get that.'

'Make it a decaf,' I instructed him, and flashed a tight smile at Jessie.

'I'll skip the drink,' she answered flatly.

'I'll get you one anyway, just in case.' Marcus fluttered

out of the room without awaiting further instruction, and I thought he was likely grateful for something to do. He'd lived through three pregnancies with his own wife and, from his entrance with Jessie, I thought he must remember first-hand how testy these final weeks were. I hadn't seen much of Jessie in the last few weeks, admittedly, but from her frosty entrance it was clear she was a mother on the edge.

'How are the twins?'

She rolled her eyes. 'Fine. They're fine. It's...' she trailed off, as though uncertain whether to continue. 'It's Tyler that's the bloody problem. Not the problem, it's just – Christ.' She rubbed her forehead. 'Sometimes it's like having three children already. And when it isn't like that, it's like having my mother living with me.'

'I see.' I leaned back in the chair. 'Difficult daddy issues?'

'I think he's finding it hard to tread a line between being involved and– I don't know, something else. Not being involved enough, I guess.'

Marcus reappeared with a takeaway cup. 'Decaf, skimmed milk, in a takeaway in case you change your mind but also want to leave.' He rushed the explanation out and then gave a curt nod. I wondered whether he'd recited the drink details from the kitchen to my office, to make sure he got everything just right – with minimal potential for offence.

Jessie smiled. 'Thank you.'

'No bother at all. You take care now.'

I waited for Marcus to hurry from the office before I asked, 'So, here about Tyler?'

'Actually, here about the party.'

I threw her a quizzical look.

'I thought as much,' she added.

'Did I miss something in the group chat?' I was reaching for my phone as I asked the question. But I saw Jessie give a shake of the head. 'Ah shit, has the party already happened?'

'I went to your flat before I came here.' *Ah, shit indeed.* Whatever face I made was telling enough for Jessie to continue. 'The doorman let me in, because I didn't know your code. Actually, I thought I knew your code, but apparently you've asked for it to be changed more regularly now? He recognised me, though.' Each flat had an individual passcode for the building – plus the generic 'deliveries' button that was available to any old intruder. I'd requested some time ago that my personal code – that was logged in a system somewhere every time I used it – was changed more often. The new code was text through to me whenever the system generated it. But I couldn't exactly stop the deliveries coming.

'He did say he was surprised to see me, though,' Jessie continued with her monologue. 'Given that you haven't really been around much. He wondered, maybe, whether you'd moved out completely. And I thought, no, Sarah wouldn't *move* without saying something.'

Landon knew. So, I pacified myself with that knowledge. But given the growing flare in Jessie's tone, I decided it was information best kept to myself. I hadn't moved out of the flat, and if all went to plan then I wouldn't. But I hadn't been sleeping there for the last few weeks either. I went back often enough, I thought – to check the post and any voicemails – but there was an anonymous place on the other side of the city where I'd been spending my time outside of work. Landon knew I wasn't at home, but even he didn't know the details of where I was sleeping – or rather, where I was working, and occasionally passing out. But the last three letters before the move had been hand-delivered to the flat, and the closing proximity had felt too much at last.

'I haven't moved,' I said plainly.

'But you aren't sleeping at the flat.' It wasn't a question, but I gave a slow nod all the same. 'What's going on, Sar?'

I half-sighed. 'I'm working on a new book. Actually, I'm nearly finished with a new book.' I tried to inject excitement into the announcement. 'But there are more distractions at home, and, I just thought I'd work better out of the flat. I'm renting a place, still in the city, though, and it really isn't permanent. It's a week a time thing.' I kept adding details until Jessie's eyebrow lowered back to its natural resting place.

'How dangerous is it, Sarah?'

I nearly laughed. 'Mama bear, look, it isn't dangerous but–'

She held up a hand to stop me. 'Don't, okay? Over the last year, I've made my peace with the fact that there's shit you don't tell me anymore. I don't know whether it's me, or because of the kids, or – I don't know, Sarah, maybe you're really trying that hard to keep us safe. That's the option I prefer to believe.' She fumbled with the zip of her bag as she spoke and pulled out a white envelope. I felt my stomach muscles knot with worry. 'Whatever the reason for that distance, you're still one of the most important people in *my* life,' her emphasis felt like a cut, 'so I'd really like it if you were there.' She slid the envelope across but didn't wait for me to open it. 'Tyler and I weren't going to tell anyone. But we thought, I don't know, it might just be a nice thing, as we didn't have a baby shower and all.'

I pulled apart the lips of the envelope and fished out a neat white card, splashed with watercolour marks of pink, blue and yellow.

'It's a gender reveal kind of thing. I know it's American of us.' Jessie had gone from confrontational to soft-boiled in a second turnaround. I didn't know whether it was the hormones or the topic, but either way I was thankful. 'It would mean everything if–'

'I'll be there.'

She smiled. 'I know you're busy, and away a lot.'

'I'll be there,' I repeated, and I reached for my diary. 'I'll pencil it in right now, which basically means it's chiselled in stone, and I'll be there. What can I bring?'

'You. Just bring you.'

On Jessie's way out of the office we shared an awkward hug – around the belly – and I promised that I'd see her before the gender reveal party happened. It was only three weeks away, and I think we both knew I'd likely just told a lie – but I hoped that Jessie would see the kindness of thought was there at least. After she'd left, I opened the top drawer of my desk – the opposite side to where the cigarettes were stashed – and pulled out my second diary, hidden right at the back of the space. I placed the two books side by side and flicked through the pages of the second one until the dates married with the first. I was meant to be out of the city that weekend – for him. But a lot could happen in three weeks. *I might catch him*, I thought. *Or he might even catch me.*

47

Jessie must have sent the invite in the last week or two, if not longer. It wasn't until she'd gone that I did the maths, and realised how long it really must have been since I was last at home. On the way home from the office, then, I decided to detour to the old place to collect post and check messages – and to tell the doorman not to tell people I was probably moving. It had been a while since I walked through the city as the sky was closing in. On my best days it was a nice enough activity. But on the worst days, I wondered whether every man, woman and person-who-could-pass-as-a-child might know something I didn't. It was paranoia; objectively, I knew, but subjectively the concerns were hard to shake. By the time I'd got to the front door of my old building I'd managed to steady my breathing into something close to normal. My watch had vibrated twice to alert me of a worrying heartrate, but things looked more stable now as I keyed in the door code and pushed in.

The front desk was unmanned – 'Back in twenty minutes' – so the chat with the doorman would have to wait. I climbed the stairs, to avoid the closeness a lift would create, and took a look left, right, then left again when I pushed through into the corridor. Landon had guessed why I was leaving. 'He knows where you live, doesn't he?' he'd asked, plainly. I'd brushed it off, instead leaning on the lie that it was a matter of wanting to get the book finished before the year was out, and not having the self-control to do it at home.

'You're never *at* home, Sarah. You're always crime fighting in a different city.'

'I am not crime fighting,' I spat back, trying to borrow from his aggression. But I'd been too tired for the argument. And when Landon pulled me into a too tight hug, I knew he'd seen the tiredness, too. 'I'm sorry,' I had said into his shoulder, 'but I have to do this.'

'Whatever this is, just try to bring my best friend back from it, would you?'

I shook away the last of our conversation as I slid my key in the door. It budged an inch, but I had to lean my shoulder against it to move it the rest of the way. However long it had been, the post had piled up while I was gone. I flicked through the first few things on the pile – and spotted Tyler's scrawl on the party invitation – and then arrived at a handwritten envelope that made the back of my throat burn with worry. He'd carried on sending things here, but he knew I wouldn't get them. From the letters he'd sent to work already it was clear he knew I was living elsewhere. But he either didn't know, or hadn't yet gone to the trouble of finding out, where the new place was. I wedged my thumbnail under the corner of the envelope as I trod through the hallway, still juggling the other items: flyers; advertisements; bills. In the living room, I landed hard on the sofa and took the paper from its sheath. But then dropped both the letter and envelope on the coffee table.

I doubled over with it, the feeling of blood rushing to my ears in panic. With my elbows sitting awkwardly on my knees, I took a deep breath in – counted to three – and then another out.

On my fourth belly breath – that's what Mum had always called them – I felt a tear roll from duct to nose, before dropping on the floor. When one had come, it wasn't long before others followed, and I found that my forearms were leaning against my knees, then, while my shoulders juddered like a skipping record.

'I just miss you both so much,' I howled to no one at all. And I cried until I physically couldn't cry anymore. And after that, I slept.

When I woke up hours later the only light in the place was an atmospheric throw-off from a street light outside. I checked my phone for the time and saw that I'd slept through two messages from Landon – the first asking me for dinner, the second asking whether I was alive – and a phone call from Wren. She'd left a voicemail, but after the breakdown earlier in the day I couldn't decide whether it was a today-problem, or something best left for my next spin on the earth. It was late, after all, and she likely wasn't expecting a call back.

I put my phone on the table next to the letter, with my voicemail server on the screen. I was a button away from hearing her. It would be the first time since we stopped sleeping together, though, and I wondered what sort of a change in tone that might cause. The optimist in me wondered whether there would be a change in tone at all. But given that we'd managed to avoid each other personally and professionally for the last six months, it seemed unlikely that she was calling for a catch up.

'You don't have to push me away, do you know that, Sarah?' She'd been trying for supportive, but somewhere her feelings had got mixed up and she came over as angry. 'Like, not everyone is going to up and die on you.' She clamped a hand on her forehead after she'd said it. 'I'm sorry, I– I'm just– I'm frustrated.'

'I can see.'

'What do you want from this, Sarah? What do you want from me?'

'Why should I want anything different to what I've wanted all along?'

'Because– because you've lost Madison, and you cared for her, and all you've done since is– is shut down on me, bit by bit. So, what, do you want us to carry on like we always have? Sleep together and avoid talking about work and– Christ, avoid talking about our feelings while we're at it?' She ran a hand through her hair and paced the length of the living room. I looked from one end of the room to the other as though I could see her all over again; as though we were still having the argument. 'Are you fucking me because you like me, even, or just because you want to overhear leads?'

My eyes had stretched wide, then, but they clamped shut at the memory.

'I think you should leave,' I'd told her.

And I ignored all her good reasons for why she should stay.

I leaned forward and tapped the play button, then dropped back on the sofa.

'You have one new message. First message. Sarah, it's DS Brooks here...'

The formality made me wince. 'You've seen me naked.' I covered my eyes.

'...I know it's been some time since there was anything to report regarding your mother's case. But I think, given some recent developments, it may be worth you and I having a talk. If you can give me a call back at the office when you have a second, and we can arrange for a time for you to visit the station, I'd be grateful.' There was a long pause before she added, 'I hope you're okay, Sarah...'

'End of message.'

I listened to the recording four times before I deleted it. She'd be at home by now. But that '...give me a call back at the office...' rang in my ears. She didn't want me to call her at home. I turned my phone off in case temptation simmered over into action. Then I balled up and went back to sleep wedged into the corner of the sofa.

48

It took me two days to return Wren Brooks' voicemail, and she called me four times. After that many missed calls, it crossed my mind I was in dangerous territory for her arriving at the office unannounced. So I called at 5.15pm on day two, in the hope that it would be too late to schedule a meeting. But I should have known better. She answered – 'Sarah, finally.' – without the courtesy of a polite hello, on the second ring, as though she'd been sitting on the handset. I would have made a joke out of it. But it sounded like we weren't in that sort of place anymore.

'I've been busy.'

'Of course. Thanks for getting back to me,' she said, as though making a concerted effort to soften her tone. 'I really need a catch up with you, though, busy-ness aside. Can we talk, face to face? Sooner rather than later?'

There were cracks of worry in her questions. 'What's he done?'

A rookie officer who didn't know my history escorted me to Brooks' office, from front desk through to her closed door. I wondered whether Brooks had requested that door-to-door accompaniment, in case something spooked me along the way. The junior officer tapped twice with knuckles and awaited instructions – 'Yep.' – before opening the door and stepping aside for me to walk in first, throwing me into the wide-open mouth of the lion.

Brooks looked up with a fierce expression that at least became a touch more neutral when she saw me. I flashed a tight smile and looked to my side, to gauge whether the junior was likely to hang about.

She looked at him. 'Thanks.' It worked as though she'd barked a complete instruction at him. He gave her a curt nod and left the room, pulling the door to with a click behind him.

'Do you want a seat?' she asked, gesturing opposite her.

'That depends. How anxious are you about to make me?'

She smiled. 'Straight down to business.'

'You always liked that about me if I remember right.' I sat down, then, and raised an eyebrow when she looked at me. It was a knee-jerk reaction to flirt with her.

Brooks moved about her desk like I hadn't spoken. She opened a cardboard folder and withdrew a plastic wallet, inside which there was what looked to be a handwritten letter. The whole meeting had a touch of the uncanny to it; the letter itself was familiar but sharing the experience with someone else wasn't something I'd been able to enjoy before. I shook my head. It wasn't enjoyment.

'Are you okay?' she asked, setting the letter down.

'Of course, absolutely,' I lied. 'He sent a letter?'

She handed it over. The plastic creased and crackled as I pinched its corner.

'You're welcome to read it for yourself but the basic idea is that there are more victims than the ones we already know about.' I skimmed the letter while she spoke and tried to uphold a poker face. There were more victims than *they* knew about.

But nothing in the opening of the letter was a surprise to me. 'The reason I thought you should be filled in about all of this, though, is because–'

'He's named Mum,' I said as I arrived at the bottom of the page.

The handwriting was shaky. But it was unmistakably his. Every letter that had a tail looped all the way down to the line below it; every capital took up two allotted spaces on the page. The tone of familiarity was the same, too, with the occasional splash of something patronising. If the physical markers weren't proof enough for me, though, the content gave him way further. He mentioned Herefordshire, Cardiff; the missed opportunity in Oxford, even, although he didn't mention his spouse, and I wondered whether that was for his own protection, or whether some things really were sacred between the two of us.

'Do you know why he'd say something like that about her?'

I read the comment on repeat: '"Evelyn was a truly special one…"'

'I don't know.' I shook my head, then, and looked up at her. 'I'm sorry.'

'As far as I can see,' she said, talking to me like I was a suspect for something, 'the thing that makes Evelyn special, out of all the women we know about – and even the ones we didn't know about – is you.'

'Me?' I feigned surprise.

'Nice try, Sarah, but I know you.'

'Knew me. A slip of the tense there, DS Brooks,' I snapped back. 'These women, or these murders, what do you know about them?'

'We're in the process of liaising with other police forces, to find out where they are in terms of their investigations into the deaths. Of course, this is the first whisper we've had of the murders all being connected across the years,' she let out a half-laugh, 'and across a bullet-point list of locations. So, it's taking some effort to collate them, and there's an added importance to some of the cases that wasn't there before.'

I flashed a tight smile. 'Because perish the thought that a woman get justice if it's only a one-off murder.'

She shifted uncomfortably. But it wasn't because of what I said, I realised, but because of what she was about to ask. 'How much of this is new information to you?'

'I'm sorry?'

'Don't play act with me, Sarah. I need to know what you knew.'

I rolled around the possibilities, then asked, 'How much shit will I get?'

'None. None at all. I won't even call you out on it.'

It was a hard decision. But I chose to believe her. 'I knew everything.'

Brooks leaned back in her chair and sighed. She opened her mouth two, three times to speak but then thought better of it every time. Instead, she pushed both hands back through her hair, and I thought of the last time I'd done that for her.

'Why didn't you tell me?' she eventually asked.

'Because I didn't know whether I was telling DS Brooks, or Wren.'

She nodded. 'Okay, okay, that makes sense.'

'I'm happy to co-operate with you however you need me to from now on,' I lied. 'I understand you'll likely have follow-up questions and, if he happens to write again, then I'll obviously be as involved as you need me to be.'

Without a word, Brooks stood up from the desk and crossed to the doorway of her office. I wondered whether I was about to be kicked out. But instead she opened the door, stuck her head around the doorway into the space outside, and took a good look around. As though seeing something that satisfied her, she closed the door and walked back around to the right side of her desk. She opened the same folder as earlier and pulled out a white envelope.

'He already wrote again.' She placed the envelope flat on the desk and pushed it towards me. 'This was inside the larger envelope, that the other letter came in...'

And there it was in his cursive: *Dear Wren.*

49

Dear Wren,

I hope you don't mind me writing, Wren. Although in many ways it feels a little overdue that I contact you. I thought I'd include both letters together, to save the cost of a stamp. It looked especially likely, from your media presence these days, that the letter(s) wouldn't be seen by anyone but you to begin with anyway, so I could rest easy in knowing we'd have some privacy.

I wonder, though, whether you'll tell anyone about this, Wren, or whether you'll be too worried of the judgement that might spill from it. Because there would certainly be some raised eyebrows, wouldn't there, if people were to find out about your relationship with Sarah. Given that you've done so well for yourself, in terms of your career, through trying to hunt me down over the years, although there were other contributing cases, I'm sure. But still, some might say you'd taken advantage of a witness. I don't mind admitting I was a little surprised when I saw you skulking out of her home late one evening. It took some time to break that barrier, didn't it, Wren? For her to let you keep her for an entire evening, I mean. Then it all fell apart anyway. Sad, really, after you'd tried so hard to spend that time getting to know her. Sarah doesn't like people getting *to know her, though, Wren, or at least I don't think she does. I think I may have taken that from her.*

For all your closeness with her, though, Wren, I'd be willing to bet she didn't tell you about me. Sarah and I have a special kind of relationship, you see. I don't know that either of us fully understand it. Although, as these weeks stretch out, it feels to me like that relationship might be drawing to an end somehow. I can't quite put my finger on my reasons for thinking it, Wren. Maybe it's intuitive – a feeling of worry that I haven't had before. Whatever it is, I think Sarah might tire of all this soon. Who knows what she'll do then, Wren? But there are times when I think when all this comes to an end, you might find yourself surprised at which one of us you're arresting.

She's changed, hasn't she, our Sarah?

You'll see from my other letter that I'm being open and honest with you in terms of the women I've spent time with over the years. It's a bit like pulling a starting pistol years too late, because Sarah really is on her fourth or fifth lap around the course now. Maybe you'll catch up with her, though, and then you'll be able to publicly reel me in. Then, think of the letters they'll put before your name, Wren. Wouldn't it be worth catching me before she can, if only for that?

I look forward to the news coverage of my other letter. Be seeing you, Wren – on the ten o'clock news, I suspect. For now, though, do take care, and keep an eye on Sarah...

Sincerely, yours –

50

I didn't know what it was meant to do. But the letter brought Wren and I closer – for an hour or two, at least. She went back and forth in pacing, leaving track marks in the carpet behind her desk that ran the length of the room. 'I can't declare this, Sarah, it could ruin me,' she eventually announced, once I'd read the letter through another two times.

'Okay,' I agreed flatly. She'd looked surprised, but I didn't know what she'd been expecting. It was her letter; she could do with it what she wanted. I had to have that attitude, I decided, because look at what I'd done with mine...

'You need to be careful. He knows us.' She winced. 'You, he knows you.'

Between us we drank four and half cups of coffee in the ninety minutes that followed. I told her he was right: things would be over soon. She just needed to wait.

'For what?'

I shrugged. 'A sign? You'll probably know when it's over.'

She asked me to let her know my whereabouts – in an unofficial capacity. She didn't say as much, but she wanted to know I was breathing; upright and walking through the city still.

After everything, it seemed a reasonable request. During that same conversation I told her about the flat, and how I'd come to spend less and less time there. But it didn't seem worth it anymore.

'Why not?'

We were walking from her office when she asked, nearing the end of the closeness.

'Because getting myself out of the way was never intended to put someone else in the firing line.' I flashed a tight smile and risked leaning in to kiss her cheek. She didn't pull away. 'He knows where all of you are. And I'm not letting it happen again.'

Sleep was an abstract concept that night. Instead of lying awake and staring into the ether of an unfamiliar flat, though, I decided to start packing. Most of my clothes had never left the bag they'd been brought over in. But the living space – which was much more like an office space – would take some careful attention. There were corkboards balanced around the walls, with a year's worth of work and then some. I had the canonical victims' pictures pinned to a board on the right-hand side of the room; although Mum was missing. She wouldn't approve of this, I didn't think, and the imagined disappointment had been enough to leave me bent double in the room late one evening. I wrote her name instead. It wasn't like I couldn't call her face to mind whenever I needed a reminder of what this was for.

On a corkboard to the left-hand side of the room, there were the non-canonical victims. Their deaths had caused flickers of interest in their respective cities. But nowhere near the interest that I imagined they'd get when Wren released the letter to the press; assuming she was given authorisation to make that move. For now, though, I had what little information the newspapers in different locations had provided. That, at least, had been enough to know names: find social media profiles; learn professions; make the women back into humans. Their faces hung in chronological order with details scribbled and pinned beneath. They were all markedly similar in appearance, still, which hadn't been a surprise. The same could be said of the women on the opposite side of the room.

They all had an average body-type. Mum had loved food, but she'd also loved her morning runs and her weekend rambles around hillsides. The other women were the same, I imagined; although I hadn't been able to find definitive evidence of it. None of them wore glasses – although I couldn't say whether contact lenses were being worn in any of the pictures – and none of them wore especially heavy make-up. They looked – natural, untouched. Their hair was dark brown, some were slightly darker shades than others, but all wore it long, with a wisp or a curl. If I span around the room I could make a kaleidoscope of their faces.

I took great care in unpinning them and packing them in an order that would make sense when I found them again further down the line. Each box was marked up on the outside with no more than three names, and then a number. When the victims' boards were empty, there were four cardboard containers, their lids lifting with the stored information, stacked by the front door of the apartment. The boxes were stacked in couples, and it was the closest I'd come to having furniture in the place. It was an empty apartment when I rented it, on a month-by-month lease, and I hadn't been the least bit interested in making the space a home.

The remaining boards in the living room – another three in total – were taken up by letters. I'd scanned and printed copies of them, too many times over to remember, to highlight, annotate, circle key words. The only thing missing from it all was a network of red string tying one piece of information to another, and I would have been a private eye from a classic detective film.

In the year since Madison, he'd been more open than before. I didn't know whether it was a deliberate decision, or whether things had started to slip out. After this long, though, perhaps it was more surprising that he hadn't told me more about himself sooner. But now, across the hazy photocopies of letters that had been staggered over a ten-month window, I thought I knew enough. I unpinned them carefully, as though they were precious artefacts; in some ways they were. I imagined these things becoming a kind of legacy – I just didn't know what for. One letter at a time, I reread the highlighted snippets...

...Work has made it too easy for me to leave the city. You might have guessed already, Sarah. There are times when I long to be in this city, though, in our city for longer than I've been allowed. Although, I suppose, in many ways that's worked to my advantage. No one even knows about the other cities, Sarah, no one has pieced it all together. It's only you...

I layered them in their respective boxes and tried to keep them bunched by topic. In March, there had been three letters that arrived close together – closer than he'd ever written things before. The first had arrived before Mother's Day – a day I steadfastly ignored in every calendar I owned – and the second two just after.

...It must be a hard time of year for you, Sarah. I think of you so often during the weeks up to Mothering Sunday. Do you miss her, I wonder? Of course, it's a silly question. Perhaps, I more wonder whether you've got used to life without her...

...I think it's a blessing, parenthood, one that not everyone is fortunate enough to come by in their lives...

He showed too much in the second letter, I thought. I realised then that he likely wasn't a father and I wondered why that was: was it a missed opportunity, or was he physically unable? *What kind of dad would you even make?* I wondered, as I packed another sheet away. Then, there was the final letter from that month.

...My own mother wasn't a special person. The woman who cared for me after my mother was, though, Sarah, and that's why you must understand I had nothing to do with Madison. What I said, in that earlier letter, I harbour a lot of ill-feeling toward myself for that, Sarah, truly. I never would have taken one mother. I certainly wouldn't have robbed you twice...

I skimmed through the middle portion to rush to the last paragraph.

...I was glad to be rid of my own, in many ways. The woman who cared for me, though, I'll carry her always.

There was a burn of bile rising to the back of my throat and I swallowed hard to push it down. I didn't read the rest of the letters, only packed them neatly like grim soldiers into their boxes, and then added the containers to the stacks by the front door. They were a morbid scrapbook, and reading them through in a near-empty flat with bare bulbs overhead made for a sorry show – and an uncomfortable swell of emotion that formed a lead weight in me. When they were physically out of sight I felt better. But even then there was still a final thing or two to pack away. Most significantly, the revised comeback tour...

I stood a safe distance from the map of Birmingham tacked to the board in front of me. There were several street addresses circled; bar one, that was looped around with a bright red circle and marked with a black cross. *The last stop*, I thought when my eyes landed on it. I looked from point to point, then, each of them adorned with a fluorescent orange Post-it note beneath to detail the significance of the street name. To start with, there was the police station; that was the letter to Wren, I guessed. It wasn't quite the same as leaving a body behind; he was still looking to cause damage, though. Alongside that there was my office; Landon's office; Landon's home. I pulled in a greedy mouthful of air and tapped at my collarbone as I moved around the city. Jessie and Tyler's address, Wren's. And, finally, marked with the black X: Madison's.

'Where it all ends,' I told the room, as I unpinned the top right corner of the map.

51

I dialled Landon's number and let it ring once when I arrived outside the studio. Nearly a full minute passed when he pushed the back door open and emerged with a cigarette hanging from his mouth. He raised an eyebrow and offered me one. I'd been trying to quit for months on end, but it wasn't sticking – and now hardly seemed like a good time for it to. I admitted defeat and pinched the offering from him. While I was sparking up, he fumbled with half a brick between the door and its frame to wedge the entryway open.

'I was starting to think you were AI,' he said as he flicked his lighter.

I exhaled upward. 'AI?'

'Do you know this is the first show we've done in three months where we've actually been in the same room as each other for it?' He lit his cigarette and took a deep pull. I thought I heard his chest crackle. 'I missed your face, Wainwright.'

I grabbed him tight against me and kept my right arm outstretched to keep the burning cigarette a distance away. Neither of us said anything for the hug.

'I read your notes for tonight's show,' he said when I pulled away. I was trying to judge his feelings from his tone, but he sounded too steady for me to know anything. He waited a full in- and exhale before he carried on. 'Are you sure this is a nest you want to kick?'

'You don't?'

'It's not about me.'

Wren had held a press conference two days ago to reveal the contents of the letter. Since then, a very public discussion had started about the non-canonical victims of the so-called Sincerely Yours killer. I imagined he quite liked the moniker.

The news reports had been patchy. But Marcus had started to hold my calls at the office because, never mind being able to cover the story, there had been umpteen requests for me to be a part of it. Brooks had hardly finished the press conference and there were other newspapers – local and national alike – contacting me with interview requests.

I'd forewarned Tina, too, that a story was about to break and when she'd watched the coverage she called me with her firm hand and kind advice: 'Do nothing that doesn't serve you, honey, do you hear me?' She told me people would ask about the second book: 'Is this the long-awaited sequel? I can hear them now, honey. You be careful what you say about that.'

'I want to cover the story with Landon, for Canonical.' I floated the idea, not knowing which way she'd land on it. The podcast had generated and upheld interest in the first book over the years though. I didn't see a reason why I shouldn't be using it to build a foundation for the second.

'You're a good thinker, honey,' Tina said. 'Use it. Be careful.'

I'd sent an outline over to Landon within the hour and asked whether we could record.

'Look, I'm game for it, if you are,' he said, after an uncomfortably long silence had passed between us. 'I've always imagined I might die young and pretty anyway.'

'Oh, shut up.' I flattened my cigarette against a wall. 'There's nothing in that outline that isn't true.'

He pulled me into a second hug and set a hard kiss on my forehead. 'That's what scares me a bit, Sarah, that's all.' He moved away, then, and turned to kick the makeshift doorstop out of the way. 'But if you need this, or want it, or– fuck, I don't know, if you'll benefit from it, I'm in. Just make sure I get an acknowledgement in that book you won't tell me anything about.'

'Hey,' I said, following him in, 'you might even be in it.'

We sat at opposite ends of the table in the recording space. While I fumbled with my headphones, Landon did the customary count-in with three fingers held high to let me know when recording would kick in. He walked through the advertisement on his own – something about a clothing store that had opened on the other side of the city – and then our usual introduction jingle followed.

'Welcome to Canonical,' Landon announced as the music faded. He sounded confident, at least, and I wondered whether he was – or whether it was something that came with years of practice in front of a microphone. Despite having engineered the interview, I had enough nerves then for the both of us. 'I'm your host for the evening, Landon Hughes and, in a schedule that runs slightly different to usual, Sarah actually won't be hosting this episode with me. Instead – and turn up those headphones, folks, because you want to hear this right – Sarah will be giving a Canonical exclusive interview about the Sincerely Yours killer and his victims, canonical and otherwise.' He hit a button on the keyboard in front of him and a burst of dramatic music followed. *That wasn't in the plan*, I thought with a raised eyebrow. But he had a flair for the dramatics that listeners had always enjoyed. 'Sarah Wainright is the closest thing living, that we know of, at least, to being a survivor of the Sincerely

Yours killer. A man who's been active up and down the country for longer than the police might care to admit...'

Also not in the script, I thought with a sigh.

'...investigations have now started into the sheer number of victims that he might have collected during his time as an active killer. And, on the top of him being an active killer, his career looks to have a longer lifespan, too, than we were previously led to believe. Sarah, why are you in a position to tell us about the Sincerely Yours killer? I'm right in thinking you've been– what, keeping an eye on him?'

I laughed. 'That's one way of phrasing it, I suppose.'

'For people who don't know, although I'm sure most of our listeners do, your own mother was one of the canonical victims of this killer.'

'She was.' It felt different, hearing it all in someone else's voice. I wasn't sure I liked it. 'Mum was the second victim in a cluster of three–'

'And he killed in threes initially, is that right?'

'Yes. Three victims, in different cities. But when he broke his pattern, he became harder for the police to track, I suspect.' I paused for a tactical sip of water. 'I can't stress this enough, though, the police really haven't done anything wrong here.'

'It doesn't seem like they've done a massive amount right, though, either?'

'Landon, I think that's unfair.' He was going off-script already; I'd counted on it happening, but perhaps not so soon. 'This man has made himself difficult to track in so many ways. He doesn't leave behind evidence, either, which adds to the mystery of who he is. There's no sign, for example, of this being a sexual thing–'

'Why do you say that?' he interrupted me.

'The women aren't interfered with.' I felt a prickle of something at the back of my throat. 'I watched– I watched what he did to Mum, and there wasn't a sexual thing in that. He just– he only wanted to kill her.'

'You're a brave woman to be able to say that, about your own mother.' His words were cracking, and I saw a swell of feeling flush his face. I hadn't thought how hard this all might be for him, too. 'Aren't you angry, though, that she– that what happened to your mum happened so early in this case history, and they're only now finding the man responsible?'

'Well, they haven't found him yet.'

'And doesn't that pi–'

'It pisses me off every day,' I finished. 'But what can I do other than what I've been doing?'

'And there's the crux of the interview, Sarah. What is it that you *have* been doing?'

I pulled in a greedy amount of air. 'The killer's behaviour changed midway through his career and the police misinterpreted that change to mean that he was no longer active. I didn't believe he'd given in quite so easily, though, and I started looking for signs that he wasn't inactive but had simply changed tactics.'

'Is it common, for a serial killer to do that?'

'I'm really not well-versed enough to say. I assume not, given that the police didn't entertain the idea themselves. Maybe it comes down to my personal attachment to the case, as to why I didn't want to let go of the possibility that he might still be out there somewhere – or, I don't know, that he might still be catchable.'

I tapped my watch and Landon nodded.

'Do you believe he is catchable?'

'What I do believe, Landon, is that he's taking up a little too much airtime for my liking.' We shared a half-laugh. 'I think there are more important people to talk about as part of this interview, if you don't mind me steering a little?'

'Please, Sarah, take the wheel. Are we starting with canonical?'

I took another sip of water and tried to steady my breathing. 'We're not, no. We're starting with the victims the police haven't found yet...'

52

Wren had called me thirteen times on my mobile alone since Canonical had aired. She'd left four messages through work, too, but Marcus was under strict instructions to put her on the screening list. He'd shifted awkwardly and muttered something about withholding information from the police. I'd only laughed and told him not to worry. Wren wasn't about to throw me under the bus for what could turn out to be hearsay. I knew she was worried that what I'd said on air was true – which it was – but I didn't know if she was more worried about that, or the letter she was no doubt carrying around in her back pocket still. It came down to which concern took priority.

Given that she hadn't pulled me in for questioning in an official capacity – nor had she turned up at the office, or at home – I took an educated guess that the letter felt most important. Nothing like having your career dangled in front of you; something the killer had been counting on when he'd written to her. That, and he'd wanted to out me to her. But I hadn't worked out the logic behind that yet.

I leaned back against my car and pulled a half-empty packet of cigarettes out of my coat pocket. It had been a while since I'd had to drive out of the city for a social occasion. I was meant to be in Chester for the weekend; not for a social occasion, but because he'd told me he would be there: 'A weekend away. There's nothing sinister in it, Sarah.' But I couldn't decide why he'd tell me something so inconsequential unless there really was menace it in. I'd planned to go up there after him; to chase ghosts for two days. Much like I'd done for the best part of my early twenties. But Jessie's gender reveal party had taken priority. Landon had gone as far to call me the day before and remind me.

'Yes, *I'm* going,' I said in mock outrage. 'Are *you*?'

A gender reveal party wasn't exactly Landon's thing. But his car was parked 200 yards up the street from mine, so I knew he'd made it.

'Those'll kill you one day, you know?'

I looked up in time to catch Tyler dumping something into the recycling bin. 'Wrapping paper. Wrapping paper, everywhere.' He closed the gap between us and came at me with outstretched arms. 'We didn't know whether you'd come,' he said into the knit of my scarf. It seemed to be a running theme; my friends not knowing whether they could count on me for things anymore. I didn't like that too much.

'I wouldn't have let you both down.'

He shrugged like the occasion was nothing. 'We know you're busy.'

'Not too busy.' I held out the packet. 'Tempt you?'

He pushed them away. 'I'm a changed man. But I'll crack if they're in front of me for too long.' I laughed and pocketed the box. 'Oh, Sar, don't let me stop you. I'm not one of *those* ex-smokers. I'll even keep you company.' He leaned back on the car next to me. 'And I'll suck in all of that second-hand smoke while I'm at it.'

'You said you were throwing away wrapping paper. Did I miss presents?'

'Christ, we've got presents for days.'

I opened the passenger door of my car and pulled out two gift bags. 'One for you, one for Jessie.' He took them but with a questioning look. 'Don't hate me, but I thought the baby probably had enough stuff, and I'm really not so good at getting what kids need.'

He laughed. 'This is perfect.'

'You don't know what it is yet.'

'As long as it's not a breast pump or a diaper genie, then I'm grateful.'

'Breast pump?' I raised an eyebrow.

He tucked an arm around my shoulders and steered me towards the front door. 'Breast pumps for days, Sarah.'

I was checking my phone religiously throughout the party. It wasn't to see whether anyone had called – Brooks, another two times – but to check the time. The room was packed with people I hardly knew, and they didn't look like the types of people Jessie and Tyler might know either. But they shot shifty looks in my direction every time my position changed. I wanted to reassure them that you couldn't catch trauma, but it didn't feel like the right time for an argument with anyone. Landon was propping up the room from an opposite corner, and every now and then he threw me a look that made me think he must be feeling the same. I took a sad comfort in that, at least.

'Hey,' a male voice pulled me around, 'you're Sarah, right?'

I held out a hand, which he took for a shake. 'Right.'

'I listen to your show. To the podcast.' He pointed to Landon. 'You two work really well together. That episode the other night, though, man, that was some deep stuff. Big accusations.' He laughed, and I wondered whether it was nerves or whether he was so untouched by violence that he could find it funny. 'Hey,' he moved a little closer, 'how much of that stuff is true?'

'I'm sorry?'

'On the show, about the victims. About the Yours Sincerely guy, I mean.'

'Sincerely Yours,' I corrected him.

'That's the one.' He clicked his fingers. 'You're what – embellishing?'

'Fin.' Jessie's hand landed heavy on his shoulder; her fingers bloated by pregnancy hormones, and her mood notably soured. 'I'm pretty sure Georgina was looking for you, maybe out in the garden?'

He rolled his eyes. 'Nice to meet you,' he said before disappearing.

'You're welcome,' Jessie said when Fin was out of earshot. She tried to hug me side-on. 'I opened your present.'

'It wasn't in bad taste?'

'Are you kidding me? Gin and cheese are the best presents for a pregnant woman.' She tapped her belly. 'Not long now and I'll be throwing this one out, then it's Tyler's turn to step up while I get drunk and eat stuff with mould on.'

I laughed. 'I'm glad. So,' I nodded to the cake on the coffee table, 'a girl.'

'Honestly, Sarah, I would have been happy with whatever, as long as there's just one.' As though taking a cue, the twins tore past us; one darted between us and one cruised straight into Jessie's legs before bouncing back and following her sibling. 'Oh, the joys. Remind me why I'm doing this again?'

'I heard it was because Tyler forgot to pay the TV licence.' Landon appeared behind us. 'You've got to do something when you can't watch *Strictly*.'

'Please, we're a *Britain's Got Talent* household, and we have Netflix anyway.'

'In which case you have no excuse.' He turned to me. 'Smoke?'

'You two,' Jessie started, and I clenched for a reprimand about the dangers of cigarettes. 'You smashed that episode of Canonical the other night. I'm glad to get you both together to say it. Are you feeling okay?' She made the question sound general, but I could guess that it was pointed at me.

'It's a hard, weird time, isn't it?'

'You've got that right. Have you heard from the police at all?'

'She's heard from Brooks,' Landon answered for me.

'Brooks is hounding you?'

'She wants to know the truth of what I said, that's all.' I brushed off the worry in Jessie's voice. 'I mean, it would help with their case and all, so–'

'So, why aren't you talking to her?'

Because then I might lose the chance to catch him myself. 'I will,' I lied.

Jessie turned to get a better look at me but, as though shifting weight had disturbed her balance too much, she landed hard on the wall behind her. Before I could grab her, though, Landon tucked an arm behind her back and pulled her up.

'You all right there, mama bear?'

She smiled. 'Light-headed. But I'm fine, Land, I'm fine.' She tried to wiggle free from him, but he kept a firm hold.

'Nice try, but I'll believe you're fine when you're sat down.' He started to steer her. 'Sofa, please, and I'll even throw a cup of tea into the mix. Decaf.'

'Oh, good,' she half-laughed, 'my favourite thing about being pregnant.'

It took them nearly a minute to cross the room. Landon walked close behind Jessie with a hand on either side of her, gripped tight just beneath her bra-line. I guessed he was aiming for her waist. He ushered people out of the walk-space and, when Tyler saw them, he joined in – 'Clear out, people, mother's coming through.' – and started to shift pillows out of Jessie's way, so she could drop easily into the cradle of the sofa.

When she was sitting, Landon continued with his offers of tea. 'You're sure, Jess? I know you hate decaf, but what about peppermint?'

Tyler fell to his knees in front of her. 'You're okay? This isn't it?'

Jessie moved between both, batting away kind offers in one direction while offering reassurances in the other. They looked like children playing at being grown-ups, and I felt a swell of love rise from the pit of my belly. But there was also a strange kiss of relief at the sight of them managing without me.

Whatever happened next, I decided, they'd all be fine.

53

Dear Sarah,

I heard the show. But you knew I would. It surprised me that you gave away so much of our privacy like that, Sarah. I wonder what Wren had to say about it. I expected an official statement from her by now. You might have set them all busy worrying, though, Sarah, trawling through their back catalogues of no-never-mind murders in their cities. Is that what you wanted, something that would keep them busy?

You've been busy, haven't you, Sarah? The lights are back on in the flat, which must mean you feel safe again. That, or you no longer mind feeling in danger. The recording with the boy was live, for the podcast, wasn't it? You were in the same room together. I could tell from the tones of your voices, the lack of a lag in your conversation. Did you tell him what to ask, Sarah, or is he really that curious all by himself? Then, there was the girl and her party. I cancelled my own plans, too, so I could make it. I saw you standing outside their palace, outlandishly decorated with their 'It's a baby' balloons and banners. It didn't seem like something you'd give time to, Sarah, not with everything else going on. But you care about them, I know, and I've been able to see that over the years. Why now, though, Sarah?

That's what's got me wondering. Why not quality time months ago – after Madison, for instance?

I've been tying up loose ends, too, in some ways. The woman I've shared my life with expects me to go away for an extended period soon, for work, which in some ways is true. Although this feels more vocational now. But telling her would cut me down the centre. Work think I'll be taking a break, too, and it occurred to me this must have been the sort of lifestyle we've both been living for so long – you and I, Sarah. Because for every city I've skulked away to, you've come running after me. The lies we must have told to our nearest and most important people over the years, all for the luxury of nearly spending time together. Now here we are, tying up loose ends.

Is that what you're doing, Sarah, tying up loose ends? Getting ready?

Be seeing you, then.

Sincerely, yours –

54

Marcus stepped back into the room with a takeaway coffee cup in each hand. He used his foot to nudge closed the door behind him. But he stood on the opposite side of the space long enough to make me look up from our work. I threw him a quizzical glance.

'Yes?'

He hesitated. 'The police officer standing out the front of the building?'

'Brooks told me she might do that.' I looked back down to the applications that were splayed across Marcus' desk. 'She, he won't bother anyone. It's nothing, really.' I waved away his discovery and went back to reading. Marcus and I had started working two hours earlier than everyone else in the office, in the interest of wading through the early applications for intern positions at the paper, generally, but at the crime desk, too.

'Sarah, don't think me rude,' he set a cup down in front of me, 'but I feel like I may have missed something.'

He had. After another seven missed calls, I finally plucked up courage enough to call Brooks back. When she'd finished reprimanding me – 'Totally selfish of you, Sarah, completely.' –

she changed her tone to one of concern: 'You're antagonising him, first and foremost, but also the police. What are you playing at?'

In the interest of easing her worries – and getting her to quieten down – I promised a first look at (some of) the files I'd been putting together on the killer. 'I don't know how much it'll help,' I'd said, trying to downplay the documents I was dragging into a zip folder as we spoke. While we were on the phone I'd sent her enough information to substantiate the claims I'd made on the podcast – a copy of the comeback tour being the most significant piece of evidence I could give her, and it felt generous to have done that, although she was outraged I hadn't done it sooner – and since then she, her team, and teams around the country had been wading through their recent and historical murder cases for fear that even *I* might have missed something. He would have told me, though, if there were more.

'You should be in police protection by now,' she said when the documents arrived on her screen, 'it's ridiculous that you aren't.' I told her it wasn't necessary, and she'd threatened a bodyguard instead...

'So, he's looking out for you?' Marcus repeated, when I finished explaining.

I took a sip of my drink and shrugged. 'I guess.'

He fidgeted awkwardly next to me and then said, 'May I speak out of turn?'

'You're my boss.' I leaned back in my chair. 'I don't know that that's something you should worry about necessarily.'

'I am your boss, but I'd like to speak to you as a friend.'

I took a long blink to try to stifle an eye roll. *Everyone's talking to me as a friend these days*, I thought as I reached over for my drink again.

'I'm worried about you, Sarah, that you're putting yourself in danger here. I don't know – I mean, I don't know if it's for the book or publicity or,' he shrugged, 'Christ even if it's for the interest it's creating in the paper, but nothing in your life should come at this price. You know that?'

I nodded. 'It isn't for the paper.' His shoulders dropped with a sigh and I assumed I'd missed the point he'd been trying to make, so I took a second run at reassuring him. 'This guy took Mum away from me. He's got a weird fixation with me now, but that's all this is. I'm not prepared to put my life on hold for some nutcase with a grudge or a– I don't know, axe that needs grinding over something–'

'Too violent on your idiom choice.'

I smiled. 'I'm not going to stop living for him.'

'And I get that, I do, and I'm genuinely glad to hear it. But if he's coming for you–'

'He isn't.' *I'm coming for him.* I reached across and gave Marcus' hand a squeeze. It was the closest we'd ever come to unprofessional contact. 'He isn't coming for me, I'm sure.'

He squeezed back. 'I just don't know how you can be sure of that.'

Because he's letting me find him. I flashed a tight smile and looked back at the paperwork in front of us. 'I know we're talking about the armed guard and all, but I really feel like that's a tomorrow problem, and the intern paperwork is maybe a today-problem.'

'Is he armed?'

I laughed. 'I don't know, but maybe I can leave first today and then you can get a good look while he follows me home.' I turned back to face the applications. 'Because nothing turns off a serial killer like knowing your target is already being stalked.'

'Not funny, Sarah, not even a little...'

It took three more hours to narrow down a shortlist of five interns.

'You should get Sheila in here,' I said, as Marcus started to pack away the papers.

He paused. 'Why?'

'Because she's also involved on the crime desk, and it would be good to get her input.' I pushed away from the table and tried to sound nonchalant. 'What if she ends up working with them at any point?'

'Well, she hasn't had anything to do with interns to date so...' he petered. His face dropped, and I wondered what he'd started to piece together. 'You're thinking of leaving the paper, aren't you?'

'No,' I spluttered, already laughing. 'Not at all.'

'So, why would Sheila need to be involved with the interns?'

My hand was already clutching the doorhandle. 'Forget I said anything.'

For the rest of the day Marcus shot me a worried look whenever he saw me. I avoided locking eyes with him in case one of us cracked into tears; it would have been him. When I saw him talking to Sheila, though, I wondered whether he'd taken my advice. But I wasn't prepared to walk close enough to their conversation to find out for certain. Safe in the knowledge that Marcus was occupied, I slipped back into my office for fifteen minutes of solitude before the staff meeting. I hadn't yet had the chance to check through my letter-tray, so I perched on the edge of my desk and thumbed through the deliveries from that morning. There wasn't anything suspicious, though, and my heart sank. The last letter he'd sent made it sound as though he were ready for something – although I didn't know what – but no matter what I shared with the police, or what the police reported back through the media, he didn't look to be shifting forward anymore. *I'm going to need something*, I thought, tearing into the first letter from the pile. *Something but*–

'Knock, knock.' Marcus stood in the doorway holding an

embarrassingly big bouquet. 'Is the reason Sheila might be working with the interns actually because you're going to be whisked away on romantic trips more often?'

'I'm sorry?'

'For you.' He held the flowers out. 'Just delivered.'

'Who delivered them?' I crossed the room.

'I don't know. A florist? Some kid, he just asked to be buzzed in and I intercepted him because I'm nosy.' He handed the flowers to me. 'Although I'm a journalist at my core, so it's literally my job to be nosy.'

'You don't have to justify yourself to me.' I was facing away from him. I set the flowers down on my desk and fished through them to find a card. The handwriting was bulbous, squat and unfamiliar; not his.

Marcus hovered until I'd opened the card. 'I'm dying to know.'

'No name, just a kiss.'

'Well, that's... creepy. Are you okay?'

I laughed off his concern. 'If it were someone to worry about then it would be a bouquet of something much more sinister than flowers. It's a super-fan or something. You know me with all my celebrity status.' I kept my tone deadpan. 'Go and answer an email or something. I'll see you in the staff meeting later.'

'Sometimes I wonder who's the boss around here...' his jovial tone trailed out of my office behind him. I waited until the pad of his footsteps was out of earshot. Then I opened the card again.

'Soon.' It read. 'Sincerely, yours –'

55

Before I left the flat I filed everything away: stray letters; Post-it notes of ideas; rough theories I hadn't been able to prove. I'd made copies and put them onto a fresh external hard drive for Tina; she'd have it in her hands before the day was out, thanks to a ridiculously expensive courier service. But at least I knew the information was where it needed to be. While I crawled through the city's traffic, I tried to guess at whether enough time had passed for me to call Tina and beg for her thoughts – or her validation, I wasn't sure which. I waited until I could put the handbrake on and then keyed her number into my phone. The ringer echoed through the Bluetooth system and I turned the volume down, for fear of becoming one of those people who has a private conversation aired. It went through to her voicemail after five rings, though, so I disconnected. I reached across to the passenger seat and freed my cigarettes from my coat pocket; I didn't manage to spark up before the phone started to ring.

'Tina.'

'Sarah, honey, I'm sorry I missed you. I was reading.'

Fuck it, I reasoned, *no point in being prissy.* 'My pages?'

'Your chapter notes. This is nearly a full draft you've sent?'

The final chapter was missing – maybe two chapters at a push. But I'd given Tina a rough idea of what should go into them. 'Nearly.'

'Honey, isn't this a step too far?'

'You don't think it'll sell?' I felt a swell of disappointment.

'That's not what I said.' I heard the shuffle of paper in the background. If she'd printed things to read, then she must have been making notes already. From experience, I knew that could only be a good sign. 'It'll sell, and it'll sell well. But I'm genuinely nervous about what you're putting on the line for this.'

The version of likely events that I'd told Tina was nothing in comparison to what was actually on the line. I tried to make a non-committal noise. 'I'm heading to Madison's for a few days. There are some things of Mum's there that I need. I think they'll help with the last chapter. When I'm back maybe we can talk again?'

'Are you taking your police escort?'

She sounded serious but I managed a laugh. 'No, I gave him the night off.'

Brooks had had someone tailing me for nearly a week without anything happening. I'd already told her I was leaving the city, and I'd been well-behaved enough to tell her where I'd be, too. We agreed a healthy middle-ground might be for me to have a police car drive by Madison's house every few hours as part of a regular patrol.

'The occasional text wouldn't go amiss,' Tina replied.

'Of course.' I had a template ready; an 'I'm fine' message to go to Brooks, and now Tina, too. 'Like I said, it shouldn't be more than a few days.'

'Keep in touch, honey. I hope you get what you need.'

I inched forward along the bypass. *If he takes the bait I'll be fine...*

Madison died here. It was my first thought when I pushed open the front door. The hinges howled from nearly a full year of no use. There'd been talk of putting the house on the market soon after Madison died. But there was no need for it. I didn't need the money – which was also my reason for not renting the place out – but I did need the emotional connection.

'If you can afford it, keep it,' Landon suggested one evening, after three bottles of wine and two packets of cigarettes had passed between us.

It had been a good idea, though, and the morning after I'd call the solicitor handling Madison's affairs to let him know that was my plan. Stepping back into the place after so long caused a wave of something, though, nausea and panic and – soft feelings, too. I thought I felt the prickle of tears but it could have just as easily been the dust of the hallway floating up to greet me.

The bedrooms were still made up, as though neither of us had ever left. But I decided to sleep on the sofa in the front room. I wanted to be close to any noise pollution as it happened, and the sofa was the best spot for noticing things. The company of the television would have been welcome, but I avoided Netflix for the same reason that I avoided the comfort of a bed. Instead, I read. The only noise that first night was the sound of pages turning at regular intervals, broken up by the ping of the microwave and the scrape of cutlery on crockery as I ate dinner in silence. I thought of unpacking. But there were things I wanted to have to hand, just in case. So, I kept my overnight bag within reaching distance. On the first night there, I fell asleep with my hand buried between the open lips of the bag and woke up in the same position, too.

After a second night, and an inquiring text from Landon – 'Any news / still alive?' – I started to wonder whether I'd misplaced my bets. Madison's house had been the X-marks-the-spot on the map he'd sent me. *All roads lead to home*, I'd thought when this final plan fell together, then, and I thought my being there might force his hand into being there, too. From the letters I'd assumed he'd been watching me all along, so would notice. But what if he wasn't watching? He had a life away from this, I reminded myself; a wife away from this. I half-laughed into the empty room and cut through the quiet; it felt like being the other woman, I realised. It felt like being juggled with a real life and one that he liked the idea of. *But what is there to like the idea of here?* I wondered, staring into the darkness of late autumn. The room had never held the light well. With that memory, there came a flood of others: watching films with Madison; eating popcorn; crying over– I couldn't remember what, but something that had felt desperately important at the time.

All the memories were tucked away at different points around the room, as though the space were shock absorbent for the kind times spent there.

I lay back and stretched my arm out to the overnight bag again. It had become my sleeping position. My head fell hard against the arm of the sofa and I clamped my eyes closed. The same memories became a film reel behind my lids, though, and I felt a tear escape.

'How the fuck did you get here, Wainwright?' I asked the room and, as though answering, I heard a crack echo through from the hallway. It could have come from any number of places: the kitchen; bathroom; dining room. I'd deliberately left all the doors open. But that meant that working out the direction of a noise was harder. It became easier, though, with the second noise, and the third – and the footsteps.

I sucked in hard and held my breath. In those seconds I heard every reprimand from Mum – 'Sarah, what on God's green are you playing at?' – and Madison – 'Darling girl, you don't need to be doing this.' I thought of Landon, lying half-drunk at home no doubt, swiping right at regular intervals; of Jessie and Tyler, taking it in turns to explain where babies come from to the twins. Finally, I thought of Wren.

When a shadow appeared in the doorway, I shrank back into the fabric of the sofa like it might swallow me whole. I didn't know whether these nerves were normal – whether there was a baseline level of nerves to feel when you were seconds away from facing off against a serial killer. I swallowed hard at the phrasing, even though they were words I'd paired together a hundred times over and then some. *Serial killer, serial killer, serial killer*. The letters chased each other around at such a speed, while the shadow hovered on the boundary of the room. *Serial killer, serial killer, serial killer*. The syllables started to knock together, and the cycles lasted so long I wondered whether I'd imagined the ghost in the room but...

'Sarah.'

He snapped the light on. And he wasn't a ghost anymore.

In all this time, I'd never been able to settle on an idea of what the man might look like. I felt as though he was nothing like I'd expected, but what had I been anticipating? It was unlikely that he'd be a hooded, axe-wielding, wide-eyed caricature; although something that glaring would have made these years easier. Instead of that obvious evil, though, he was something more subtle; a man who I would have walked by on the street on any given day, without giving him a second thought when I got home. He hovered in the doorway as though waiting for an invitation. His posture was slightly hunched over – from age, I wondered, because his hair was greying, too. The overhead lights were unforgiving in this room, though, Madison had always said that. An audible gulp rose from my throat at combining the two worlds: him and Madison in the same train of thought. He was wearing dark clothes – deep grey jeans, a black T-shirt, and dark brown jacket over the top – and although he wasn't wearing glasses I thought I could see the indentations where nose pads had recently been. He looked like a nobody.

'Sarah,' he said again, and I realised I'd never thought what his voice might sound like either. He took a nervous step into the room, and I couldn't make sense of his demeanour. He'd killed my mother; what did *he* have to be nervous about?

When he was a fraction closer, I swung myself upright on the sofa but perched on the edge of the seat. I nodded towards the other sofa, opposite my own, and he took the invitation. The couch moaned under the weight of him and he smiled.

'I can't believe we're here,' he said.

I reached into the overnight bag and wrapped my fingers around the warm metal. It had been snug in my hand for nearly an hour before this; the weapon felt like a natural extension of me now. I pulled it out and set it on the coffee table that separated us. 'No, I can't believe it either.' My hand stayed in place, a finger flirting with the trigger but not quite making it there. He kept quiet for a few seconds and I watched as his eyebrows pulled together, like he was struggling to work it all out. 'You didn't think I'd bring protection to this?'

'But, Sarah,' he started, and I thought he sounded saddened. 'A gun?'

'I'm an inner-city crime reporter. You think I don't know who to call for a gun?'

It had been easier than I'd expected. I'd tallied up a number of good sources over the years; I paid them well and I kept my mouth quiet about their names. It turned out I had a good reputation, and that made me a good person to sell a firearm to.

'Did anyone teach you how to use it, Sarah?' He leaned back into the sofa, as though he were making himself comfortable, and I felt an overwhelming urge to hurt him. Instead, I lifted the gun into good view and flicked the safety catch.

'Why don't we see...'

56

He was either too nervous to speak or he didn't have anything to say. The latter seemed unlikely, though, so I assumed it was a lingering shock at seeing a gun that kept him quiet. I asked him whether he had a mobile on him and he only nodded. When I told him to throw it over to me, he did it without a fight. It landed heavy in the seat next to me; I powered it down without looking, to keep my eyes firmly on him, and then I put the dead handset on the table. It was next to my own, which was very much alive – with 999 already keyed in, in case things got out of hand. I heard Mum, then, 'Sweetheart, aren't things already out of hand?' Whatever facial expression accompanied my thought made him look back at me in confusion.

'Are you okay?' he asked, almost whispering, and I laughed.

'You killed my mother.'

'And I'm sorry about that.' He half-laughed, too. 'This is ridiculous. Of course, I'm sorry, but I never would have killed her, Sarah, if I'd known about you. I just wouldn't, it wouldn't have been right–'

'None of them were right.'

He winced. 'I know that, of course.'

'Stop saying "of course".'

He held his hands up in a defensive gesture, then, and edged forwards in his seat. 'You have things that you want to know now, don't you? So why not ask – now we've got the chance, and this time? Now we can really talk, Sarah.'

I pulled the gun closer to me along the table. 'This isn't a social occasion.'

'No, apparently it's a hostage situation.' He looked at the weapon.

'If you play the victim prematurely, I'll shoot you.'

'And how will you explain that, Sarah, to Wren, for instance?'

'Don't.' I looked from him to the gun and back again. 'Don't bring her into this. You've dragged enough people into this mess, this – Christ, this lifestyle of yours. You've made it sound like something you *need*, like doughnuts or vodka.'

'It is something I need, Sarah,' he said plainly. 'I know you won't understand that, most won't, but it's true.'

'Cassie,' I said, and I saw his eyes narrow at my use of the name. 'Does Cassie understand it, or are you still lying to her?' He tilted his head and looked at me hard, as though he were trying to work something out. 'You used her name in a letter, once.' It was one of many things I'd banked: first that he was married; second that he was lying to his wife. Mum had told me once that that was something all men did. This, though, I thought, this was something extra. 'Let me guess, she just doesn't understand you?' I said, my tone mocking. 'Show me a married man whose wife–'

'Cassie is a special woman,' he interrupted me.

'Special enough to kill?' I raised an eyebrow. 'Or too special to kill? I'm never really sure how it works with you.'

He pinched at the fabric of his jeans around his knees and then stood. 'I don't have to stay here, Sarah.'

I picked the gun up. 'Yeah, you do.'

'You'll kill me?'

'I think you'll find I'll defend myself against you.'

He laughed; a real, smile-cracking laugh. 'I thought better of you.'

'Then I guess we're both doomed to disappointment.' I gestured with the handgun. 'Sit.' He followed the instruction, and I left a long enough silence for him to start shifting with awkwardness. 'What's your name?' He opened his mouth but before an answer arrived I decided to clarify my question, 'Not the name the media has given you. Your actual name. The one that Cassie calls out when you get home every night. Except, you know, not on the weekends when you're away murdering innocent women.'

He swallowed hard. 'Patrick. My name is Patrick. Cassie sometimes calls me Pat.'

'Your job. You're in the city?'

'I'm an advertising scout. I'm part of a company that liaises with bigger companies for advertisement campaigns.' He shook his head; the admissions looked physically painful to him, and I wondered how much more hurt I could find if I looked hard enough. 'I'm part of the national team.'

'Which is why it's easy to leave the city so often?' He nodded. 'Tell me about your mother.' He snapped his head up and stared into me. 'You know about mine.'

'She wasn't a very nice woman.' He shifted awkwardly. 'She– when I was younger, she often hurt me. Not sexually,' he rushed to add. 'But she did everything– I didn't have a father. No, I did have one. But I didn't have one who was around. My mother had to do everything on her own, which she– I don't know, I suppose she found difficult. She took some of the frustration out on me. When I was being boyish, or, I don't know, troublesome, as boys often are. She didn't appreciate my antics.'

'She beat you?' I asked flatly and he winced. There was a knee-jerk reaction in me to apologise, until I remembered who I was speaking to. 'Cassie can't have children?'

He was visibly thrown by the question. He moved to answer two, three times before rubbing hard at his eyes and avoiding my stare. 'Me. I'm the one who can't have children. There was an accident, incident when I was younger. My mother pushed me.' He looked up, then, and spoke to the ceiling; anywhere but directly at me. 'She said she didn't. She told everyone that I was clumsy, I fell, it wasn't her. But she pushed me and– I don't know, I must have landed at an awkward angle.' He nearly laughed. 'Severely awkward angle. Part of my pelvis was damaged, part of my left leg,' he tapped the limb as he spoke, 'and my right arm was broken. After that, I developed as I should have, but inwardly – there was something wrong on the inside.'

I laughed – and swallowed another apology for it. 'The woman who was like a mother,' I prompted him.

'She took me in after the fall happened. I spent most of my time there anyway, when Mum allowed it.' He took a long pause that I chose not to fill; I wasn't going to let him off with a half-story. He pulled in a greedy mouthful of air before he started to talk again. 'She was Mum's best friend. She was her Madison, I suppose, Sarah.'

'Don't compare our stories.'

'There are similarities.'

'Did someone kill your mother?'

He narrowed his eyes at the question and stared into a fixed spot on the floor. 'Me.' I let the admission hang; it hadn't been entirely surprising. Since Mum, I'd read enough true crime to know where these things start. 'No one ever knew.' He smiled, then, and looked at me. 'You're the only person in the whole world to know that, Sarah. I was older, she was drinking more by then. It was a nudge, more than a push. But

I watched her tumble, saw her neck land at a fantasy angle, and I just – in those few seconds looking down at her, I just knew.' His eyes had glazed over in the memory; it didn't feel like he was speaking to me anymore. 'I didn't even call anyone, Sarah, I just left. Someone called me, maybe a day or two later, to say a friend had found her. Tessa, she's the woman – the woman my mother should have been. She called to ask when I'd last seen Mum. I never knew whether she knew or not. Some women know, don't they, Sarah?' He looked like he was back in the room with me, then. 'Some women have a gut for it.'

It felt like a pointed comment. I tried to keep my face neutral. 'People letting you get away with it isn't the same as it being an acceptable thing to do. We're not talking about the odd bit of gaslighting, or forgetting the turkey at Christmas, Patrick.' I leaned hard on his name. 'Your mother was your first?' I asked, and he nodded. 'When?'

'2008. It was a difficult time for me, after she died.'

'After you killed her,' I corrected him.

'I lost my way for a while. I was... I don't know, distracted. It always felt like there was something missing in me, after Mum.' He was staring at the spot on the floor again and I didn't like it. I wanted him to look me in the eye while he did this; I wanted it to be harder for him. Instead, it felt like a purge. He'd made me an emotional accessory and it made me hate him even more. 'Jada, I met her while I was on a work thing. We were out together as a team and I sort of – I don't know, I drifted towards her.'

'Tell me about Mum.'

'Sarah–'

I clutched the gun tighter. 'It wasn't a question.'

'I was rushing– rushing everything. I was new to it all and panicking because– I don't know.' There seemed to be a lot he didn't know. 'I felt like I needed to do something, I just hadn't worked out what it was.'

'So, killing women was a filler activity?'

He frowned. 'No. No, it always meant more than that, Sarah. Your mother – whenever I saw her, she seemed so kind and open with people. She was everything I'd never had, when I was younger, and something about that – Christ, it made me angry and sad and – it just happened, from there.'

'Why weren't you killing cruel women, women who reminded you of her?'

He smiled. 'I was killing women who reminded me of her. Every time, I was...' he petered out, and I hated the thought that he might be remembering them.

'After Mum, you kept in touch with me.'

'I had to.'

'You chose to. I know that's something you're struggling with. But everything you've done, everything that led you here,' I tapped the coffee table with the metal, 'all of that was your choice. Why did you choose to keep in touch with me?'

He shrugged. 'You'd seen me. You were the only person ever to see me like this, as I am. I thought I'd be able to let that go, Sarah, I truly did. But then I saw how well you were doing, and then I saw what you were telling people, how you– I suppose how you were shaping your whole life around– well, me.' My face changed and he noticed. 'I was so flattered, Sarah. And then, when I saw you were reaching out to me, too, with the podcast and the obituary and – all these other tiny things you thought maybe I wouldn't notice.' He smiled; wide enough for me to see his teeth. 'I noticed, Sarah. I saw you back.'

'You know nothing about me, Patrick.'

'I know enough. We've got a bond, you and I, Sarah. I don't know what it means or what we can do with it, but there's something, isn't there? Something you feel–'

'Don't make this into something it isn't.'

'Okay.' He sat back. 'What is it, Sarah?'

I drew a line along the table with the tip of the barrel; the metal grated against the wood grain and the sound filled the room. 'An ending.'

'I see,' he spoke slowly. 'What kind of ending though?' Without warning he stood up and spread his arms in a way that looked sacrificial. 'Murder or mercy, Sarah?'

My mobile was still flat on the table in front of me. I kept the gun in one hand, and reached for the handset with the other. My thumbprint unlocked the screen and there were the three digits, still, waiting for an emergency. I looked up at him. 'Can I have one on sport?'

'You haven't decided yet, have you?' He moved closer, then, and although he was still a safe distance the change in proximity was stifling. I let my breathing spiral into something that sounded ragged. 'What if I decide for you?' He crouched, which brought him into my eyeline, and I felt my chest rise and fall at an unnatural rate.

I hit the bright green telephone and pressed my iPhone to my ear.

'Operator...'

'Should I sit with you and wait for them to come, Sarah? Would you like that?'

I swallowed hard and thought of Mum. 'Help me.' My voice cracked with the memories of her – of Madison, too. There were times when the three of us would have been in this room, talking about what life might be like when I was this age. 'Help me, please, someone's broken into my home...' They always joked that I'd be a man-eater; human-eater, Mum once said, because she didn't want to shoebox me. '...I can hear him downstairs.'

Patrick's eyes spread.

'Okay, I need you to breathe deeply for me, Miss...'

'Please, send someone. I'm – I'm Sarah Wainwright, I'm worried it's him...'

He sat back down on the sofa, then, and watched.

'DS Brooks, in the Major Incident Team,' I name-dropped, 'she knows...'

'Okay, Sarah. I need your address...'

'23 Hurston Street. Please, he's downstairs, please hurry...'

He smiled and slowly nodded. And I thought: *He must have realised, now.*

PART VI

57

2019

I'd been staying at Madison's home for a few nights. I was – I write with a bitter twist of irony – there to get some of Mum's things, so I could write what I originally planned to be the final chapter(s) of this very book. Little did I know that my time at Madison's would change so drastically – as would the closing of this story.

Patrick Haber arrived on my third night in the house. In his letters prior to this he'd implied that he was following me. But my time – both alone, and under police protection – had been uneventful. As a result of that I, like others close to me, had assumed his comments were empty ones. There was nothing specific written in any of the letters to suggest he actually knew where I'd been, or where I might be going. Although – with further irony, perhaps – I now know he'd been following me for some time, whenever an opportunity presented itself to. It was in following me that he knew where I'd be on the night of his final attack. He knew I'd be alone. He knew he might add me to his growing list of victims.

What he didn't know, was the sheer strength and

determination instilled in me by the two women who raised me...

58

Tina had copies of the letters, and the maps. But she was the only other person to have seen them in full. We agreed it was best – for me, for the book – if it stayed that way. 'No sense incriminating yourself for no good reason,' she said, feeding sheets of paper through a shredder in the corner of her office. 'The digital files are locked, and they'll stay that way. But rest assured it's just in case you lose your copies,' she told me, and I believed her. We'd written most of the final chapter of the book together; not to fabricate details, but to tread the line between what had been made public by the police and what was being brought by me, as a Sarah Wainwright exclusive. After I'd finished talking detectives through how Patrick had broken into the house – with a handgun, no less – I could talk Tina through it, too, as well as several other head figures from the publishing house. *Who knew self-defence would open so many doors*, I thought, each time Tina introduced me to a new face.

Nearly a full year of elbow-brushing and official statements had passed when the book was signed off as finished. Tina sent it to me as a courtesy, and for one final proofread. This was my last chance to change any details, too, but given that I'd recited my statement to the police like it was a gospel passage, it seemed an unwise move to start changing things. Instead, I read the book chapter at a time. The earlier parts were about Mum, and I read them slowly, with my legs tucked beneath me and hot tea to hand. The later parts were about him and, although I knew I needed to pay closer attention, I found myself rushing through them.

'Maybe you're just done with it,' Landon said, when I told him about my hurry.

I smiled. 'Maybe I am.'

'Does this mean we get another book launch?' Jessie asked from behind her pint.

Tyler laughed. 'One of us gets a book launch,' he looked at Jessie, 'one of us gets to stay home and babysit.'

'Aren't they old enough to look after themselves, though, really?' Landon asked.

'Yes,' Tyler replied, 'Dot is nearly one, after all.'

We were doing this, spending more time together. After what happened with Patrick, we made a quiet vow to be more involved in each other's lives – on the off-chance any of us were targeted by a serial killer again. But it had been a communal kindness to have these evenings out; or, more often, evenings in. Jessie and Tyler found it difficult to track down a babysitter brave enough to take on three children, so our nights together typically saw us crowded around their dining table with open pizza boxes and board games. That's how we'd evolved from teenagers getting drunk in the local woodlands before stumbling home to Mum's. But on this rare evening when Tyler's Mum had been bold enough to tackle her own grandchildren, we'd flocked to a nearby pub.

'I should make a move,' I said, pushing my empty glass away.

'Nonsense.' Landon drummed the table. 'Isn't it your round?'

'Ah, it's your round,' Jessie corrected him, 'but we should

make a move, too.' Tyler took the signal and reached around to slip his coat off the back of his chair. 'I'm too worried to get hammered on a school night these days.'

'Worried for the kids?' Tyler asked and Jessie laughed.

'Worried for your mum.'

In the bustle of the smoking area, we said our goodbyes. It had been three months since I'd had a cigarette. But when I pulled Landon in for his farewell hug, I still took a deeper than usual inhale on his clothing. He knew, too, which is why he held me for a beat longer than the others. He waited it out for a taxi – a long enough wait for him to enjoy his smoke in peace – while Jessie, Tyler and I went our separate ways. It took me twenty minutes to walk home, and I hoped that in that time my head would be clear enough to read through the final chapter one last time...

Before she said anything, I knew she was there. Wren had taken to watching me while I worked. I didn't know whether she enjoyed the view, or whether she was waiting for a breakdown. Since Patrick, though, we'd been able to break the golden rule on not discussing work. I'd confided in her several times over about the experience of reading the book back through; although I hadn't managed to confide in her much of the truth about having written it. Still, all relationships had their secrets, I reasoned.

She kept a safe distance until I pulled up my emails; then she knew it was time. She crossed the room and stood behind me, kneading my shoulders while I typed to Tina: 'All present and accounted for. No typos. No regrets. Sx.' And when I hit send Wren leaned over to plant a kiss on the crown of my head.

'Another best-selling piece of true crime from Sarah Wainwright.' She spun my office chair around and crouched level with me. 'What's next?'

'For life or...?'

In the dead of night, after a shared bottle of wine, Wren and I had made fantastical plans about what life might be like, when the book was written and the case was closed, and our relationship – as it was called now – was out in the open. I wondered whether she was about to initiate the conversation that we'd spent months tactfully avoiding. But instead she only laughed, stood and rested her hands on my shoulders again.

'Let's start small. How about for writing?'

I thought of the lies I'd told to get here. She pressed her thumbs into the balls of my shoulders, and I shrugged under her hands. 'I don't know.'

'I don't think I believe that.'

My email alert chimed, and I turned back to my monitor. It was confirmation from Tina – 'Safe and sound. T.' – and Wren let out a laugh as I skimmed it.

'A workaholic like you, and you want me to believe you've got nothing planned?'

I read and reread Tina's email before I turned back to Wren. 'Okay,' I admitted, 'maybe I'll try my hand at fiction...'

THE END

ACKNOWLEDGEMENTS

Sincerely, Yours is the first book I've ever personally offered ARCs for. The response to my social media call-out was kind and encouraging, and I've loved being able to share snippets of Sarah's story in a sneak preview fashion with this new group of readers. So thank you to those kind enough to give this book time in advance – and for putting up with my occasional pictures of Benji (which I realise may not really be too much of a chore).

Thank you, too, to my fellow hounds: for the retweets, the support and for swapping war stories from the writing world.

Finally, Beth, I owe you thanks in every single book I've written and this one is no exception. You're a truly excellent human bean and friend, and as much a part of the process as French Vanilla candles. I will forever be grateful for the time – and the emojis. If I could, I would send you a whole ocean of boats and a safety pin.

A NOTE FROM THE PUBLISHER

Thank you for reading this book. If you enjoyed it please do consider leaving a review on Amazon to help others find it too.

We hate typos. All of our books have been rigorously edited and proofread, but sometimes mistakes do slip through. If you have spotted a typo, please do let us know and we can get it amended within hours.

info@bloodhoundbooks.com

Printed in Great Britain
by Amazon